THE BODY AT ROOKERY BARN

KATE HARDY

Storm
PUBLISHING

Copyright © Kate Hardy, 2023

The moral right of the author has been asserted.

Ebook ISBN: 978-1-80508-083-1
Paperback ISBN: 978-1-80508-084-8

Cover design by: Lisa Brewster
Cover images by: Shutterstock

Published by Storm Publishing.
For further information, visit:
www.stormpublishing.co

Dedicated to the memory of my grandmother, Doris Camp, who taught me to read at a ridiculously early age; my mum, Sandra Sewell, who told me stories, encouraged me to write my own, and bought me my first typewriter; and my cousin, Terri Baker, who was always the first to celebrate with me. Love you and miss you all so very much.

ONE

'I really wouldn't go in there if I were you.'

Halfway through putting the key in the Yale lock of the front door, and with one hand still on the cast-iron thumb-latch, Georgina looked round. She couldn't see the woman who was talking. When she'd walked down from her farmhouse to the flint-and-brick converted barn she rented out as a holiday cottage, the shingled drive had been completely empty. The little flagstone courtyard by Rookery Barn was empty, too, apart from the odd bee buzzing lazily across the tulips and forget-me-nots that foamed over the edges of the terracotta troughs along the front of the barn.

'I mean it. Don't go in,' the voice continued.

With that slight Norfolk accent, the woman had to be someone local, but it wasn't a voice Georgina recognised.

'Call the police and the ambulance.'

What? This didn't make sense. Why could she hear someone but not see them – particularly as it was usually the other way round?

'Who's there? Are you hurt?' Georgina asked, narrowing her eyes.

There was no answer.

Maybe it was her new hearing aids. The audiologist had run through all the usual tests at the fitting appointment this morning and checked that the connection to her phone worked. Maybe she'd accidentally switched on a radio app broadcasting a drama, in the same way that you could 'pocket-dial' someone, and the radio had connected to her hearing aids. The mobile signal around Little Wenborough could be a bit patchy, which would explain why bits of the drama were cutting out. Of course there wasn't anyone actually here. She would've heard footsteps crunching on the shingle; or the rooks who gave their name to the farmhouse and the barn would've seen and yelled about it from the little copse of oak trees at the bottom of the garden where they nested.

Brushing aside her unease, Georgina decided to switch over to a music station when she started cleaning the barn, now that Roland Garnett, the Classics lecturer who'd been staying there for the last three weeks working on his book, had left. Knowing that her hospital appointment was first thing on Friday morning and she wouldn't see her guest before his departure, she'd dropped in yesterday afternoon to say goodbye, confirm what he needed to do with the keys after he'd locked up and wish him a safe journey home.

She'd felt slightly mean about it, but at the same time she'd been relieved that the man was finally going back to Cambridge. Dr Garnett had started out perfectly charming, but within three days he'd become the most demanding guest she'd ever had. The mobile phone signal was spotty and the Wi-Fi was slow. (What did he expect, in a rural area?) There wasn't anyone around here who delivered takeaways. (Ditto.) The oven didn't work. (It did – he just hadn't bothered reading the instructions in the folder of information she'd left for guests.) Then he'd upset Jodie, who usually cleaned the barn but had refused flatly to do anything there while he was in residence; he'd also upset

Francesca, who ran the farm shop, so she had insisted on delivering Dr Garnett's orders to Georgina at the farmhouse rather than to the guest in the barn. Neither of them would say what he'd actually done, but they'd both warned her to be careful around him. Georgina assumed that it had involved wandering hands or unwanted comments: probably both.

Although she didn't have a booking for the coming week, she wanted to get the chores out of the way. Changeover day meant fresh bedding, doing the laundry and making sure the barn was clean and ready for the next guests. Jodie usually did it but, in the circumstances, Georgina wanted to deal with the cleaning herself today. Though she still intended to pay Jodie her usual fee; Georgina considered her cleaner a friend as well as a colleague, and she didn't want the obnoxious behaviour of a guest causing problems between them.

'I'm warning you, this is a really bad idea,' the voice said again as Georgina finished unlocking the door.

Whatever radio station she was connected to, the signal was definitely patchy, because Georgina only seemed to be picking up one of the cast talking. Ignoring the voice, she picked up the cleaning caddy, pushed the door open and walked into the kitchen.

She regretted it immediately when the smell hit her, strong and sour: stale vomit. She couldn't help gagging, and covered her nose and mouth with one hand to block the smell while she dropped the cleaning caddy onto the stainless-steel draining board.

'I did *tell* you not to open the door,' the voice said plaintively.

Georgina took her phone from her pocket to switch off the annoying drama, only to discover that the radio app wasn't playing.

If the voice wasn't coming from her phone, then logically it must be coming from a person. Someone who trod lightly enough on the shingle for her not to hear them. Someone who hadn't spooked the rooks. Someone who was hiding. *Someone who was watching her.* Georgina's skin crawled, and for the first time she was aware of just how isolated the farmhouse and the barn were. If she screamed, nobody would hear her. Except the rooks – and who, in the countryside, would be bothered by a bunch of rooks kicking up a fuss?

She tried her best to keep her voice steady. 'Who are you? What do you want?'

There was no answer, and Georgina shook off the feeling of dread.

Maybe she was going mad. Maybe everyone was right, and she shouldn't have spent the past year living on the edge of a small village, alone apart from visits by her children and old friends, occasional interactions with the guests who stayed in the holiday cottage and the weekly Pilates class in the village hall that Francesca had talked her into joining. Or maybe the simple explanation was that her new hearing aids were somehow picking up signals from a neighbour's radio, and she'd have to go to the drop-in repair clinic next week to get the settings fixed.

The most urgent thing right now was to find out where that smell was coming from. Had her guest been taken ill overnight and unable to call for help? 'Dr Garnett?' she called loudly. 'Are you all right?'

There was no answer.

Leaving the kitchen door open so the fresh air would dispel at least some of the stench – and thinking that maybe the smell would make whoever was outside think twice about coming in – she shoved her phone back into her pocket and opened the door to the living room. Roland Garnett wasn't there, but his laptop sat on the pine dining table and there were books spread everywhere around it, as well as an untidy heap of papers scattered across the wooden flooring.

Clearly he hadn't left this morning, as planned. 'Dr Garnett?' she called again.

There was still no answer.

She checked the bathroom next, rapping on the door first. He wasn't there, but his things were strewn across the glass shelf by the sink and on the corner of the bath.

Which left only the bedroom.

And the smell was getting stronger.

Her fingers tingled with adrenalin as she twisted the round brass handle and opened the door. The smell of sick was over-powering now, and she could see a body lying on the bed; the duvet was pushed back and there was vomit all over the pillows and the sheet. Georgina's stomach lurched, and she had to swallow hard to stop herself throwing up, too.

'Dr Garnett?' she asked. 'Are you all right?' Stupid question. Obviously he wasn't all right, or he would've called out earlier – and he wouldn't be lying there in a pool of his own vomit.

Unconscious... or *dead*?

Georgina wrapped her arms round herself, suddenly cold.

Please don't let him be dead.

Please don't let this be like when she'd found Stephen on the floor in the living room, two summers ago. Cold. No pulse. No booming voice, from treading the boards for years before he'd switched to directing. All that larger-than-life personality snuffed out. Her beautiful husband, gone. No chance to say goodbye. No last 'I love you'.

Ophelia's haunting song – from the last production Stephen had directed before his death – slid into her head. *He is dead and gone, lady, he is dead and gone...*

Dr Garnett hadn't even closed the curtains or taken his clothes off. Had he, like Stephen, suffered a heart attack? Had he died alone and in pain, the way Georgina's beloved husband had? Or had he drunk himself into a stupor and choked on his own vomit?

She didn't want to go any nearer to the motionless body. Didn't want to have to face this. But there wasn't anyone else here to deal with things. She'd just have to block out the memories and get on with it. *Screw your courage to the sticking place...*

Shaking, she forced herself to walk over to the bed; she touched Roland Garnett's forehead, avoiding the dried splashes of liquid on his face. His skin felt cold. She moved her fingertips to his wrist, but she couldn't find a pulse. She couldn't see any trace of colour in his face, either: none of the usual signs of life.

Ohgodohgodohgod.

Dead.

Her teeth chattered, and she wrapped her arms round herself again. Right at that moment, all Georgina wanted was to curl into a ball and sob her heart out, though she knew that wasn't going to be of any use whatsoever.

'Call nine-nine-nine. Police. Ambulance,' the voice in her ear said, and Georgina jumped.

That voice again.

Was it just some kind of weird coincidence – or was there someone there? Someone who could see what was going on and that Georgina was lost in the past instead of reacting to the situation like a normal person would?

Either it was the radio signal she was picking up and nobody would reply; or someone really *was* there and she needed to deal with it. Feeling awkward, worried and annoyed all at the same time, Georgina said, 'Whoever you are, either show yourself and do something to help, or just piss off and leave me alone.'

'I want to help. I'm not hiding.' There was a sigh. 'Look, I'll explain later. But right now you need to pull yourself together and call nine-nine-nine.'

So it was a real person.

Georgina knew the woman had a point. Grimly, and trying hard not to think about the time when she'd had to do this before, she took her phone from her pocket and dialled. Unable to bear the smell of the vomit any longer and needing fresh air, she headed outside while the call connected.

'Which service do you require?'

It was hard to think straight. Police or ambulance? But it was too late for an ambulance to help Dr Garnett now. 'Police, please.'

'Can you give me your name, number and location, please?'

Georgina did so. 'I've... found a body in my holiday cottage. I think he's dead.'

'All right, love. We'll put you through to the paramedics while you're waiting and send the police out,' the call handler reassured her.

There was a pause, followed by a series of clicks, and then finally she was connected.

'My name's Josh, and I'm a paramedic. Is the patient breathing and conscious?'

Georgina leaned against the flint-and-brick wall next to the kitchen door, glad of the solid mass behind her. 'He's not a patient. And I'm pretty sure he's dead,' she said. 'He's cold and he doesn't have a pulse.'

'We might still be in time to resuscitate him. Let me talk you through the —'

'I don't think anything will work,' Georgina cut in. 'There's a lot of vomit and his face is an odd colour. It looks as if he's been dead for more than a few minutes. I'm pretty sure CPR isn't going to revive him.' *Just as it had been too late for Stephen.*

'Ah.' There was a pause. 'The police are on their way, and I'll make sure an ambulance comes out. Are you all right?'

'Yes,' she lied.

'OK, love. Try not to worry. They'll be with you as soon as they can.'

'Thank you.' It was hard to talk. Hard to swallow. Hard to breathe.

What now?

She definitely didn't want to wait in the cottage with a dead body. Plus there was nothing else she could do until the police and the ambulance got here. 'You weren't a very nice man, Dr Garnett,' she said quietly, 'but I'm sorry you ended up like this. Nobody deserves to die alone.' Not wanting to go back into the cottage, she locked the kitchen door and slid the keys into her pocket before heading for the farmhouse. She barely noticed the tumble of cottage garden plants that usually had her dawdling and reaching for her camera. All she could think about was the dead body in the barn – and how she was on her own.

Should she call her daughter? It would take Bea at least twenty minutes on the tube from Camden to Liverpool Street, then however long she'd have to wait until the next train to Norwich, followed by two hours on the train and another half an hour by taxi to the village. By then, the police would be here. Her son, Will, in Salisbury, was even further away. Anyway, by now he'd be in his lab with his phone switched off. She couldn't drag him here on a four-hour drive just because she was a bit spooked. Her friends in London or Brighton were all too far away to help, too.

Someone local? Her neighbours on one side were out at work, and the other side had gone away for a long weekend. Francesca would be up to her eyes in the farm shop, and Georgina was pretty sure that Jodie would've found something to replace her usual Friday shift cleaning the barn. Sybbie was probably out to lunch. Young Tom, who looked after her garden, would be busy with another client right now; it wouldn't be fair to drag any of them away from work when there wasn't really anything they could do in any case.

Which left Georgina here, alone.

'Oh, Stephen. I wish you were here,' she whispered. Not that she needed him to deal with this for her – she was perfectly capable of handling the situation on her own – but she missed her late husband so badly. And she really couldn't let finding a dead body push her back into the black hole she'd dragged herself from over the last year. She'd weaned herself off the anti-depressants, and she absolutely wasn't going back there.

She went over to the butler's sink in her own kitchen, turned on the tap and splashed her face with cold water. The shock of the cold against her skin helped steady her nerves.

'Make a list,' she told herself, and grabbed a pen and the spiral-bound reporter's notebook from the middle drawer of the oak dresser. Bea and Will both teased her about being old-school but, when she was working with lists or ideas, she found that paper and pen freed her thoughts better than typing notes on a screen.

Contact RG next of kin, she wrote, sitting down at the table next to the dresser. Though she'd need to find out who they were, first. The agency which handled the holiday bookings for her only sent her the barest details of the clients: name, address, email address, phone number. Maybe the police would be able to tell her. Or the college where he'd worked.

What next?

She stared at the paper, her head full of nothing.

'Put the kettle on. Make yourself some tea. Put a bit of sugar in it, because it's good for shock,' the voice said.

Oh, dear God, would that voice not leave her alone?

She checked her phone again. All the apps were closed. So who was talking to her? Georgina could see the entire kitchen, and nobody else was there. The cream-painted Shaker-style cupboards weren't big enough for anyone to hide in, and neither was the oak dresser; the mismatched chairs were all neatly in their places at the ancient oak table, and she couldn't see anyone hiding there. The old-fashioned casement windows behind her and next to the sink were both closed; the cast-iron thumb-latches on the cottage-style plank doors to the hallway and the utility room tended to stick, so she would've seen or heard someone trying to close a door behind them.

Who was speaking to her? Was she going mad? Or had she simply missed something obvious? Right at that moment, she was so flustered by finding the dead body that she couldn't think straight.

'All right. I've had enough now. Don't make a horrible day even worse. Finding a dead body is bad enough, without someone playing mind games with me. Whoever you are, please just come out where I can see you,' she demanded.

'That might be a bit, um, tricky,' the voice confided.

'Why?' Georgina asked.

'One thing at a time,' the voice said. 'My name's Doris. Doris Beauchamp.' She sang a snatch of 'Que Sera, Sera'. 'My mum loved Doris Day's films and named me after her. Though I think she was secretly disappointed that my hair was red, not blonde.'

So it *was* a person. But where was she hiding? And, whoever the voice belonged to, Georgina thought grimly, her sanity was definitely in question. 'OK, Doris. Wherever you are, please just come out so I can see you,' she said, keeping her voice very calm and very neutral. With a dead body in Rookery Barn, the last thing she needed now was —

And then she went cold. Was Doris responsible for Dr Garnett's death? Would *she* be Doris's next victim? Would the police arrive to find two dead bodies instead of the one that she'd just reported?

She dug her fingernails into her palms, willing herself not to panic.

'As I said, it's a bit tricky,' Doris said. 'You know the Sherlock Holmes quote about eliminating the impossible and then whatever's left has to be the truth, even if it seems improbable?'

'Ye-es.'

'Well, it's that.' There was a pause. 'Can you look up some-thing for me on the internet?'

If she could just keep this Doris person talking until the police arrived, Georgina thought, maybe that would keep her safe. 'OK.' The window was behind her; she pushed her chair back as she reached for her laptop, so she'd have quick access to the kitchen door if she needed it. Better than using the desktop computer in her office, where she could end up being trapped.

As Georgina opened the lid of the laptop, Doris rattled off an address for a genealogy website that offered a free search of the births, marriage and deaths index.

This was all familiar stuff: when she was 'resting', Georgina's daughter worked for a probate genealogy company, and had also done some work on their own family tree. Bea had taught Georgina how to look up records, saying that it would be fascinating to go a bit further into their family tree – and maybe Georgina would find something interesting in the history of Rookery Farm. Not that Georgina had even made a start on researching the house. Without Stephen, everything felt too hard.

'Tick the deaths index. Surname Beauchamp.' Doris spelled it out. 'First name Doris. Date range January to March 1971.'

Just over half a century ago. If Georgina had picked that date range in the births index and typed in her first name and maiden name, she knew her own details would've come up. Trying to ignore the chill of fear seeping through her, she typed in the details and pressed 'find'.

One record came up.

'Click on that, and then on "view",' Doris directed.

Wherever she was, Doris could clearly see the screen.

She's behind you...

Georgina tried to steady her breathing. Of course nobody was behind her. Just the wall and a window that was too small for anyone bigger than a ten-year-old to climb through – and they'd have to flick the casement stay off its pins and undo the monkey-tail window catch first, which wasn't possible from the outside.

She clicked on 'view'. A scanned page of a book came up, listing all the people in the country with the surname Beauchamp who'd died in January to March 1971. Doris Elizabeth Beauchamp was the second one down. Date of birth November 1952. She'd died at the age of eighteen.

'What does this mean?'

Doris sighed. 'I'm trying to show you who I am and why you can't see me.'

'You seriously want me to believe I'm talking to someone who died fifty-odd years ago?' Georgina winced even as she said it; how stupid, to challenge someone who was clearly unhinged. She needed to humour the woman until someone from the emergency services arrived.

'I did *say* about the Sherlock Holmes thing,' Doris said plaintively.

Even with hearing aids, Georgina found it hard to work out which direction sounds came from. And she still couldn't see a person or their reflection. 'Are you trying to tell me you're a ghost?' she asked in disbelief.

'Yes.'

'Then why can I hear you?'

'I've no idea,' Doris said. 'You're the first person I've talked to in a very long time – well, apart from the odd small child or dog who notices me. A dog can't talk; and who's going to take notice of what a little kid says?' She paused. 'Maybe you're psychic or something. Did you have invisible friends when you were little?'

'No.' Georgina frowned. 'And I've lived here for just over a year, so why is today the first time I've heard you?'

'I don't know. I've tried talking to you before,' Doris said. 'When you first came here. When you cried yourself to sleep every night. When you reached for the packet of antidepressants first thing in the morning then put them down again because you were trying to come off them.'

Georgina's breath hitched and she glanced at the back door. She could be outside in about three seconds, but what if Doris followed her? 'You've been watching me for a whole year?'

'No! That sounds *creepy*. I'm not stalking you and I don't mean you any kind of harm. I *live* here,' Doris said. 'When someone's sharing your house and sobbing themselves to sleep every night, you kind of want to comfort them. Except, being what I am, I couldn't make you a mug of hot chocolate, give you a hug and tell you that eventually you'd get through this and you'd be all right.'

It was too much for Georgina. 'Look, Doris, or whoever you are, I'm sorry, but I don't believe in ghosts.' The words burst out of her. 'If there's life after death, then Stephen would still be here with me. Talking to me. Close to me. And he's *not*.'

'I'm sorry,' Doris said, sounding forlorn. 'He's not here. There's just me. And I really haven't been spying on you or stalking you, Georgina.'

The 'ghost' knew her name, then. Georgina steadied herself against the table. 'I am not having a conversation with someone I can't even see,' she said through gritted teeth.

'Technically, you do when you're on the telephone,' Doris pointed out. 'If it's not a video call.'

Crazy. Georgina was obviously the one going crazy. Hearing things.

She must've spoken out loud, because Doris said, 'That's it. Not that you're crazy, I mean – that you're hearing things. You're hearing *me*.'

'I don't believe in the supernatural,' Georgina said.

'All right. What if I tell you things about you? Your children are William and Beatrice – named after Shakespeare himself and your favourite Shakespeare heroine.'

'That's public record,' Georgina said. Stephen had given plenty of interviews during his career, naming his wife and his children.

'It's obvious when they call you that they both worry about you.'

'As any child would worry about their middle-aged parent, particularly one who'd been recently widowed.' Georgina folded her arms. This wasn't good enough. 'Tell me something that isn't either public record or simple cold reading.'

There was a pause. 'Apart from photographing Sybbie at the manor house, because Cesca talked you into it, you've turned down every single offer of a shoot from magazines since you've been here.'

Georgina felt her eyes narrow. 'So you've hacked my phone or my email?'

'The only things you've photographed since you've been here are the flowers in your garden and the moon. You haven't wanted to photograph people and I think a bit of you is scared you never will again, that you've lost your skill. You talk to Stephen, even though he's not here, and you know he'd be furious with you for moping and missing him instead of living life to the full. You fake it when your children or your friends come to stay. You make the excuse that you're busy, when you're not – except for Pilates, because Cesca made you go with her that time for moral support and you think you'd be letting her down if you didn't keep going. And, if it wasn't for the guests staying in the barn, you wouldn't have any contact with Cesca or Jodie, and barely any with the outside world.'

That stung, because Georgina knew it was all true.

But the detail that stood out for her was the fact that Georgina had only taken photographs of the garden and the moon. The only way anyone could possibly know that was if they'd been in the house with her – specifically, in the darkroom with her.

For the most part, she'd been alone in the house; even when people came to stay, nobody went into her darkroom. Not even her children. Everyone knew her darkroom was sacrosanct.

'OK,' she said. 'That's not public record, or cold reading.' And it made all the hairs stand up on her arms. Who was 'Doris' and what did she want?

'I think you've lost your way, just as I'm lost,' Doris said quietly. 'And I think that's maybe why you can hear me. But I've talked to you every day since you've been here, and today's the first time you've been able to hear me. I don't understand. Why today?'

'I had new hearing aids fitted this morning,' Georgina said. 'Bluetooth ones that connect to my phone. I thought maybe they'd accidentally connected to the radio – like the way you might call someone without meaning to when you shove your phone in your pocket – and I assumed I was hearing a play when I went to the barn and heard someone telling me not to go in.'

'It wasn't the radio. It was me. You can hear *me*.' Doris's voice was full of wonder. 'This is amazing. Oh, my God. You can actually hear me. You can answer me. I'm not alone anymore.'

Not alone anymore.

Georgina had felt alone for the last year. It was partly her own fault, she knew, for moving to the middle of nowhere; but even in a crowd in London she'd felt lonely, without Stephen. She still didn't think she was talking to a ghost, but maybe Doris was elderly and muddled. And when you were vulnerable you could feel very, very lonely. 'How long have you been here?' she asked.

'As a ghost? Since Valentine's Day 1971.'

'The day I was born.' The words blurted out before Georgina could stop them.

'It's the day I died.'

Did that mean there was some weird connection between them? Either Doris was delusional; or, given that Georgina still hadn't seen any sign of her, maybe Doris really was a ghost. *There are more things in heaven and earth, Horatio*, as Stephen had been fond of quoting. 'If I was born on the day you died, does that mean I used to be you?' Georgina asked.

'No – I'm still here, aren't I? I know some cultures think that there's an endless cycle of death and rebirth, but I don't believe that. It's just a very big coincidence. Or maybe,' Doris said thoughtfully, 'the fact I died on the day you were born is the connection that means you can actually hear me.'

'Then why can't I hear Stephen?' Georgina shook her head. 'Surely I have a deeper connection with the man I was married to for more than twenty-five years than with someone I've never even heard of until today?'

Doris didn't answer. Weirdly, Georgina felt she'd been unkind to the 'ghost'. 'I'm sorry. I didn't mean to take it out on you,' she said, guilt prickling her skin.

'You just miss him. And it feels like a lifetime since you last held him close.'

That sounded personal, as well as being exactly how Georgina felt. 'Does everyone become a ghost when they die?' she asked quietly.

'I don't think so,' Doris said. 'Or this house would be full of everyone who'd ever lived here, wouldn't it? And it's not. Right now, there's just you and me.'

This time, it didn't feel like a threat. 'Why do you think you're here?' Georgina asked.

'I'm stuck,' Doris said. 'I think there must be something unfinished – something I need to do here before I can move on to... well, wherever.'

Hope flared for a moment and Georgina could hardly breathe. If this woman really was a ghost, and there really was an afterlife... She gripped the edge of the table. 'Are you here to reunite me with Stephen?'

'No. It took me a while to work it out, but I'm a ghost. I'm definitely not a medium. To be honest, I'm not entirely sure mediums really exist.'

Georgina felt the colour flood into her face. 'I spoke to a medium. After Stephen...' She couldn't bear to say the d-word. But she'd been so desperate to talk to him, one last time. To tell him she loved him. To know that, wherever he was now, he was all right.

'My mum got in touch with a medium after I died. Though the woman she spoke to couldn't see me or feel my presence, not even when I sat on the arm of her chair and blew into her face and put my hand on her shoulder. She didn't even feel a change in temperature. It was hopeless.' Doris sighed. 'I don't think she was the kind of con woman who was only in it for the money, though. I think she just wanted to make my mum feel better. She told Mum what she wanted to hear.'

Georgina winced. Doris might've been describing her own experience. 'Did it help your mum, talking to a medium?'

'Sort of. Did it help you?'

If only it had. 'No.'

'I'm sorry,' Doris said. 'I wish I could contact Stephen for you. If I could, I would. But I'm stuck here. In this house, and the grounds.'

'Is this—? Sorry. No. That's an unfair question.' Georgina shook her head.

'Where I died? Yes. I fell down the stairs and hit my head in the wrong place,' Doris said. 'It was an accident. I *think*. I don't know for sure, because it's all a bit hazy.'

'You think someone pushed you?'

'I don't know. The stairs are steep, but I grew up here and I was used to them. I don't understand how I fell. I don't remember what happened, just that I suddenly saw myself in the hall and Mum was there next to me, on her knees, cradling me and crying.'

Tears prickled Georgina's eyes. She couldn't imagine anything worse than losing your child. Right at that moment, she was desperate to hold both of her children tightly and tell them she loved them. 'I'm sorry,' she said. Doris clearly couldn't remember what had happened, but maybe Georgina could find out. Bea would know where to start looking for the evidence.

Though she still couldn't quite get her head round the idea that she was talking to a ghost.

'What does a ghost do all day?' she asked.

'I don't sit there clanking chains, chanting "whoo, whoo" or making things move, if that's what you mean.' Doris's tone was decidedly waspish. 'Dickens has a lot to answer for, as well as for being a total arse to his wife. That's not ghostly stuff, in my experience. There's no walking through walls. No floating at random and tapping on windowpanes and wailing – I'm no Cathy Earnshaw, either. And sadly there are no dinner parties where I get to sit chatting to Shakespeare and Chaucer about human nature, and then Freddie Mercury gets up and does a duet with Mozart on the piano to entertain everyone after the coffee and petits fours.'

'OK. Got it,' Georgina soothed. 'I didn't mean to offend you. I was just curious. When I'm taking a portrait, I ask my subject a lot of questions beforehand, so I've got a better idea of their personality and what I want to capture through the lens.'

'I'm not offend— hang on. Could you take a photograph of me?'

'Every photograph of a ghost ever published has turned out to be a fake,' Georgina said. 'The images have all been caused by a long exposure, a double exposure, or an anomaly in a camera.'

'Oh.' The word was filled with a mixture of disappointment – and was that annoyance?

Georgina shuffled in her chair. She was supposed to be mollifying Doris, not making her angry. 'Maybe we could try later today. Once I've got more of a picture of you in my head. What do you do with your days?'

'I wait, and I try to work out why I'm stuck here,' Doris said, sounding sad. 'I listen to other people's conversations. I watch TV when they do, or surf the internet or listen to music – and, if I'm really lucky, I get to listen to an audiobook. Even though I don't actually get to choose anything, other people's choices are better than being stuck listening to the house creaking or the rooks cawing.'

'If you could choose a song, what would you choose?' Georgina asked.

'George Harrison. "My Sweet Lord",' Doris said promptly. 'It was number one, the week I died.'

'The week I was born. It's why my mum called me Georgina. George was her favourite Beatle,' Georgina said, smiling.

'Mine, too.'

That was good: a mutual interest. Maybe, if she could find some more points in common, she could keep Doris talking until the police arrived. Georgina switched into the music player on her phone, her fingers weak with relief, and chose 'My Sweet Lord'.

Doris sang along with the harmonies, though Georgina noticed that her voice was wobbly.

'That was so kind of you,' Doris said when the song ended.

'Are you crying?' Georgina asked.

'Yeah. Sorry. But I love that song. I never got to see the Beatles – I was too young when they played the Grosvenor in Norwich, and Dad wouldn't let me go to see them in London – but I was hoping George might play somewhere in London when I was a student, and I could go and see him. Except,' Doris said softly, 'I never got to be a student.'

'This is surreal,' Georgina said. 'I'm waiting for the police to come and see a dead body in the barn. And I'm chatting to a ghost about George Harrison.'

'Trust me, it's just as weird for me. I'm sitting chatting to a woman who talks back to me,' Doris said dryly. 'Let me try an experiment.' There was a pause. 'Can you feel that?'

'Feel what?'

'The weight of my hand on top of yours. A drop in temperature. *Anything*.'

'No,' Georgina said. 'I can hear you, but –'

A rap on the front door cut through the rest of her words.

'It's probably the police,' Doris said. 'You'd better answer that. Pretend I'm not here.'

As Georgina walked through the kitchen into the hallway, then opened the door to the little porch, she wished she'd asked the police to bring a dog with them. It would sort this out one way or another. If 'Doris' was a real-life intruder, the dog would find her. Alternatively, didn't they say that dogs could sense ghosts? At least, they could hear more sound frequencies than humans and from further away, their sense of smell was a thousand times better than humans', and they could detect changes in temperature.

But, even without a dog, maybe the police could do a quick check for intruders. Footprints. Anything.

Though how did you ask the police to check for a ghost?

TWO

'Mrs Georgina Drake?' the policeman standing at the front door asked.

'Yes.'

'I'm Sergeant Ian Kennedy,' he said, 'and this is my colleague, PC Sarita Khan.'

Sergeant Kennedy was big and burly, but there was a wide gap between his front teeth which made him look slightly less formidable. PC Khan, by contrast, was petite and slender, and her smile was kind.

'Thank you both for coming so quickly.' Georgina took a deep breath. 'Shall I take you to see the...?' She stopped, unable to finish the sentence because saying the words aloud made everything feel so much more real.

'The body,' the sergeant said gently. 'If you would.'

'Be warned, the cottage smells really vile.' She closed the front door behind her and took the police down the side of the farmhouse and onto the path that led through the garden to Rookery Barn.

'Has anyone else been here since you found the body?' Sergeant Kennedy asked.

Only someone who claimed to be a ghost. Though how could she say that in a way that would make the police take her seriously? At least her surreal conversation with Doris had distracted her from the knowledge that there was a dead body in the barn – and stopped her thinking about how she'd found Stephen. 'Not as far as I know,' Georgina said. 'I thought Dr Garnett had left the holiday cottage this morning, while I was out. I was going to clean the cottage, ready for the next guests. And then I opened the door, and...' She grimaced as she repeated her actions. 'You can smell for yourself.'

'Not pleasant,' PC Khan agreed as the stench wafted out.

She ushered them into the barn's kitchen. 'I called out as soon as I walked into the cottage, but nobody answered. It's not exactly huge; there's just the kitchen, the living room, a bathroom and a bedroom.' She indicated the narrow hallway that led to the bathroom and bedroom, and the plain wooden door that led to the living room. 'I found Dr Garnett lying dead in bed, in a pool of vomit, and I came straight out again to call you.'

'And the front door was locked when you got here?' PC Khan asked. At Georgina's nod, she checked, 'Have you closed any windows?'

'No. I left everything exactly how it was when I found him – well, almost. I left the cleaning stuff on the draining board,' Georgina said, indicating the caddy, 'because I wanted to get out of here as fast as possible. In the bedroom, I touched his forehead to see if he was still warm and his wrist to see if I could find a pulse, so I could try to resuscitate him, but there wasn't one. I came out to call the emergency services and I locked the door behind me.'

Sergeant Kennedy went into the bedroom and came out a few moments later. 'As you said, there's no pulse, he's cold, and it looks to me as if he's been dead for a while. Did he say anything to you about being ill, Mrs Drake?'

'No.' Georgina wrapped her arms round herself. 'My

husband died from a heart attack, two years ago. I came home from work and found him. Finding Dr Garnett was...' She couldn't finish the sentence, because it made her stomach hurt.

PC Khan gave her sympathetic look. 'It must've been a shock.'

Yes. One which was only just beginning to hit her.

'Obviously with this being an unexpected death, we will need to document everything,' Sergeant Kennedy said. 'Can you tell us, is there anything missing from the cottage?'

'You think a burglar killed him?' Georgina asked.

'We're just running through a checklist,' PC Khan said. 'Was there anything missing from the cottage?'

'I didn't notice,' Georgina said. 'I haven't touched anything – well, no, obviously I touched the door handles when I checked the rooms, and I've already told you I touched his forehead and his wrist. But nothing else.'

'Thank you, Mrs Drake,' Sergeant Kennedy said. 'We'll need to fingerprint you so we can eliminate your prints from the scene.'

Between them, the police officers checked the body and the rooms, made notes and took photographs, and Sergeant Kennedy made a couple of phone calls.

'We've got a local doctor coming out but, unless the deceased attended the practice, we'll need a pathologist to confirm the cause of death,' Sergeant Kennedy said. 'And I'm afraid we'll need to treat this as a suspicious death until it's proven otherwise.'

'You mean, you really think someone *killed* him?' Georgina stared at him, shocked. 'It wasn't a heart attack or something like that?'

'We mean we don't know what caused his death. Until the cause is identified, we have to treat it as suspicious,' PC Khan clarified. 'We're going to need to secure the property until the Scenes of Crime team gets here. May I have your keys, please?'

'Yes, of course.' Georgina detached the two keys to the barn from her keyring and handed them to PC Khan. 'The Yale key is for the kitchen door, and the other key is for the French doors.'

'Are there any other keys to the barn?' Sergeant Kennedy asked.

'Jodie – who cleans for me – has a set of keys. And there are the ones that Dr Garnett used while he was staying here. I assume they're still somewhere in the house.' She frowned. 'It wouldn't make sense for him to put them in the key safe by the front door while he was still in the house.'

'Can you open the key safe for us, please, so we can check?' PC Khan asked.

Georgina pressed four numbers on the keypad. The door clicked open, revealing an empty space. 'They're not here,' she said, feeling that she was stating the obvious.

'We'd better wait here until the SOCO team arrives,' PC Khan said.

Georgina bit her lip. 'Can I get you a cup of tea or anything?'

'No, we're all right,' Sergeant Kennedy said. 'Perhaps we can have a chat while we're waiting.'

'Is this a formal interview? Do I need to...?' She raked a hand through her hair. 'Sorry. I'm not thinking straight.'

'Finding a body is always a shock,' PC Khan said sympathetically.

'It's an informal chat,' Sergeant Kennedy said. 'At the moment we're gathering information. What can you tell us about the deceased?'

'His name's Roland Garnett – *Dr* Garnett,' Georgina emphasised. 'He was very particular about using his title. He teaches – taught,' she corrected herself, 'Classics at St Bene't's College, Cambridge. He was writing a book about food and drink in Ancient Greece, and he booked his stay at Rookery

Barn through the agency I use to handle bookings. He was staying here for three weeks on a retreat, so he could finish writing the book.'

'Wasn't that something he could have done in his office at the university?' Sergeant Kennedy asked.

Georgina shrugged. 'I have writer friends who go on retreats to finish a book. They say when you're out of your usual environment, you can avoid the things that normally distract you and concentrate on your work. Maybe it's the same for academics.'

She noticed that PC Khan was making notes as she talked.

'Where's his car?' Sergeant Kennedy asked.

'He didn't have one. He arrived in a taxi. He said he caught it at the station, so I assume it was one of the black cabs,' Georgina said. 'I don't know who he'd booked to take him back to the station, because I wasn't here this morning when it would've arrived, but there's a list of local taxis in the information folder I leave for guests. Unless Dr Garnett moved it, the folder should be in the kitchen drawer next to the sink. It might be worth checking with the taxi firms on the list.'

'Has he had any visitors?' Sergeant Kennedy asked.

'The only ones I know for definite are Jodie and Cesca. Jodie Fulcher cleans the barn for me. She came as usual after the first week of his stay, but she refused to come back again while he was still here, so I've done the weekly cleaning and linen change myself. As far as he'd let me clean, that is. Dr Garnett was very fussy about people not touching his paperwork. Though, as you probably noticed from the living room and the bathroom, he wasn't the tidiest of people.'

'The kitchen was spotless,' PC Khan pointed out. 'Was he a cook?'

'I have no idea,' Georgina said. 'But he wasn't very happy when he arrived and discovered that none of the takeaway delivery services he's used to in a city can deliver out here. In the end, he bought some ready meals from Cesca Walters at the farm shop at the other end of the village, because she agreed to deliver his order as a favour to me.'

'So the only visitors to the barn were yourself, the cleaner, and the farm shop staff,' Sergeant Kennedy noted. 'Does anyone else have access to the house, the barn or the garden?'

'Young Tom – that's Tom Nichols,' Georgina said. 'He runs the local gardening business. His grandfather – Old Tom – does the garden at Little Wenborough Manor. Young Tom does my garden on Mondays and Thursdays.' She frowned. 'Actually, that's reminded me. He was mowing my lawn last week and it disturbed Dr Garnett. Young Tom apologised to me later and said it was only for a quarter of an hour.'

'I see. Does he work on his own, or does he have an assistant?' Sergeant Kennedy asked.

'A girl's been with him for the last couple of weeks, but I'm not sure if she's his assistant or his girlfriend,' Georgina said. 'I think her name's Ginny, or it might be Jenny. Young Tom's got quite a strong accent and I didn't hear it clearly. She seems very shy and I didn't want to embarrass her by asking.'

'That's helpful,' PC Khan said. 'How many times did they come out from the farm shop?'

'To Dr Garnett, once,' Georgina said. 'After that, Cesca said she'd prefer to deliver his orders via me.'

Sergeant Kennedy looked interested. 'Two female visitors, both of whom refused to return. Did they say why?'

Georgina grimaced. 'All they said was to watch myself round him. I assume it was the usual.'

'The usual?' Sergeant Kennedy repeated.

'Unwanted comments or advances,' Georgina explained. 'Cesca and Jodie are both in their twenties. Pretty. And Dr Garnett was...' She grimaced. There wasn't a nice way of saying it. And not all men were like that: just enough of them to make it a problem.

PC Khan nodded. 'Middle-aged, entitled and white. I know the type.'

When Sergeant Kennedy looked awkward, PC Khan smiled at him. 'I'm not including you, Ian. You're middle-aged and white, but you're one of the good guys.'

He reddened slightly and asked, 'Do you know if Dr Garnett had anything to do with your gardener's assistant?'

'With her being young and female, you mean? I doubt he acted the way he did towards Cesca and Jodie, because whenever I've seen her she's been almost glued to Young Tom.'

'Fair enough. Did Dr Garnett have any other visitors, Mrs Drake?'

'Not that I know of,' Georgina said. 'Though any visitors to the barn would park in the courtyard, and I can't see that area from the house.'

'But wouldn't you hear a car coming down the driveway?' he asked, gesturing to the shingle.

Georgina indicated her hearing aids. 'These are good, but no hearing aids are perfect. At my last appointment, the team discovered my hearing had deteriorated quite a bit during the last couple of years. I had new aids fitted this morning, with updated programmes, but I didn't hear your car arrive, either.' Mainly because she'd been talking to a ghost, but she didn't think it would be a good idea to bring that up right now.

'Thank you.' Sergeant Kennedy looked thoughtful. 'Did you have any problems with Dr Garnett?'

'Not in the same way as Cesca and Jodie. Maybe because I was nearer his own age, and maybe because I answered him back in Latin when he started quoting at me.' Georgina shrugged. 'He was very charming with me for the first couple of days.'

'And then what?' Sergeant Kennedy asked.

'He had...' Georgina paused, not quite sure how to phrase it. 'Exacting standards.'

'How do you mean?' the sergeant asked.

'There was a new complaint every day. The spotty mobile phone signal, the slow Wi-Fi, the lack of local facilities, the lack of a fancy coffee machine in the barn kitchen, the dawn chorus being too loud.' Georgina rolled her eyes. 'I think he expected the countryside to be like the city but prettier.'

'Then you weren't sorry to see him go?' PC Khan asked.

'I wouldn't have wished him any harm,' Georgina said, 'but I was quite relieved his stay was up, yes.'

'When did you see him last?' Sergeant Kennedy asked.

'Yesterday afternoon,' Georgina said. 'I knew I wouldn't be here when he was due to leave this morning, because of my hospital appointment. I called in to check that he was happy to put his keys in the key safe by the front door of the barn after locking up, and to wish him a safe journey home – the usual polite chat you have with your holiday guests.'

Sergeant Kennedy inclined his head. 'Right. What sort of time?'

'I'm not sure.' She thought about it. 'It must've been some-where between three and five. I have a Pilates class at six on Thursdays, at the village hall, and we normally go to the Red Lion for a drink afterwards. One of us drives and drops the others home. It was my turn to drive, this week, so I left at half past five.'

'And what time did you come back?' PC Khan asked.

'The class finished at seven, so… probably about half past eight, by the time I'd finished dropping everyone off,' she said.

'Who do you go with?' Sergeant Kennedy asked.

'Jodie, Cesca and Cesca's mother-in-law, Sybbie,' she said.

'We'll need to speak to them, if you can let us have their details,' Sergeant Kennedy said.

'Of course.' She took her phone from her pocket, checked her contacts list and gave the numbers to the police.

'When you came back, did you see or hear anything

unusual, or something you didn't expect, at the barn?' PC Khan asked.

'I can't see the barn from the house or the driveway,' Georgina said.

'And how long have you been living here?' Sergeant Kennedy asked.

'A year. As I said, my husband died two years ago. I couldn't handle living in London without him.'

'You moved from London to a remote farmhouse in a little village in Norfolk,' Sergeant Kennedy said, as if he couldn't understand why on earth someone might make that choice.

'I moved,' she said, 'to a place with no memories, where the house had enough space for a darkroom.'

'You're a photographer?' PC Khan asked.

'Freelance. I take mainly portraits for magazines – Sunday supplements and the like,' Georgina explained. 'Though I haven't really had the heart for it since Stephen – my husband – died. I've spent more time developing old negatives and fiddling with them than taking new shots.'

'Like Photoshop?' Sergeant Kennedy asked.

'A bit,' she said. 'Except it's in my darkroom, not on a computer.'

'Did Dr Garnett know about any of this?' PC Khan asked.

Georgina didn't see how it was relevant, but she thought about the question. 'I don't remember it coming up in conversation, so I don't think so.'

A car pulled up at that point. When the woman climbed out, Georgina recognised the village doctor. 'Hello, Dr Fairley.'

'You know each other?' Sergeant Kennedy asked.

'Little Wenborough is quite a small place. Everyone knows everyone round here,' Dr Fairley said with a rueful smile. 'Hello, Mrs Drake. Sorry to see you in such difficult circumstances.'

Sergeant Kennedy introduced himself and PC Khan.

'I should tell you now,' Dr Fairley said, 'we haven't treated the deceased at the practice during his stay in the village, and the death was unexpected, so I won't be able to issue a medical certificate for the cause of death. You'll need to refer the case to the coroner.'

'Which means we still have to treat the death as suspicious,' PC Khan explained to Georgina as Sergeant Kennedy took Dr Fairley to see the body.

A few minutes later, Dr Fairley and Sergeant Kennedy returned. 'I can verify that life is extinct. It was most probably asphyxia-induced cardiac arrest – the vomit blocked his airways, causing a heart attack,' she explained. 'But I'm afraid it's one for the coroner to confirm.' She nodded to Georgina as she headed for her car. 'Nice to see you, Mrs Drake.'

'Look, it feels wrong, you being here and me not giving you at least a cup of tea,' Georgina said when the doctor had left. 'Especially if you're going to be waiting around for a while.'

'Then a cup of tea would be lovely, thanks,' PC Khan said with a smile. 'Milk, no sugar, for both of us, please.'

* * *

'Roland Garnett, aged thirty-seven, university lecturer. It's an unexpected death, the building was locked from the inside and there was no sign of any open windows or forced entry, no signs of any struggle, and nothing out of the ordinary.' Inspector Colin Bradshaw looked down at his scribbled notes as he spoke. 'The village doctor can't give an official cause of death, though she thinks a heart attack caused by choking on his own vomit is the most likely reason. Our colleagues in Cambridge have spoken to his college to get the details of his next of kin. She – his ex-wife – is coming to formally identify him, though we've had preliminary confirmation from the owner of the holiday cottage. We're waiting on the coroner's representative and the scene's secured. Have I got that right?'

'Spot on, guv,' Larissa Foulkes, Colin's detective constable, said.

'Is there anything else I need to know before I go out there?'

'There's a couple of photographs of the body, guv, where they found him. I'm sending them over to your phone now,' Mo Tesfaye, Colin's detective sergeant, said.

'Thanks.' Colin flicked into his phone and looked at the pictures. 'Hopefully the pathologist can confirm the cause of death.'

A heart attack caused by choking on his own vomit.

It could so easily have been him.

Dying alone, choking on his own vomit as he felt that band round his chest get tighter and tighter...

He'd come close. The biggest cliché of all: the copper who thought he didn't need counselling after a particularly horrific case because he was coping perfectly fine. Except he'd been coping with the help of a bottle that had put its glass wall around him, too, and he'd shut out everyone close to him. Including his wife.

Marianne, tired of trying to get through to him, had eventually walked out on him. He was lucky she'd dropped in to pick up some paperwork she'd left behind and found him shortly after he'd collapsed. She'd been the one who called the ambulance.

He still had days when he wished the paramedics hadn't resuscitated him.

Drying out had been hard.

But he'd done it. It was too late for his marriage, but he hoped he still had a chance to become a decent father. He was a hundred miles away from his daughter, Cathy, and right now another man was doing a far better job of being a dad than he had. He texted Cathy every day, video-called her once a week, and saw her on Sundays when he wasn't on duty. Was it enough? Of course it wasn't. But he couldn't give any more, right now. He was just muddling through as best he could. The only thing he still knew he did well was his job.

'Right. I'd better get out there and take a look,' he said grimly.

Colin knew the rumours had followed him from London to Norfolk. How he'd almost been kicked out of the force, but they gave him a second chance after he'd agreed to go to rehab. He couldn't afford to make a single mistake. Which meant doing everything strictly by the rule book, checking a third time as well as a second, not getting involved emotionally with the case, and staying well clear of alcohol.

* * *

'They're treating it as a suspicious death,' Doris said as soon as Georgina was back in the garden, out of earshot of the police.

'You heard all that?' Georgina asked, keeping her voice low.

'Yes, but there was no point in talking to you about it. You wouldn't have been able to answer without the police asking who you were talking to, and that would've been a bit awkward,' Doris pointed out.

'It's a suspicious death until they know the cause. And you heard what Dr Fairley said.' Georgina dug her nails into her palms and forced herself to sound calm. 'It was probably a heart attack.' *Like Stephen.*

'I'm sorry to ask something that's going to hurt you, but was Stephen... like that, when you found him?'

'No.' Georgina concentrated on putting one foot in front of the other and tried not to think of Stephen lying on the floor, cold and alone. She hadn't been there because of a stupid shoot. A job she hadn't really wanted, because the subject had been a complete prima donna, but she'd done it as a favour for a friend

– and, oh, how she wished she'd made an excuse not to do it. If she'd been in London when Stephen had collapsed, she could've got help in time and he would still be alive. She'd never, ever be able to forgive herself for that.

'Sorry.' Doris sighed. 'But something about it doesn't seem right. If he got drunk and inhaled vomit in his sleep, surely the kitchen would be in a mess? Surely there'd be empty bottles and what have you?'

'I don't know. For now, we have to go with the flow.' Georgina smiled wryly. Accepting that she was talking to a ghost was definitely going with the flow. But what other explanation was there? She knew she wasn't going mad: she knew what day it was, who she was and where she was. If Doris had a physical form, the police would've heard her moving about or seen her shadow or *something*.

Unless someone had placed a bugging device in the house and was spying on her. But why on earth would someone want to do that? She was an ordinary photographer, the widow of an acclaimed theatre director. As far as she knew, the nearest she'd been to a spy was when Stephen had directed Alan Bennett's *A Question of Attribution* – and the spy in question had been an actor, playing the part of the real-life Anthony Blunt.

When she went back to the holiday cottage, carrying two mugs of tea, there was an unfamiliar grey car parked on the shingle next to the police car, and a man wearing a white forensic suit and overboots was busy putting on a pair of latex gloves.

'Mrs Georgina Drake, owner of the property; DI Colin Bradshaw, in charge of the investigation.' Sergeant Kennedy introduced them swiftly.

'Hello,' Georgina said. 'Can I get you a mug of tea, Detective Inspector?'

'No, thanks.'

Unlike the uniformed police officers, Bradshaw was

unsmiling and abrupt. The sort, Georgina thought, who knew just how good-looking he was, and was arrogant with it. Stephen would probably have cast him as Claudius.

'We need all the keys to the barn, Mrs Drake,' he said.

'You've already got my set,' Georgina said. 'I'll ask my cleaner for hers. I haven't looked for them, but I assume the ones Dr Garnett was using are somewhere in the barn.'

'Tell your cleaner to bring them now, please. And we'll need her fingerprints, as well as yours, for elimination purposes.'

His tone rubbed Georgina up the wrong way. Dr Garnett was dead, and it had nothing to do with Jodie. What difference would it make whether her keys were here in the next ten minutes, or this evening? 'I'll call her and see if she's available,' she said, narrowing her eyes at him and taking her phone from her pocket.

Jodie answered on the third ring. 'Hi, Georgina. Everything all right?'

'Um – no, actually. I need your set of keys to the barn. Could you come by and drop them off?'

'Why? What's happened? You're not sacking me because I didn't want to clean with *him* around?'

'No, nothing like that,' Georgina reassured her. 'I'm sorry, it's not good news. Dr Garnett is dead. Until the police establish what happened and the coroner's confirmed the cause of death, they have to treat it as suspicious. They need all the keys to Rookery Barn, and they'll also need your fingerprints.'

Jodie gave a sharp intake of breath. 'He's *dead*? Oh, my God. How?'

'Dr Fairley thinks he choked on his own vomit and had a fatal heart attack.' The last couple of words tasted like acid on Georgina's tongue.

'He was an arrogant twat, but even so I wouldn't wish that on him.' Jodie paused. 'Why do they want my fingerprints?'

'To eliminate us from the investigation, I presume. They're taking mine, too.'

'OK.' Jodie sounded worried. 'Georgie – what about that row I had with him? If they've got a coroner looking at him, they'll probably see the bruise where I stood on his toes and put all my weight on my heel, to make him back off and keep his hands to himself.'

'Don't worry,' Georgina said. 'I'll explain.' She was pretty sure PC Khan would be sympathetic. 'Can you bring the keys now?'

'I can't,' Jodie said. 'I'm at the Red Lion. Seeing as I'm not cleaning the barn for you today and Mike's short-handed because he's got a function on, I said I'd help him out. But the barn keys are in my bag. Can I drop them in before I pick Harry up from school?'

'The police want them now,' Georgina said. 'I'll come and collect them.'

'Would you? Thanks, Georgie.'

Georgina ended the call. 'Jodie's at the Red Lion, working for her brother. She's got the barn keys with her, so I'll go and fetch them,' she told DI Bradshaw.

He shook his head. 'One of my team will do that. They'll conduct a preliminary interview while they're there.'

She stared at him. 'Hang on. Are you implying...?' He couldn't possibly think that she or Jodie had anything to do with Roland Garnett's death, could he?

* * *

Maybe he had a suspicious mind, but that outrage was a little bit too studied for Colin's liking. And his notes had told him that Georgina Drake was the widow of a London theatre director and actor. She must've picked up some things about acting from him, over the years.

It was probably an unfair snap judgement, he acknowl-
edged, but all his instincts were telling him that this wasn't a
death from natural causes. He'd taken a look round the crime
scene, being careful not to disturb anything. On the surface, it
looked as if Roland Garnett had choked on his own vomit and
nobody else was involved with his death.

But.

But.

If Garnett had been a drinker, there would've been signs.
Empty bottles in the waste bin, or just left wherever they'd been
drained and cast off. When they knew they were on their own,
drinkers didn't bother trying to hide the booze. There was a
heap of dirty clothes on the bedroom floor, there were papers all
over the living room, and there were toiletries strewn across the
bathroom, but not a single bottle.

And the kitchen was much too clean for Colin's liking.
Even if Roland Garnett hadn't been a cook, the room should've
been messy, to match the rest of the cottage. There should've
been takeaway cartons in the bin, dirty mugs and glasses on the
work surfaces or a few days' worth of crockery in the washing-
up bowl, biscuit crumbs on the work surfaces and bits dropped
on the floor. But the room looked as if it'd been cleaned – and
cleaned *thoroughly*. Beneath the stench of vomit, Colin could
smell the telltale scent of bleach.

The team definitely needed to check the waste pipe and U-
bend of the kitchen sink, in case any evidence had lodged there
and hadn't been drowned in bleach.

What wasn't Georgina Drake telling him? He had the
impression that she was hiding something.

And she was waiting for an answer. Why wouldn't he let
her collect the keys? Because it would give her a chance to
collude with another witness. She wasn't stupid. Of course
she'd work that out for herself.

'It's routine procedure,' he said instead, schooling his expression to give nothing away.

'I see. What happens now?' she asked.

'We wait for the coroner's representative to collect the body and do their investigation,' he said coolly. 'We need to be sure the death was from natural causes before we get rid of any evidence.' If it wasn't from natural causes, he needed his team to sift through the evidence and come up with answers. Fast. The first forty-eight hours of an investigation were crucial.

'What about his family? Is someone contacting them?' she asked.

'Someone on my team will do that,' he said.

'What about his things? Will you return them to his family, or do you need me to do that?'

'We'll do it,' he confirmed. 'We'll take his laptop, phone, fitness watch and wallet back to the station with us, but we'll leave his clothes and other personal effects locked up here. If you don't mind.'

She clearly realised that he'd said the last bit purely out of courtesy, because she wasn't getting the keys back until they'd finished their investigation. 'Of course.' She bit her lip. 'Is there anything I can do?'

'I'd advise you to cancel anyone who's booked a holiday here in the next week,' he said. 'Possibly the week after, too. And maybe the week after that.'

Her hand went to cover her mouth. 'I... Thankfully there isn't anyone arriving today.'

Interesting. That led to an important question. 'If you don't have guests arriving, why did you need to clean the barn today, so soon after Dr Garnett was supposed to leave?'

Her eyes narrowed slightly. 'Routine procedure,' she said, repeating his words back to him.

Touché. He admired that; at the same time it nettled him slightly. 'Perhaps, Mrs Drake, you could give PC Khan a copy of the paperwork regarding Dr Garnett's stay here, and direct her to the Red Lion,' he said. 'And perhaps you could make sure my team can talk to you immediately if they need to.'

She'd know exactly what he meant.

He could see in her expression that she'd picked it up: as a potential suspect, she needed to stay local. 'Of course.'

'PC Khan, perhaps you could take Mrs Drake's fingerprints as well, so the SOCO team can eliminate her prints from the scene,' he said.

'Yes, sir,' PC Khan said.

THREE

This was surreal, Georgina thought. Was her barn really a crime scene? Was she a suspect because she'd been the last person known to see Roland Garnett alive, and she'd found the body? She knew she hadn't killed him; but how could she prove it when she didn't have an alibi?

PC Khan collected the mugs Georgina had brought down earlier, took a kit from the police car and escorted her back to the farmhouse.

When they were nearer to the house and out of earshot of the barn, Georgina asked, 'Can I tell you something in confidence?'

'About the case?' PC Khan asked.

'Sort of.' Georgina bit her lip. 'Jodie told me what happened when she did the cleaning. Dr Garnett grabbed her from behind, and she stood on his toes to make him let go. Quite hard, so there might still be some bruising on his toes, and she's worried it might be misinterpreted.'

'I'll have a word with her,' PC Khan said.

'But surely what she did was reasonable, if he touched her

without her consent and didn't back off when she told him to keep his hands to himself?'

'Without witnesses, I'm afraid it's one person's word against another's – and Dr Garnett can't exactly give us his version of events,' PC Khan said grimly. 'Don't worry. I'll talk to her.'

Georgina found the paperwork for Roland Garnett's stay so PC Khan could photograph the details. Then she had her fingerprints taken at her kitchen table.

'This makes me feel like a criminal,' she said.

'It's routine. It's your barn, your prints will be in the place, and so will Jodie's as your cleaner. This helps us eliminate both sets of prints from the scene,' PC Khan reassured her.

'What happens now?' Georgina asked.

'The pathologist will collect the body, do an examination and then give us a report. If the GP's theory was right and the pathologist agrees the death is from natural causes, then we can send Dr Garnett's things back to his family and return the keys to you, and you can carry on as usual,' PC Khan said.

If. Such a small word with such huge possible consequences, Georgina thought. 'And if it's not?'

'Then we'll have to investigate further. I can't give you any more detail than that, right now. Someone will stay at the barn until the body's been collected and forensics are done, and then make sure it's secure. And we'll return access to you as soon as we can. In the meantime, if you think of anything that might be useful, please get in touch.' PC Khan gave Georgina her card.

'Thanks. I will.'

'He's a bit of all right,' Doris informed Georgina when PC Khan had left.

'Who is?'

'The inspector. Imagine him coming out of the lake, all Mr Darcy.'

Georgina gave a short, mirthless laugh. 'He's about as snooty as Darcy. What is it with middle-aged men thinking their IQ is twenty points higher than anyone else's?' The way Colin Bradshaw had spoken to her still rankled. 'He's as bad as Dr Garnett quoting Latin at Jodie.'

'I don't think he's a show-off. I think he's damaged,' Doris corrected softly. 'There's a look in his eyes, as if he's been through the mill.'

Georgina shrugged. 'That's none of my business.'

'He does look like Colin Firth, though. You have to admit there's a Darcyness about him. He's proud, and you're prejudiced.' Doris laughed at her own joke. 'I loved that adaptation.'

'You've seen it?' Georgina asked, surprised.

'Thankfully some of the guests were really into Austen and chilled out with a bottle of wine and a P&P marathon. But Colin Firth's my favourite Darcy.' Doris sighed happily. 'I loved him in *Love Actually*, too.' She paused. 'Did you ever meet him at an actor party? Something all glitzy and glamorous?'

'No. And acting really isn't that glamorous,' Georgina said. 'Yes, you get the strutting and fretting of the hour upon the stage, but there's all the stuff behind it. Auditioning time and time again until you actually get a part, and doing a job you don't love while you're "resting" – which is most of the time. Learning lines. Blocking out a scene. Rehearsals, with all the tiny changes that make a difference and then it all has to be repeated to make sure it all still fits together. Checking the music and sound effects. Making sure the backdrops work. The lighting. The costumes. Managing the spats and the egos.'

'You miss it, don't you?' Doris asked.

'The theatre?' Georgina shook her head. 'No. I miss Stephen.'

'*And there is nothing left remarkable /Beneath the visiting moon,*' Doris quoted quietly, and Georgina recognised the line from *Antony and Cleopatra* instantly. 'I know how that feels,' Doris continued. 'Cleopatra was a selfish cow, but I think she really did love Antony.'

Tears blurred Georgina's vision and she blinked them away. 'You loved Shakespeare, too?'

'I was going to read English at University College, London,' Doris said. 'As long as I got the grades, though I was going to work hard enough to make sure I did. I would've been the first one in my family to go to uni. And I was going to teach. I was going to open the hearts and minds of my students, show them that Shakespeare's for everyone.'

Georgina swallowed hard. 'You sound like Stephen. That's how he felt about Shakespeare, too. How I do. That's how we met. I was working on the university newspaper and he was in *Macbeth* at the theatre round the corner. It was his first shot at being a director, too. I interviewed him.' She'd fallen in love with his voice. With his eyes, the colour of forget-me-nots. With his quick mind. 'The guy who was meant to take the photos was ill, so they gave me a camera and told me to take the headshot as well as do the interview. And that was that.'

'I think I would've liked your husband,' Doris said quietly. 'And I'm sorry you lost him too soon.'

'I think he would've liked you,' Georgina said, realising with surprise that it was true. If Doris had been a real person instead of a ghost, Georgina would've been friends with her. 'And I'm sorry you're stuck here. Maybe...' She shook her head. 'This is going to sound crazy, but I was thinking maybe you and I can help each other.'

'Maybe we can,' Doris said. 'I'd like to try.'

'Me, too.'

Georgina busied herself washing up the mugs. But, once that was done, she was at a loss for what to do next. All she could do was wait for the police to finish their investigations and for the body to be collected. She mooched about the house, unable to settle to reading, working on an image or doing a crossword, any of the usual things she did in the day.

'Pacing the house isn't going to make the police leave any more quickly, you know,' Doris informed her.

'I know.' But Georgina continued to walk round the kitchen. 'We have to find out what happened.'

'The coroner's verdict for me was an accidental fall,' Doris said.

Georgina frowned. 'I thought you said you weren't sure what happened?'

'It's hazy,' Doris said. 'What I do know is from putting bits and pieces together afterwards. Things I've heard other people say. I know it happened on Valentine's Day. And I remember Trev, my boyfriend. I was eighteen, so I must've been seeing him that night. I must've been getting ready.'

It sounded like a typical teenage girl planning to go out with her boyfriend.

'The bath was full. So maybe I went downstairs for something before I had my bath, and I slipped. But I can't remember falling. There's just a blank. All I know is I died.'

'What about Trev?' Georgina asked.

'I don't know,' Doris said. 'I never saw him again, and my parents never spoke about him afterwards. I don't know if he made it to uni, like we planned. But I hope he did. I hope he found someone who loved him as much as I did. I hope he's had a good life.' She dragged in a breath. 'Mum and Dad sold the farm, a year later, because they couldn't bear to live in the place where I died.'

Georgina could understand that only too well. It was the main reason why she'd moved. *The look of a room on returning thence.* The line from Thomas Hardy's *The Walk* summed it up.

She'd half-expect to see Stephen whenever she walked into a room; then it would slam into her why she wouldn't see him, and it was like losing him all over again. She hadn't been able to bear it. Here, she still missed him, but there weren't any memories to rip her scars open every single day. And, slowly, she was healing.

'I don't actually know where my family moved to.' Doris's voice was slightly wobbly. 'And I just wish...'

'Maybe I can find out for you,' Georgina said. 'Find out what happened to them, and what happened to Trev.'

'How?'

'The internet. I'm surprised you haven't tried that already.'

'It's the same with the walking-through-walls stuff. I can't physically open a laptop, switch it on, bypass the login and press the keys,' Doris said.

'How did you know about the genealogy website?'

'Because I've seen other people do it, not because I've done it myself.'

But, before Georgina got a chance to open her laptop, there was a knock on the kitchen window and Jodie stood there, waving.

'Don't say anything,' Georgina warned Doris in a low tone, and opened the back door. 'Hi! Is everything all right?'

Jodie flapped a hand. 'Sure. I wanted to check that you were OK.'

'I'm fine.' The half-truth tripped easily off Georgina's tongue. 'Come in. I'll make you a coffee. How did you get on with PC Khan?'

'She was really nice. I told her what happened. And she said not to worry about it.' Jodie jerked her head in the direction of the barn. 'I assume you know there's still a copper outside, guarding the barn.'

'He's waiting until Dr Garnett's body has been moved to the mortuary,' Georgina said.

'I can't believe he's really dead.'

'It's horrible – and it's going to get worse.' Georgina grimaced. 'When I finally get the barn back, I'm going to need a lot of bleach and I'll have to leave the windows open for a week to get rid of the smell. Not to mention getting a new mattress, new pillows and new bedding – I can't let someone sleep in a bed where someone died.'

'I know what I said,' Jodie said, 'but I'm not leaving you to clean up something like that on your own.'

'It's really not pleasant,' Georgina warned.

'I'm still not letting you do it on your own.' Jodie gave her a hug. 'And it must've been horrible, finding him. Especially after... Well, you being a widow and it not being that long ago.'

'Yes.' Georgina hadn't told anyone in Little Wenborough exactly what had happened, even Jodie and Cesca; she'd simply said that her husband had died from a heart attack, knowing they'd probably assume he'd died in hospital.

Hating having to face everyone's pity was one of the reasons that she'd moved from London. She didn't want to have to do that in her new home. Though at least she'd been spared the waiting for a coroner to confirm things because, a week before his death, Stephen had had his six-monthly blood tests to check his cholesterol, followed by a phone consultation with their GP.

Before Georgina could say anything more, there was a rap on the kitchen door. Francesca waved and opened the door at Georgina's gesture.

'Hello, Cesca.' Georgina added water to the kettle. 'Good timing. Coffee?'

'Yes, please. I brought brownies,' Francesca said. 'Are you OK, Georgie?'

It warmed Georgina that at least two people locally were concerned about her. Maybe she wasn't quite as alone as she'd thought, earlier. 'I'm fine, thanks. But I owe you an apology. I should've called to warn you that the police might want to see you. I'm sorry if I dropped you in it.'

Francesca put the cake tin in the middle of the table and removed the lid before pulling out a chair and sitting down. 'You didn't really drop me in it. PC Khan was lovely. She told

me not to worry about having had a row with Dr Garnett.' The
last two words were a savage mimicry of the lecturer's tone.

'You had a barney with him, too?' Jodie asked, sitting opposite her.

'Wandering hands and gobby mouth,' Francesca said,
rolling her eyes. 'I told him where to go. And you?'

'Snap,' Jodie said. 'I stamped on his foot. Did he try it on
with you, Georgie?'

'No. Remember, I've got a good couple of decades on the
pair of you,' Georgina said, 'and I speak Latin. Apart from the
fact he obviously didn't fancy me, he also knew I wouldn't be
impressed by his quotes.'

'I wasn't impressed by them, either,' Jodie said.

'Nor me. I answered him in Italian and told him he needed
to update his language.' Francesca rolled her eyes. 'I wish
Sybbie had been there. She would probably have corrected his
Latin and told him he wasn't up to the standard of her own
professor at Oxford.'

'I would've liked to see that, too.' Jodie grinned. 'I wish I'd
been a fly on the wall when you talked back to him, Cesca.'

'If I teach you to swear in Italian, I'll be hounded out of
Little Wenborough for being a bad influence,' Francesca said.

'No, you wouldn't,' Jodie corrected. 'Everyone within a ten-
mile radius loves your tiramisu.'

'Which I'm considering developing as an ice-cream flavour,
if you're up for testing,' Francesca said.

'Name the time and place, Cesca,' Georgina said, 'and we'll
be there.'

'Good.' Francesca paused. 'Roland Garnett was a horrible
man, though that wasn't a reason for him to die.'

'Agreed,' Jodie said. 'Is there anything we can do to help,
Georgie?'

'Not with the barn, until I'm allowed access again,'
Georgina said. 'And your guess is as good as mine as to when

that'll be. But there is *something* you might be able to help with. Your families have both lived here for years, haven't they?'

'Mike's the fourth generation in my family to run the Red Lion,' Jodie said, sounding proud.

'We all know I'm the incomer,' Francesca said, hamming up her Italian accent, 'but Giles's family have lived here for ever. I'm pretty sure his parents bought some of the land that once went with your house, Georgie. I can ask Sybbie for you.'

'Yes, please. I was thinking about researching the history of the house,' Georgina said. 'Do you know anyone who could tell me about the people who lived here, say, half a century ago?'

'Bernard' – Francesca's father-in-law – 'would still have been a child, but if there was something particular you wanted to know about then he might have an idea. Or Old Tom.' Tom Nichols was the head gardener at Little Wenborough Manor; he flatly refused to retire, despite being over seventy, because he loved the gardens so much. 'And there's the local history society,' Francesca suggested. 'Billy in the butcher's runs it. If you ask him, he'll put the word out.'

'My gran would probably know something, too. She was born at the Red Lion. She's seventy-five now,' Jodie said.

Only a couple of years older than Doris would've been, Georgina thought. Maybe she'd known Doris; and she would definitely have known about Doris dying.

'I could ask her, if you like?' Jodie suggested.

'That,' Georgina said, bringing three mugs of coffee over to the table, 'would be a brilliant start. Yes, please.' She smiled. 'I'd better go and ask the policeman if he wants a coffee.'

'I'll go,' Jodie said. 'Have one of Cesca's brownies. I bet you haven't had any lunch yet – and you need carbs.'

Jodie's coffee was almost cold by the time she got back. 'He says yes please, but he'd rather have tea with two sugars, if that's all right.' She walked over to the kettle, added more water and switched it on. 'And guess what? From what the copper just told me, it seems our charming professor's ex-wife is going to formally identify the body.'

'His next of kin is his *ex*?' Francesca blinked.

'Are you really surprised he's divorced?' Jodie asked.

'No. I'm surprised,' Francesca said, 'that someone actually married him in the first place. He reminds me of that politician – you know, the snooty one who's about two hundred years out of date.' She shuddered. 'Giles went to school with people like that. Can you imagine having to live with someone who holds ninety-nine per cent of people in contempt?'

'The man's dead,' Georgina reminded them quietly. 'And I don't think the policeman should've told us anything.'

Jodie looked chastened. 'I didn't think about that. I don't want him to get into trouble, Georgie. He's a couple of years younger than me and it's his first job.'

'I won't say anything, either,' Francesca promised. 'This whole thing's pretty horrible – and especially for you, Georgie, being the one to find him.'

'It's worse for his family,' Georgina said.

'Even if he's horrible, I guess his family will still miss him.' Jodie sighed. 'I'll take that tea out.'

* * *

'My condolences on your loss, Mrs Summers. Thank you for giving us a formal identification of the body,' Colin said. 'I know this is a difficult time, and I'm sorry to have to ask, but would you mind helping us fill in a bit of background about Dr Garnett?'

The young woman's face was pinched and Colin noticed that she was gripping her husband's hand tightly.

'I haven't seen him for nine years,' she said, 'so I'm not sure I'll be much help.'

'Anything you can tell us will be helpful,' Colin said.

'I... didn't have a happy marriage to Roland Garnett, Inspector. It took me a long time to trust people again, afterwards,' she said.

'It took her two years to agree to go out with me, and another three to marry me,' her husband put in. 'Hayley, you don't have to drag it all up again. If it's upsetting you, don't talk about him.'

She swallowed. 'I'll try. If I don't, he'll be back in my head again. He's taken enough from me.'

'Take your time, Mrs Summers,' Colin said. 'Rest assured, I won't be passing any judgement on you. Whatever you tell me is confidential, though I will need you to sign your statement to say that it's accurate.'

She was silent for a long time, but Colin had done this often enough to give her the space until she was ready to talk.

'I met him at Cambridge, when I was doing my MA,' she said. 'I wasn't one of his students, but my supervisor had the set of rooms opposite his and I bumped into him a few times in the corridor. He asked me out for a drink and kind of swept me off my feet.' She closed her eyes. 'My parents weren't very happy that I wanted to get married before I'd even finished my studies, but they came round in the end. They gave us the deposit on the house for a wedding present.'

'The house?' Colin asked.

'Nineteen Trinity Way,' she said.

Interesting, Colin thought: that was still listed as Roland Garnett's home address. Her parents had given them the deposit for the property, but Garnett had kept the house after the divorce. Had he bought Hayley out, perhaps?

'I thought everything was going to be so wonderful,' she whispered, and covered her face with her hands.

'It wasn't. He was terrible to her. Separated her from her family and her friends,' Mr Summers put in, sliding his arm round her shoulders to comfort her.

Hayley Summers dragged in a breath. 'Roland could be so, so charming when he wanted. But, once he'd got what he wanted from you, he changed. He'd make all these sly little comments – if I challenged him, he'd say I must've misheard or I was overreacting, and he'd make me believe that I was the one making a drama out of things and he'd done nothing wrong. It just chipped away at my confidence.' She looked miserable. 'In the end, it was easier not to argue.'

'He didn't even like her being friends with people at work,' Ryan Summers said.

'I'm an archivist at the county records office,' Hayley said. 'The office has moved to Ely, now, but back when I first started it was based in Shire Hall and I could walk to work from our house. Roland used to walk me to work and then meet me to go home. I thought it was because he wanted to be with me as much as he could – and maybe he did, in the early days. Maybe he wasn't a control freak.' She swallowed hard. 'Or maybe he was. And it was so subtle I didn't even notice. It always sounded so reasonable when he came up with an excuse why we couldn't see my parents or my friends. Little by little, my friends stopped asking us to join them on evenings out.'

'What about his friends?'

'That's the thing,' Hayley said. 'Now I look back, he didn't really seem to have any. It was just the two of us.'

'What about your neighbours?' Colin asked. 'How did he get on with them?'

'There was an old couple next door to us, the Ropers,' Hayley said. 'They were lovely, but he said they interfered.' She sighed. 'Maybe they did, in his eyes. But I'm glad they kept an eye out for me. Betty Roper was lovely. She... Well, I think she realised what was going on. She came round a few times, when Roland wasn't there, to check I was all right. I always lied and said I was fine, even when I wasn't. But then I fell pregnant.'

She stopped suddenly. When she started talking again, her voice was shaking. 'Sorry, I can't go on.'

Colin gave her some space, to see if she could compose herself enough to continue.

She gripped her husband's hand hard. 'It was awful, but eventually I got a divorce. I left my marriage with nothing but the clothes I was wearing.'

Yet she'd said her parents had paid the deposit on a house; even ten years ago, in Cambridge, that couldn't have been a small sum. 'You didn't want your half of the house? Or at least your deposit?'

'It was more than worth losing that,' she said, 'to get my freedom.'

'I'm sorry,' he said, 'that you had to go through that.' Colin knew Marianne had had more than enough grounds to divorce him for unreasonable behaviour, but she'd been kind. On condition he agreed to get help for his drinking, she'd divorced him on the grounds of mutual agreement and being separated for two years.

'I'm surprised I'm still down as his next of kin,' she said. 'He didn't remarry?'

'It seems not,' Colin said. 'He didn't have a parent or sibling who could be named as next of kin?'

She shook her head. 'His parents died when he was quite young. I think there were aunts and uncles, but none of them could take him in at the time. He grew up in care, and he lost contact with his family. Or maybe he didn't want to see them, because they'd let him down when he needed them. That might be why he's – he *was*,' she corrected herself, 'so possessive with people.'

Ryan looked as if he thought it was a pathetic excuse and that Roland Garnett was simply a nasty piece of work, but he was clearly keeping his mouth shut because he wanted to support his wife.

'Thank you for sharing something so difficult with me, Mrs Summers – Mr Summers. We can end here, but we may be in touch with further questions,' Colin said, wanting to acknowledge them both. 'Can I ask – again, just to help our enquiries – your whereabouts yesterday?'

'We were driving back from York,' Ryan said. 'My best friend got married in Edinburgh, last weekend, and we decided to make a holiday of it. We dropped Barney – our little boy – in York with my mum and dad, and we stayed in Edinburgh for a couple of nights.' He smiled at his wife. 'We had a romantic weekend. Then we went back to York to stay with my family. My dad loves steam trains and he was thrilled to take our Barney on his favourite ones. I'm not sure which of them was grinning most or enjoying waving a flag.'

'Like peas in a pod, the pair of them,' Hayley said, and Colin was relieved to see some of the misery drain from her face.

'We got stuck on the A1 for about an hour yesterday, about four o'clock – traffic's always a nightmare on that road, especially with the roadworks, but yesterday was worse than usual because there was an accident,' Ryan added. 'Everyone was just stuck until the road cleared.'

That would be easy enough to check, Colin thought.

'We got home about eight,' Hayley said. 'Luckily we'd been to the park in the morning, and Barney wore himself out playing football with his dad and his grandad, so he slept for most of the journey.'

Diverting to Norfolk to murder Roland Garnett would've taken them a couple of hours, and then it would've been yet another couple of hours before they got back to Cambridge. Colin made a note to check the database and then to check the traffic cameras near the Summers' house.

'Thank you,' Colin said. 'You've both been very helpful. We might need to come back to you at some point in the future, to check some points, but it should be routine. I'm just going to finish writing up your statement; if you wouldn't mind reading it through and signing it, I'd be very grateful.'

'Of course,' Hayley said.

'Let me get some tea or coffee organised for you,' Colin said, 'and I'll be as quick as I can.'

Back in his office, he had a quick confab with Mo and Larissa, his sergeant and constable, organising refreshments and making sure the Ropers were contacted before Hayley Summers had a chance to have a word with them, and checking out any vehicles registered to Ryan or Hayley Summers. There was always a chance that they'd hired a car, but he'd get the other details checked first.

Then he finished writing up their statement, ready for signature.

* * *

Later that afternoon, Colin dropped in to see Sammy Granger, the pathologist. 'The tech team's managed to get some data from the fitness watch. I know I could've emailed it to you,' he said, 'but I thought I'd see how things were going.'

'I haven't started the PM,' Sammy said. 'But Roland Garnett's the next on my list.' She took the graphs he'd printed out, spread them on her desk and pored over them.

'Look – you can see his heart rate slowing here,' Sammy said, tracing the line. 'And it stops here, somewhere between twelve and...' She squinted at the graph. 'The scale on this thing isn't great, but I'd say that it stops at around one in the morning. That's consistent with the evidence your team sent over.'

'And you think the GP's right and it was a heart attack?'

'I don't know. Yet. You can stick around while I open him up, if you like,' she offered. 'Feel free to use my desk while you're waiting.'

'Thanks. I appreciate that.' Normally, Colin would just leave the professionals to get on with their job, but he had a funny feeling about this case. On the surface, it looked like a simple death from a heart attack; but the tingle at the back of his neck said otherwise. Over the years, Colin had learned to trust his hunches.

He was working through the reports of the preliminary interviews in Cambridge when Sammy called him in.

'Take a look at this,' she said. 'There are lesions on the heart.'

'And that's unusual?' Colin asked.

'These ones are.' Sammy used a penlight torch to highlight the lesions.

'What caused them?'

'The most probable cause of lesions like this is drug poisoning. Hopefully the tox screen will pick it up.'

'What kind of drug?'

'Digoxin, I'd say, though that's not included in a standard tox screen. It's used to treat cardiac failure or atrial fibrillation in patients who can't tolerate the newer drugs.'

'Was Garnett taking it?' Colin asked.

'Not according to his medical records.'

'If he wasn't taking heart medication, how would digoxin have got into his system?'

'There aren't any puncture marks on the body, so injection's unlikely – and you'd only have injections in hospital, in any case,' Sammy said. 'It was most probably through ingestion. Could he have taken someone else's medication by mistake – say, thinking it was paracetamol?'

'Apparently he was staying at the holiday cottage on his own. It's unlikely he took someone else's meds,' Colin said.

'Digoxin is prescription-only,' Sammy said. 'But it's made from foxgloves. If he was into foraging, he might've mistaken foxgloves for borage or comfrey and cooked with the leaves – which are poisonous.'

'The woman who owns the holiday cottage said he wasn't a cook,' Colin said. 'What was his last meal?'

'According to the analysis I made earlier of the vomit, chicken curry,' Sammy said.

'Could that hide the taste of foxglove leaves?'

'If it was hot enough, you could hide the taste of practically anything in a curry,' Sammy mused.

'We need to check it and find out where he got the chicken curry. We'll check the rubbish for takeaway cartons,' Colin said, 'and, if that draws a blank, we'll try his phone and internet history for a call or an order.' He paused. 'Can you screen for digoxin and anything else that might have caused those lesions?'

'If you authorise it, yes. As I said, it's not standard,' Sammy reminded him.

'I'll sort the paperwork and authorise it,' Colin said. 'Let me know when you get the results.'

He was still no further forward. At the moment, it looked as if Roland Garnett had either eaten foxgloves or taken some kind of heart medication that wasn't meant for him. Murder or suicide? Not everyone left a note but, from what he'd learned so far of the lecturer, Colin suspected Garnett was the type who would've wanted people to know what he'd done and why, so he would've left a note. Probably in Latin.

If it was murder... Until the more detailed tox screen came through, there was no proof of method. There was also no suspect and no motive, but his instinct told him he was heading in the right direction.

The last person to see him alive was the owner of the holiday cottage, Georgina Drake.

He'd start by talking to her.

FOUR

Colin drove out to Little Wenborough. As with many of the pretty villages outside Norwich, there were flint-and-brick cottages lining the main street, all with front gardens full of spring flowers; a flint church with a round tower and a thatched roof; a large village green with a duckpond and a children's playground; a little parade of shops; and a pub. According to his satnav, the school, doctor's surgery, village hall and a housing estate were off a side road. It was the kind of place where families had lived for generations, and he'd just bet that everyone knew everything that happened in the village within seconds of it happening.

At the far end of the village, there was a shingled drive and a sign on the open white five-barred gate saying *Rookery Farm*. This time, he took the left-hand fork up to the farmhouse rather than the right-hand fork to the holiday cottage.

The farmhouse was even more picture-postcard than the converted barn, its plaster painted cream and contrasting with the both the red pantile roof with its enormous chimney stack and the weathered single-storey brick porch. The windows were small and, like the front door, painted Chartwell green.

On either side of the door was a large terracotta pot planted with rosebushes that would obviously climb up the trellis around the doorway later in the summer. The house looked old enough to be heavily beamed inside, and he was sure that it would be furnished expensively. Georgina Drake clearly wasn't short of money.

But, as far as he knew, she was the last person to see Roland Garnett alive; she was also the one who'd found the body, and she'd been on her own at the time. Added together, those facts made her a person of interest.

As the owner of the holiday cottage and its neighbouring farmhouse, Georgina had the opportunity to kill Garnett. She might well have also had the means and, although he wasn't clear about the motive, he knew from the reports he'd read that she'd admitted to disliking her guest. Though other people in the village who'd come across Garnett had also disliked him, and simple dislike wasn't enough of a motive for murder.

Strictly speaking, Colin should have left the questioning to a junior; an inspector was meant to work on the strategy rather than the nuts and bolts of an investigation. But he wanted to see Georgina Drake's reactions for himself. He climbed out of his car, used the heavy cast-iron knocker on the front door and waited.

Silence.

PC Khan had said she'd advised Georgina Drake to stay local. Her car was parked on the shingle in front of the house. Maybe she'd gone for a walk. Or maybe she hadn't heard him knock.

He knocked again, this time a bit harder. Still nothing. Irritated, he took his mobile phone out of his pocket and was about to try calling her when the door opened.

'Detective Inspector.' She looked worried. 'Has the pathologist confirmed the cause of death?'

'Not yet,' he said, annoyed that she was questioning him

when it should be the other way round. 'Could I have a word, Mrs Drake?'

'Of course. Come in.' She ushered him through the hallway – a stripped wooden floor with an expensive-looking runner, cream walls hung with framed photographs and watercolour prints and with beams running across the ceiling, as he'd expected – into the kitchen. 'Can I offer you a cup of tea or coffee?'

'Thank you, but no.'

'Do take a seat.' When he made to pull one of the mismatched chairs back, she winced slightly. 'Would you mind sitting on the opposite side of the table?' His surprise must've shown on his face, because she said, 'I wear hearing aids, but your voice is deep enough to be in my difficult range, and it's easier for me to lipread you if your face is in the light. That'll save us both time and patience when you're talking to me.'

He liked that she was so matter of fact about her hearing difficulty, neither making a big fuss about it nor pretending that everything was fine when it clearly wasn't. 'Of course,' he said. 'If you need me to repeat anything, just say.'

'Thank you. And thank you also for not shouting,' she added, 'or talking super-slowly, as if I'm too stupid to understand.'

Was that what people usually did? That would really irritate him, in her shoes. He tried not to scrape the chair against the red pamment flooring as he pulled it away from the table, then sat down and flipped open his notebook. 'I'd like to ask you a few questions, if I may.' At her nod, he continued, 'Do you live here on your own?'

'Most of the time,' she said, sitting opposite him. 'I'm widowed.'

She was young to be a widow, he thought.

'My son lives in Salisbury and my daughter lives in London,

but they each have a room when they come to stay. And there's a couple of spare rooms for friends.'

Which meant she must fairly rattle around the farmhouse on her own. He found it hard enough in the small two-bedroomed riverside flat he rented in Norwich. This place would give him way too much room for thought. 'No pets?'

'No. Will and Bea – my children – think I need a dog, but I can hardly take a puppy on a shoot.'

'Shoot?' he asked, his tone slightly sharper than he'd intended.

'I'm a photographer,' she said. 'Mainly portrait.'

Of course. Shooting film, not bullets. Maybe he'd spent too long in this job. 'Where does the rubbish from the barn go?'

She didn't seem fazed by his abruptness. 'The guests have two bins at the side of the barn,' she said. 'Green for recycling, black for everything else. They're collected at the same time as mine.'

She was a good witness, giving thorough answers, Colin thought. Unless it was clever misdirection. 'When were the bins last collected?'

'Wednesday morning.'

Garnett had died on Thursday, so if the curry had been bought from a takeaway or a supermarket then the packaging was probably still in the bin.

'It was the recycling bin, this week; they're collected on alternate weeks,' she added. 'Is there a problem?'

'I'm afraid I can't discuss anything at the moment. However, I'll need to take the contents of both bins.'

She nodded. 'I've got some bin bags, if you need them. They're the sturdy sort – I use them for garden waste.'

Garden. He'd need to check that for foxgloves. 'Thank you, but I already have bags,' he said. 'I know you've already been through everything with Sergeant Kennedy and PC Khan, but could you talk me through it again?'

'Of course.' She paused. 'Look, I'm going to put the kettle on for myself. Are you sure I can't offer you a drink?'

Maybe drinking a mug of coffee with him would make her relax enough to tell him things she might not have realised she'd forgotten. 'Coffee, then, thanks. Black, no sugar.'

She busied herself making the drinks, then put the mug in front of him together with a plate of brownies before taking her seat opposite him again. 'Help yourself. Cesca from the farm shop brought them over earlier this afternoon.'

He thought about it – they looked and smelled wonderful – and then remembered the conversation he'd had with the practice nurse about his blood sugar levels at his six-monthly checkup. Swapping alcohol for sugar hadn't been a good solution. 'Thank you, but I'll pass. When was your first contact with Dr Garnett?'

'When he arrived here. He booked a three-week stay through the agency I use to let the holiday cottage, and they handle all the details. I get a note of the guests' names, address and contact details – oh, and any dietary requirements.'

'Dietary requirements?' he asked.

'I leave my guests a welcome pack,' she explained. 'Tea, coffee, milk, a loaf of bread and some biscuits. If anyone's gluten-free or dairy-free, then I tweak the welcome pack to suit.'

Kind and thoughtful: that didn't sit with being a murderer. Then again, didn't they say you could kill with kindness? 'Did Dr Garnett have any dietary requirements?'

'No.'

'Did he mention any kind of health issues or ask where the nearest pharmacy was?'

'No,' she said, 'though I've included the phone number of the pharmacy and the doctor's surgery in the barn's welcome pack.'

Colin made a note. 'What information do your guests receive before they come here?'

'My name and mobile number, directions to the barn and the number for the key safe,' she said.

'Do you use the same number for the key safe every time?'

Georgina shook her head. 'I change it with every new set of guests.'

Good. So she had some idea of security – even though he'd noticed that the kitchen windows didn't have locks, and the back door had a rim lock but no deadbolt. He'd get one of the team to have a quiet word with her about improving security. Although PC Kennedy had already asked the question, he thought it was worth double-checking. 'Who has access to the cottage, besides the guests?'

'Me, obviously; and Jodie, who cleans the barn for me. You've already got her keys. Young Tom, who does my garden, doesn't need access to the barn, but he spends a few minutes in the barn's courtyard every week to keep the troughs looking nice.'

He made another note. 'When did Dr Garnett arrive?'

'On Friday afternoon, three weeks ago. Fridays are changeover days. We ask guests to arrive after three and leave before eleven, so we can make sure the cottage has been thoroughly cleaned between bookings.'

Which made sense, and he remembered her comment earlier that day about cleaning being routine. 'Was Dr Garnett happy in his stay here?'

'He was disappointed,' she said, 'because I think he was expecting to have city amenities in a very rural area, and he wasn't expecting birdsong to be quite as loud as it is.'

Either Roland Garnett had been an academic who didn't live in the real world, or he'd been arrogant and obnoxious. Probably the latter, Colin thought, given both Hayley Summers' revelations and the fact that Garnett had clashed with other people since being here. 'What were the issues with your cleaner and the farm shop?'

'Dr Garnett,' Georgina said resignedly, 'was the sort of man who didn't respect personal space. Particularly that of young, pretty women – which was why they didn't want to be alone with him.'

Colin knew the sort. If anyone had treated his Cathy like that, he'd want to rip them apart with his bare hands. 'Did he behave like that towards you?'

'No. But I'm not a pretty girl in my twenties,' she said.

He looked at her, guessing that she was close to his own age, late forties or perhaps early fifties. But she was definitely pretty, with light-brown hair cut in a bob, green eyes and a heart-shaped face. She wasn't wearing make-up, and in his opinion she didn't need to.

'Plus,' she said, 'I understand if someone quotes Latin at me.' She fluttered her eyelashes. 'Amazingly, for a mere woman, I can even quote Latin back.'

He had to suppress a smile, knowing exactly what point she was making. Garnett had clearly been the type who liked to put people down with his erudite comments, particularly women. Colin was pretty sure that Georgina Drake had been scrupulously polite to her guest but had also made it clear that her intellect equalled his.

'Where would someone buy a curry around here?' he asked, watching her closely for the minutest flicker of guilt.

She looked surprised, then considered her answer. 'We're out of area for the takeaway delivery apps. There's an Indian takeaway in the next village – which is about five miles down the road – but you'd have to collect the food yourself. Or maybe buy a ready meal in the supermarket that you could stick in the microwave.'

It seemed unlikely that she was the cook, then. Or was she protecting someone? 'I understand that Roland bought ready meals from the farm shop. Could they have sold him a curry?'

She frowned. 'Is that what killed him? Curry?'

'It hasn't been confirmed,' he said.

'You wouldn't be asking me about curry specifically, unless the pathologist had told you that he'd eaten it,' she pointed out.

She was sharp-witted; he'd need to be careful.

'I have no idea what Cesca sold him – I didn't look in the delivery bag before I handed it over,' she continued, 'but the farm shop has a top hygiene rating and they're really careful about allergens, so I very much doubt they sold him anything that would've made him ill, let alone killed him.'

That definitely sounded protective. He'd need to have a word with Francesca Walters. 'Is there anywhere else locally where he could've eaten out?'

'There's at least one pub or restaurant that offers food in every village in a ten-mile radius, plus Norwich itself,' she said, 'but he would have needed transport to get there and back. I can give you the list of local taxi firms that I put in the holiday cottage information pack. I'm sure they'd be able to tell you whether he booked them.'

'Were you aware of any other visitors to the cottage?'

'No. As I told Sergeant Kennedy and PC Khan, even with hearing aids in my hearing isn't great, and I didn't hear any cars on the driveway. Anyone who visits the barn would park there, and a car wouldn't be visible from here.'

He made a note to check. 'When did you last see Roland?'

'Alive, yesterday afternoon. I had a hospital appointment this morning, so I knew I wouldn't be here when he left. I called in to wish him a safe journey home – as I do to all my guests – and to confirm where he'd need to leave the keys this morning.'

Colin noted she'd made the distinction about seeing him alive yesterday; she'd also been the one to find him dead this morning. 'Can you run me through your movements, this morning?'

'I drove to the hospital just outside Norwich for my appointment, and I picked up some groceries from the super-

market on the way home. I can give you the number of the audiology department if you want to confirm that, and forward you
the email with the electronic receipt from the shop.'

'Yes, to both, please,' he said. Though he'd watch her
forward the message, to make sure she didn't change anything
on it.

She picked up her phone. 'What's your email address?' she
asked.

He told her, and she forwarded him the receipt.

'Thank you. What happened next?'

'I put my shopping away. And then I went to clean the barn,
to get the bulk of the chores out of the way before lunch.' She
swallowed hard. 'When I opened the kitchen door, I could
smell vomit.'

It was a distinctive smell; he didn't bother quizzing her
further.

'I called out, thinking Dr Garnett might have been taken ill,
but he didn't answer – at least, not so I could hear him. I looked
in the living room, and his things were still there; his things
were also still in the bathroom. I found him in the bedroom. He
didn't have a pulse and he was cold, so there was no point in
even trying CPR. I came outside again and called the emergency services.'

Her story was identical to the notes he'd read. Either she'd
had time to learn her story off pat, or she was telling the truth.
So what was he missing?

'What do you know about chemicals?' he asked, hoping to
catch her off guard. He could ask her straight out about digoxin
– but what if another poison was similar? He'd start with a
general question and then narrow it down.

'What sort of chemicals?'

'Any,' he said.

'My son, Will, is a chemist,' she said. 'But I'm afraid I can't
actually tell you what he does. He works at Porton Down.'

Which, Colin knew, meant that whatever Will Drake did was covered by the Official Secrets Act. But, if Will was close to his mother, would she have picked up knowledge about chemicals and poisons through him? Could he have brought something to the house that had ended up in Roland Garnett's curry, accidentally or otherwise?

'I see. Anything else?'

'I use the same kind of household ones that everyone does, though I use eco versions where I can,' she said. 'And I develop my own black-and-white pictures; I keep the photographic chemicals in my darkroom.'

Were they anything that could mimic the effects of digoxin, if ingested? 'What kind of chemicals?' he asked.

'Let me show you,' she said, standing up. 'It's the one thing I've changed about the house. A local builder made me a darkroom out of a corner of the utility room.' She led him through one of the oak plank doors into a cream-painted room with the same pamment flooring as the kitchen and similar cream-painted cupboards, along with a washing machine and a tumble dryer.

One window looked out towards the front of the house – where you might see a car driving up to the farm from the road – and the other looked across the fields to the side. Colin wandered over casually and glanced out. He could see the garden, but not the barn.

'If you want to look in the cupboard where I keep my photographic paper, I'll need to close the door behind us and use a safe light,' she said, 'otherwise the paper will all be ruined. Or you can just take my word for it and look at the chemicals.'

'I need to be thorough,' he said.

'In that case, I'll need you to keep your phone in your pocket, to avoid any leaks of light.' She removed the fitness watch from her wrist and put it on the worktop next to the sink. 'I hate this thing. It's useful because it buzzes on my wrist when my phone rings, so I know someone's calling me – but it also lights up the room at random.'

He felt exactly the same way about fitness watches. He'd bought one after the nurse had given him a sheet on an effective exercise routine, but the watch's constant nagging about doing more steps with its cheery 'time to move!' message had made him dump it in the back of a drawer within a week. Now he just walked along the river every evening after work and tried not to think.

Georgina opened the plank door to a small windowless room, ushered him inside, then turned on a red lamp before closing the door behind them.

'No light comes in through the door?' he asked, surprised.

'The planks, you mean?' She shook her head. 'I wanted the outside of the door to look in place with the rest of the house, but the inside is lined properly so I can work here.'

The room was very sparsely furnished, and immaculately tidy. There was a sink; a bench with a bit of equipment he didn't recognise, a manual timer and three different-coloured lidded trays with matching tongs; a cupboard; and what looked like a washing line with some clips on it.

'Let me give you the quick and dirty guide to developing photographs,' she said. 'You need to process the film, first, but the chemicals are pretty much the same. Once you've processed the film, you can make your prints. You start with an enlarger.' She indicated the equipment with a lens. 'You use that to project the negative onto the paper. The tray nearest to the enlarger contains the developer, which makes the image appear on the paper; the next one's the stop, which stops the image developing any further; and the final one's the fixative, which keeps the image in place. Once you've exposed the image on the paper, you put it through each tray of chemical in turn – setting the timer accordingly – then wash it and hang it up to dry.' She gestured to the cupboard. 'Paper's in the left side, chemicals and equipment in the right. I'll spare you the lecture about different sorts of paper; I can bore for England on the subject.'

She thought she was boring? She could read the phone book out to him and he wouldn't get tired of her voice. He quickly squashed the thought. This was work and, as the owner of the place where Roland Garnett had died, she was involved in the case. He duly opened the cupboard and checked the paper, the bottles of chemicals and the small box of equipment. 'What's all this for?'

'A cap remover to take the end off the film cylinder, a spiral to put the film on, scissors to cut the film off the cylinder and the light-safe developer tank to process the film – that's the bit you do in complete darkness, because even a safe light will wreck the film,' she explained. 'You can do everything else with the light on.'

'Can I have samples of the chemicals?' he asked.

'Yes. I tend to use the liquid form, which is a bit less hazardous than mixing powder. Don't get the chemicals on your hands, because they're irritants,' she said. 'I use tongs when I'm transferring the paper between baths, as well as wearing goggles and gloves.'

She seemed very aware of the hazards of her chemicals, he thought. 'Could anyone have accidentally drunk any of these chemicals?'

'No. Apart from the fact that I'm the only one who uses this room, I keep everything in the original packaging. Nobody could mistake developing solution or what have you for a soft drink or alcohol,' she said. 'If you take photographs of the labels, you can see the hazard symbols and the precise contents. I've been experimenting with homemade eco products as alternatives, but they're basically household chemicals – white vinegar, salt and the like.'

'And the chemicals in your trays on the bench – do they stay there all the time?'

'You use them until they stop working,' she said. 'It's more eco.'

'I'd expect chemicals to smell.'

She smiled. 'If I didn't have a good ventilation system, they would. It's a vinegary smell – not that I'd advise taking a big sniff from an opened bottle.' She closed the cupboard where the paper was kept. 'Do you have containers for the samples?'

'I do,' he said. 'In the car.'

'I assume you want me to accompany you while you fetch them, so you can be sure I haven't tampered with the contents of my darkroom in your absence,' she said.

'Have you worked with the police before?' he asked.

'No, but it's common sense. If I'm the last person who saw Roland Garnett alive, and you're not certain what killed him, everything's suspicious.'

Was that really calm common sense talking, or was she double bluffing?

'Where do you want me to decant the chemicals?' he asked.

'I assume you want to sample the chemicals in the trays as well as the opened bottles,' she said, 'so the darkroom's the obvious choice. Though I'd ask you to use separate pipettes for each kind, please, so you don't contaminate the trays.'

That sounded reasonable. He went out to his car with her to collect his sampling kit, then followed her back into the dark-room to collect and label the samples in turn. Because he wasn't going inspect the cupboard with her photographic paper again, she turned on the overhead light rather than the safe light, this time, so he could photograph the labels of the bottles easily.

'Is there anything else I should know about?' he asked.

'Are you asking me under caution?'

Colin felt his eyes widen. She'd said she hadn't worked with the police before, but maybe he'd asked the wrong question. 'Do you have police experience?'

'No, but my daughter's an actor and had a small part in a

police drama, last year,' she said. 'Let's just say she researches her roles thoroughly, and I helped her learn her lines with a read-through of the script.'

He nodded. 'I'm not asking you under caution. I haven't arrested you.' And he could see from her expression that she'd picked up the unspoken 'yet'.

'Apart from the stuff in the darkroom, there's just the household stuff I told you about. You're welcome to take samples of those, too.'

Until he knew precisely what had killed Roland Garnett, everything was on the possible list. 'Yes, please.'

Once he'd taken the samples, labelled them and put them in evidence bags, he looked at her. 'I'll go and collect the bins. If you could give me that list of taxis, too, I'd be grateful.'

'Of course.' She paused. 'Actually, can I ask you something?'

'I might not be able to answer,' he warned.

'It's not to do with Dr Garnett or the investigation,' she added hastily. 'I was wondering where's the best place to find inquest reports?'

'The coroner's office would be the best place to start. The reports for the last seventy-five years are closed to the public, however – unless you have a valid reason for hearing a recording or seeing a transcript, and the coroner will decide that,' he said. 'Why?'

'I'm looking into the history of the house. I know there was an accident here, about fifty years ago, and I wanted to find out some more information about it.'

Given that she'd asked about an inquest, the accident must have been fatal; though it was unlikely to have anything to do with the death of Roland Garnett. 'Unless you have a direct connection to the case, you're unlikely to get access to the coroner's records,' he said. 'You could try the local newspaper records instead. They have to report what was said accurately, though there are some things they're not allowed to report at all.'

'Thank you. I'll print out the list of taxis and bring it out to you,' she said.

Colin checked the view from the kitchen side window; it was the same as the utility room. The back door and the window over the sink overlooked the garden. He'd check the garden once he'd collected the evidence.

He'd just finished bagging up the contents of the bins when Georgina walked into the courtyard and handed him a folded sheet of paper. 'The taxis,' she said.

'Thank you,' he said. 'Last thing. Could you show me round your garden?'

'Sure. I can't tell you what all the plants are, because it was put together by the previous owner of the house. I don't have particularly green fingers, so Sybbie – Lady Wyatt – put me in touch with Young Tom. He's her gardener's grandson. If you need information, he's probably the best one to ask. I can give you his details, if you like.'

'Yes, please.'

She wasn't wrong about being a lacklustre tour guide; he probably knew more of the plant names than she did. There were plenty of pretty cottage-garden plants, drifts of bright blue forget-me-nots nestled around clumps of red tulips, plus rose bushes and lavender that would clearly make the garden smell amazing when they bloomed in the summer. There was a weathered brick wall around two sides of the garden that supported a lean-to wooden greenhouse full of pots containing tomato plants, cucumbers and peppers; the rest of the walls were taken up with espaliered apple trees and more roses. The vegetable patch was organised a bit like an old-fashioned knot garden, with raised beds and gravel borders; Colin could see carrots, potatoes and a large clump of rhubarb, plus some canes that were clearly there to support runner beans and the like.

But no foxgloves.

'Do you have any herbs?' he asked.

'I have pots of parsley, basil, thyme and coriander on the kitchen windowsill. They're the ones I tend to use most,' she said.

No comfrey or borage, he noted, the other things that Sammy Granger had mentioned. But Georgina was clearly a cook. 'Do the guests have access to your garden?'

'No. Well, I suppose they could walk up the path from the barn through the garden to my house – but, unless there's a problem with the cottage, they wouldn't need to,' she said. 'They'd call me, first.'

'Thank you. You've been very helpful. If you can send me your gardener's details, I'd appreciate it,' he said. 'I'm sorry. I know it's not very nice that you can't clean up.'

Her mouth thinned. 'It's rather worse for Dr Garnett's family, because they've lost him.'

He remembered she was a widow; she was clearly talking from recent experience. 'I'm sorry,' he said again, knowing the words were completely inadequate. 'We'll be in touch as soon as we can.'

She inclined her head. 'Thank you.'

'One last thing,' he said. 'Do you take any medication?'

'Is that relevant?'

'It might be,' he said.

She grimaced. 'I was on antidepressants, when I first came here, but I've weaned myself off them and I don't have any in the house, anymore. The only medication I do have is some paracetamol, and that might not be in date.'

No kind of heart medication, then. Unless she was lying – and he didn't think she was – that ruled that out as a line of enquiry. 'I appreciate your help, Mrs Drake.'

'You're welcome, Inspector Bradshaw.'

FIVE

'I still think he's hot,' Doris said when Georgina came back into the kitchen and tidied up, tipping the inspector's half-drunk coffee down the sink before washing up. 'Tall, dark and gorgeous. And those eyes!'

Georgina couldn't help smiling, even though the visit had unsettled her. 'That's probably because his first name's Colin. Though I should remind you that his surname isn't Firth. Or Darcy.'

'No.' Doris's voice sobered. 'I was standing behind him when he was writing notes. Something about asking Young Tom about foxgloves.'

'Why?' Georgina asked. 'Surely he doesn't think that Young Tom has anything to do with Dr Garnett's death?'

'At the moment, I don't think he's ruled out anyone. He took all those chemical samples from you.'

'I didn't kill Roland Garnett. I didn't like him, but he was meant to be leaving this morning – so even if I had wanted to kill him, it would've been a bit pointless because I didn't have to put up with him for much longer.'

'I guess,' Doris said. 'What happens now?'

'I have to wait for them to finish doing their investigations,' Georgina said.

Doris coughed. 'I know it's selfish, but I didn't mean that.'

'You mean your situation?' Of course she should've thought about that. 'Jodie's going to have a word with her grandmother to see if she remembers anything – I've told her I'm researching the house history. In the meantime, I'll find out what I can from the internet. I assume you heard what Inspector Bradshaw said about the coroner's report.'

'Yes. We'll have to start with the newspaper archive – or, rather, you will, because I won't be able to go with you.'

'Unless it's been digitised and it's available online. I'll ask Bea what other sources we can use, and we'll make a list of what we need to know.' Georgina paused. 'Do you mind me looking you up, Doris?'

'It feels strange,' Doris said, 'but I suppose it's the only way you're going to get any information.'

'Apart from what you can tell me,' Georgina said. 'And then I'll find a paper trail to back it up – not that I don't believe a word you tell me, but if we have to talk to someone else, we'll need proof.'

'And you can hardly tell them that a ghost told you,' Doris said. 'A ghost you can't see.'

'And who doesn't clank chains, say "whoo, whoo" or walk through walls,' Georgina added.

'All right. My parents are Elizabeth – everyone called her Lizzy – and Albert, and my brother's Jack.'

'Hang on. Let me make notes.' Georgina sketched a rough family tree in her reporter's notebook. 'Dates of birth, marriage and death would be helpful. Maiden names, if you know them, and middle names.'

Doris duly gave her the details. 'When we were small, our grandparents lived here, too – Edward and May. My dad took over the farm when his father retired, and Jack was going to take over from Dad.' Doris paused. 'Except, after I died, Dad sold up. The people who bought the place, the Norton family, stayed here until 2001, when they lost their stock to foot-and-mouth. The farm was empty for a year or so, and then the land and the house were sold in separate lots. The house was renovated and sold again about ten years ago, to the people you bought from – they're the ones who got planning permission to use the old dairy as holiday accommodation and turned it into Rookery Barn.'

'As well as revamping the garden.'

'In my day,' Doris said, 'the greenhouse was there, but the vegetable garden was a lot bigger and without any gravel, and there were half a dozen apple trees. Three Bramleys and three eating apples – Coxes, I think. The rest of it was lawn. Mum had a couple of rosebushes but, between the farm and looking after us, she didn't have a lot of time for flowers.'

Georgina finished making notes. 'Thank you. That's a great starting point.' She tapped her pen on the page. 'I really need to let the kids know about what's happened here,' she said. 'Though forgive me if I don't mention you. Will'll be worried, and Bea will rush straight here.'

'I'm still not entirely sure that you believe me,' Doris said. 'I can't push a glass off a table, or make a door bang, or give you any other sign to prove that I'm here.' She paused. 'Do you know anyone with the same hearing aids as yours? What if they could hear me? Or if someone listened through yours – would they hear me?'

'I don't know anyone else with these ones,' Georgina said. 'And I think the answer's probably not, though. Inside the hearing aid is this tiny computer that's programmed specifically to match my pattern of hearing loss, which they find when they do the audiology tests. If the aids are switched on and not in my ears, all people can hear is this loud, screechy whistling noise. But it was a good question. Maybe I can try it with Bea or Will, next time they come to stay. But, in the meantime, I'll ask Bea for some help.' She typed a quick message into her phone. *Video call tonight at seven? Nothing to worry about, but I need to talk to you both. Love you, Mum xx* She sent the message to Bea and Will, then added a second message to Bea. *Finally researching the history of the house. Where's the best place to start? Any online local newspapers? Love you, Mum xx*

'It might be a while before Bea gets back to me,' she warned Doris. 'If she's at an audition or doing a shift for the probate genealogy people, she won't pick up any messages until she's finished.'

'I've waited fifty years. Waiting a few more hours isn't going to make much difference,' Doris said.

'Are there likely to be any photos of you online?' Georgina asked. 'School photos, or anything like that?'

'I doubt it. If you can find my brother, he might have some,' Doris said. 'Or you could try taking a photo of me.'

'I can't see you, so it's highly unlikely a camera lens can,' Georgina said, wanting to let Doris down gently.

'What about those ghost-hunter programmes? They said that ghosts show up as orbs or spots on a photograph.'

Georgina bit her lip, hating the fact that she was going to burst Doris's bubble but having no other option. 'That's their sales pitch, Doris. There's a more practical explanation.'

'Which is?'

'Either a lens flare – the reflection of a light, that causes streaks and polygons – or something that's out of focus so it turns into a blurry shape,' Georgina said. 'If it's a circle, it's probably dust or an insect; if it's an oval, it's likely to be a rain-drop or snowflake; and if it's a random shape, it'll be dust or a hair on the camera's lens or sensor.'

'Right.' Doris sounded disappointed. 'What about those photos where you see a hand where it shouldn't be, or there's a figure sitting in the back of the car?'

'For the hand, it'd be a long exposure, and the person moved; for the person in the car, it'd be either a reflection or a double exposure.'

'Or the ones where there's a blurry face in the background?'

'Pareidolia – the human mind sees patterns and tries to make them into something that makes sense. Like the face in Cydonia on Mars,' Georgina said.

'The what face?' Doris asked.

'The supposed face in pictures taken by the Viking Orbiter in the 1970s – it's all to do with the light and the angle of viewing, and the pictures being low-resolution. Here.' Georgina flicked into her laptop and brought up the photographs, along with more modern high-resolution images.

'When you see it properly, it's not a face at all.' Doris sounded hugely disappointed. 'So you can't take a picture of me.'

No. But Georgina felt oddly protective of the teenager whose life had been cut tragically short. 'I can try,' she said. She took one of the chairs and placed it against the kitchen cabinets. 'We'll do a few shots against a light background, and then I'll tuck a tablecloth inside the top cabinets and shut the doors so it drapes down behind you as a dark background.' She opened a drawer and took out a dark red tablecloth. 'Let me know when you're sitting in the chair. I'll use my film camera as well as my digital one – and my phone, so we cover all possibilities.'

'OK.' Doris's voice sounded slightly quavery. 'I'm sitting. Do you want me to smile?'

It wouldn't make a scrap of difference because Georgina knew the photograph would be of an empty chair. And how ridiculous was it that she was trying to reassure a ghost, the way she'd get a client to relax? At the same time, Georgina knew that if today was the first time she'd had a real conversation with anyone for fifty years, she'd be all over the place emotionally.

She understood exactly where Doris was coming from. 'Relax. Imagine you're seeing Trev.'

She heard a muffled sob, and knew she'd react the same way if someone told her to imagine she was seeing Stephen again: she'd feel that same black hole of loss, knowing that imagination was the only thing she'd ever have now. They needed a safer subject to make Doris relax. Given that Doris had wanted to teach English, books might be better. 'What's your favourite poem?'

'Shakespeare. Sonnet 130.' Doris's voice still sounded wobbly.

'Hold that thought,' Georgina said gently. 'I'm going to get my cameras. Then I want you to read me the poem while I take the photographs. Can you do that?'

'Yes. I don't need a book. I know it off by heart.' There was a pause. 'I wanted Dad to read Shakespeare at my wedding.'

'Mine read Sonnet 116,' Georgina said, her eyes pricking with tears at the memory. Twenty-seven years ago. She'd lost both her father and her husband, since then.

'That's the one I wanted mine to read,' Doris said. 'You and me – I think we're a lot alike.'

A ghost and a lonely woman who worked with images that looked like ghosts as they developed in a tray. 'You're right. We are,' Georgina said softly.

She fetched her cameras and a mini tripod, and set them on the kitchen table next to her phone. 'I'm going to try a range of exposures, and I'm going to do a set with infra-red film, using my first ever SLR camera. Ready?'

'*My mistress' eyes are nothing like the sun,*' was the answer.

Georgina smiled. 'Keep going, Doris. We have work to do.' And she clicked the first shot.

* * *

Georgina spent the rest of the afternoon in the darkroom; even though she could see nothing in the prints but the still life of the chair against the ancient pamment flooring and the kitchen cabinets or the tablecloth, she enjoyed the discipline of developing the films, making test prints to check the exposure, then printing all the negatives before hanging them up to dry. Apart from the shoot that had introduced her to Francesca and Sybbie, it was the first time she'd really enjoyed working since she'd moved here – and that was all thanks to Doris.

She'd just finished in the darkroom and had put the kettle on in the kitchen when her watch vibrated to signal an incoming call on her mobile.

Shocked, she realised it was gone seven o'clock – when she'd said she'd call the children.

'Mum? Is everything all right?' Will asked when Georgina answered the video call.

'Sorry. I was in the darkroom and lost track of time,' she said, switching off the kettle so the noise of the boiling water didn't drown out Bea and Will's voices.

'Did you shoot anything interesting?' Bea asked.

'Still life. Messing about with arty stuff,' Georgina said. It wasn't a complete fib. But she wasn't ready to tell her children that she'd spent the afternoon talking to a ghost; she didn't want them thinking she'd gone mad.

'What did you want to talk to us about?' Will asked.

She took a deep breath and sat down at the kitchen table, propping her phone against a mug and changing the display so she could see both her children on the screen. 'First off, I don't want either of you to start worrying, OK?'

'That in itself is worrying, Mum,' Bea pointed out. 'What's happened?'

'Dr Garnett – the guest staying in the barn – died,' Georgina said. 'The police think it was a heart attack brought on by choking on his own vomit.' Vomit caused by a poisoned chicken curry, given DI Bradshaw's questions about curry, chemicals and foxgloves, but Bea and Will didn't need to know that. 'But, because he hadn't been seeing a doctor, it means they have to treat it as a suspicious death. The barn's sealed off until the pathologist's finished doing the autopsy and all the tests are back.'

'If I leave now, I can be with you before midnight,' Will said, his mouth thinning.

'Honestly, love, there's no need to rush here,' Georgina said. 'And that goes for you, too, Bea. I found him in the barn this morning –'

'This *morning*? And you left it until *now* to tell us?' Bea interrupted, looking horrified.

'You were both at work, and there was nothing either of you could have done,' Georgina pointed out.

'We could've supported you,' Will said. 'How come you were the one to find him?'

'I went to clean the barn, and it was obvious something had happened,' Georgina admitted.

'Oh, Mum. That must've been so hard.' Bea's voice thickened. 'Are you all right? And I mean *really* all right, not putting a brave face on it.'

'I'm fine,' Georgina insisted.

'But you're on your own, and someone's died. At least let one of us come down for the weekend and be with you,' Will said.

'It's fine. Don't drag yourselves all the way up to Norfolk. You've got your own lives to lead, and I have no intention of being one of these helpless old ladies who depend on their children to do everything for them and expect them to be around virtually all the time,' Georgina said.

'You're never going to be a helpless old lady, Mum,' Bea said, laughing. She sobered. 'But this isn't a normal weekend. You found a dead body.'

'I promise you don't need to worry about me. And I'm not on my own, Will. Cesca and Jodie are looking in on me.' Georgina decided not to mention Doris. 'If I need anything, I can call one of them.'

'I wish you had a dog,' Will said. 'It'd make you safer.'

'Oh, Will, stop nagging. We've been through this. It wouldn't be fair to dump the poor dog in kennels every time I had to go on location for a shoot,' Georgina pointed out.

'When was the last time you even went on a shoot?' Bea asked. 'I know you did that session with Lady Wyatt, but have you done any portraits since?'

'Yes,' Georgina said, knowing that it was technically true and false at the same time. How could she admit to trying to take a portrait of a ghost, a couple of hours ago?

'If you had a rescue dog, one that was already housetrained and reliable, it could go on shoots with you,' Will said. 'And then Bea and I wouldn't worry about you so much. It'd be company for you, too.'

'A dog would be great,' Doris chipped in. 'We used to have Labradors.'

Georgina sincerely hoped that neither of her children had heard the other resident of the house talking.

'Think about it, Mum,' Bea said, and Georgina almost sagged with relief that her daughter clearly hadn't heard Doris.

'I'll think about it,' she promised, purely to mollify them. 'I just wanted to explain the situation here and reassure you both that everything's fine.'

'Hmm,' Will said.

'And, as I messaged you earlier, Bea, I'm going to start researching the history of the house,' Georgina added. 'That'll keep me busy.'

'At last! I'm sending you some links in an email, to give you some ideas where to start,' Bea promised.

'Thank you. That'd be really helpful.' Georgina established

that everything was fine in Salisbury and London, and Bea had an audition next week. After wishing her daughter luck, promising both children that she'd be in touch if she was worried about anything, and telling them she loved them, she ended the call.

'They're nice kids,' Doris said. 'You're close to them.'

Georgina nodded. 'They were close to their dad, too.'

'If my mum had been more like you...' Doris sighed. 'Sorry. Technically, I'm old enough to be your mum.'

'And yet at the same time you're eighteen, which makes you younger than my children,' Georgina said. 'I wish things had been different for you, but I'll do my best to help.'

'You already are, with the photographs. Did you see any sign of me?' Doris asked hopefully.

'I haven't looked at them properly, yet. Let me go and get them.' Georgina fetched the prints and spread them across the table in columns. 'OK. These are the ones from my digital camera.'

'No orbs. No streaks. Nothing,' Doris said.

'These ones are from the film camera.' Again, there were no anomalies on the photographs. 'And here are the infra-red shots.'

'There's just the chair – and there isn't even a dent in the cushion.' Doris sounded miserable.

Georgina checked the photos on her phone, transferring them to her laptop and enlarging them. 'No anomalies on the phone pics, either. I'm sorry. I know that's disappointing.'

'Right now,' Doris said, 'I don't think I want to talk.'

'I understand.' Georgina paused. 'If I could see you and touch you, Doris, I'd give you a hug, make you a hot chocolate and one of Bea's chocolate mug cakes, and put on a film to cheer you up. I can't do most of that, but if you want to sit on the sofa with me and watch a film of your choice, it's probably the nearest I can get to making you feel a bit better.'

There was silence, and for a moment she thought Doris had gone.

But then there was an audible gulp. 'I can't remember the last time someone was kind to me, before today. The days all blur into one. But you've been amazing.'

'I'll do whatever I can to help you,' Georgina promised. 'Let me make myself a cup of tea and a sandwich, and in the meantime think about what you want to see.'

'I already know. It's not a film, but if you don't mind watching *Pride and Prejudice*?' Doris asked hopefully.

'And I know which version you want,' Georgina said with a smile. 'You're on. We'll do the whole lot.'

* * *

On Saturday morning, Colin was sitting in his office, checking through the timeline of the Garnett case, when his phone shrilled.

He picked it up. 'DI Bradshaw.'

'It's Sammy Granger. I've got the results back from the tox screen.'

'And it's digoxin?' Colin guessed. 'Someone, somehow, slipped him a heart drug?'

'Something a bit more unusual actually, that acts in a similar way,' Sammy said. 'I found oleandrin glycosides.'

'Which is?'

'It's a compound formed from a sugar in plants – in this case, oleander,' she said. At his silence, she continued. 'That's a large shrub. Most cases of oleander poisoning are animals – cows or horses, where the leaves have fallen into their field and the animals have eaten them. And there's a case where someone committed suicide by boiling the leaves and drinking the liquid, but the guy left notes on everything to warn whoever found him that it was poisonous. It's stable when heated – boiling it doesn't make it less toxic.' She paused. 'Though apparently it's very bitter, so you'd notice the taste.'

'But it could've been disguised in the curry?'

'Yes. The victim had also drunk vodka, which might've stopped him noticing the taste.'

He blew out a breath. 'So we could have other potential cases, depending on where he bought the curry.'

'Or he made it himself. He could've ingested it intentionally,' Sammy pointed out.

'To kill himself?'

'Not necessarily. There's a lot of dangerous nonsense on the internet,' Sammy said. 'And if people are worried about their health and either can't or don't want to see a doctor, they might turn to alternative routes. Not that I'm saying all alternative medicine's quackery but, if you don't know what you're doing and you self-medicate, you can end up in trouble.'

'Why would people take oleandrin?' Colin asked.

'According to the medical journals, it's been a folk medicine for heart problems, asthma, skin conditions and cancer, but no clinical trials have supported it. And there was some really dangerous stuff on the internet promoting it as a cure for viruses, which it absolutely isn't. The leaves, flowers, seeds and roots are all poisonous.' She paused. 'Basically, within a couple of hours after eating the stuff, he would've started suffering gastric symptoms – nausea, vomiting and abdominal pain. He might've felt dizzy, confused or had visual disturbances. If he'd taken enough of it, then his heartbeat would've slowed and gone into an arrhythmia. After that, without medical treatment, it'd progress to seizures, coma and death.'

'If he died at around one in the morning, that means he would've eaten the oleander at some point between about six and nine p.m. – vomiting would've started at say eight to eleven p.m., then it would've taken a couple more hours for him to die,'

Colin said. 'Thank you, Sammy. Where would someone buy oleandrin?'

'The internet?' she suggested. 'Unless you know someone with a plant who'll let you take a cutting.'

Roland Garnett allegedly hadn't been a cook; but had he been a gardener? Colin wondered. Sammy's information had just raised a whole new set of questions – and a few new lines of enquiry. He made a note to ask Roland Garnett's ex-wife about the gardening.

'If it was from a plant, then could it have been cooked in the curry?'

'I'll analyse his stomach contents further and let you know,' she said.

'Thanks, Sammy. That's very helpful. I'll wait for your report,' he said. And in the meantime he needed to check Roland Garnett's computer history, his bank account and his phone records.

SIX

Georgina sat at the kitchen table early on Saturday morning, her laptop open on the genealogy website Bea had recommended and a mug of coffee next to her.

'Sorry for making you stay up so late last night,' Doris said.

Georgina smiled. 'Don't apologise. I promised you the full *Pride and Prejudice* marathon.' And it had been fun, discussing books and their favourite bits of Austen. She hadn't done that for a while, and she knew that for Doris it had been even longer.

'I still feel guilty. You're a lark rather than an owl.'

'The occasional late night won't ki—' Georgina stopped. Given the fact she was talking to a ghost, and the dead body she'd found in Rookery Barn yesterday, that was definitely the wrong turn of phrase. 'You know what I mean. Nothing that an extra mug of coffee won't sort out. Now, before I start this, are you prepared for whatever I find?'

'For Mum and Dad to no longer be alive, you mean? Yes. They'd be in their early nineties now, if they're still here. But I hope Jack's doing OK.' Doris paused. 'And Trev.'

'I'll do my best, but I might not get that far today,' Georgina warned.

An hour later, she'd confirmed that Doris's father had died ten years ago and was buried in the churchyard of the village they'd moved to after leaving Little Wenborough, but there was no mention of her mother's death. Doris's brother, Jack, had married in 1980, and had two grown-up children, Matthew and Lucy.

'A niece and a nephew. That's wonderful. Though I didn't know Tracey, his wife,' Doris said, clearly reading over Georgina's shoulder. 'Can I ask you a weird favour?'

There was nothing non-weird about this whole situation, talking to a ghost and researching things for her, Georgina thought. 'Sure.'

'Would you mind taking some flowers to Dad's grave for me? I mean, I know it'll be a drive for you, because he's buried the other side of Norwich, not here in Little Wenborough, but...'

'Of course I will,' Georgina said. 'Would you like some from the garden, or shall I nip to the garden centre?'

'From the garden would be lovely,' Doris said. 'Those purple wallflowers near the greenhouse are gorgeous. He would've loved them.'

'Then that's what I'll take,' Georgina promised.

* * *

Colin checked the university website for term dates. Teaching didn't start again until Tuesday; today was Saturday, so it was pretty unlikely he'd be able to find anyone free to talk to him. All the same, he tried calling St Bene't's College, and was met with a recorded message telling him that nobody was available to take his call and there was no facility to leave a message; he could either call back during office hours, from nine to four Monday to Friday, or send an email via the college's website.

He did at least have the notes from the preliminary interviews with the Ropers. Betty Roper corroborated what Hayley Summers had said, adding that Garnett blamed them for Hayley leaving and they were barely on speaking terms with him. He would need to follow up with Hayley about that. According to her, he tormented the neighbours on the other side with loud music. They'd called the council about it, but nothing had ever happened.

Geoff Roper had said something much more interesting, though: that Garnett had poisoned their old cat a couple of years ago and he hoped Garnett would rot in hell.

It might be a coincidence that both the cat and Roland Garnett had died from poison, but Colin didn't believe in coincidences.

The PC who'd done the interview had been thorough, and had also emailed the file concerning the poisoning incident. It seemed Garnett had taken exception to the Ropers' cat doing its business in his garden. The situation had escalated, and he'd stuffed the offending cat faeces through their letter box; they'd called the police, who'd logged it as a domestic. And then, two weeks later, the Ropers had found their cat lying dead, poisoned. Again, they'd gone to the police; but, with no evidence that Garnett had administered the poison, they'd had to drop the complaint.

People tended to be very attached to their pets. Was it possible, he wondered, that the Ropers had sought revenge for their cat, by poisoning Garnett?

He'd definitely do a follow-up interview.

* * *

Albert Beauchamp, 1927—2013. Dearly loved husband, father and grandfather.

The words on the headstone were simple and understated; there was a space beneath the words, clearly waiting for his wife to join him. Georgina noticed that the headstone was kept clean from moss, and the red silk roses in the vase seemed relatively new. Given that Lizzy Beauchamp was in her nineties, Georgina guessed that Doris's brother, Jack, or his wife were the ones who tended the grave. She was glad she'd thought to bring a jam jar filled with water, and unscrewed the lid before putting the bunch of wallflowers into it.

'Doris asked me to bring these,' she said quietly. 'I hope I'll be able to reunite you.'

There was no answer, and she realised with a start that she'd half expected one. Which was probably what came of spending too much time on her own.

Quietly, she took a photograph of the grave with the flowers, followed by a couple of the flint church and the churchyard, and finally one of the sheep grazing in the field next to the church. Then she drove back to Little Wenborough. On impulse, she left her car in the church car park and wandered through the churchyard.

It took her a while, but eventually she found the grave she was looking for. *Doris Beauchamp, 3 November, 1952 – 14 February, 1971. Loved by all who knew her.* As with her father's grave, there was a vase of newish-looking silk roses – this time pink – though the grey headstone was starting to weather. Next to the roses was a plastic push-in pot, filled with pink carnations.

Someone had clearly visited the grave recently. A week to ten days ago, Georgina thought, given that the edges of some of the carnations' petals were starting to shrivel. There hadn't been fresh flowers on Albert Beauchamp's grave; surely Jack would've put fresh flowers on his father's grave as well as his sister's? Frowning slightly, she took a snap of the grave, then headed back to the farmhouse.

'Well?' Doris barely gave her the chance to get through the kitchen door. 'Did you find Dad's grave?'

'Are you sure this isn't going to upset you?' Georgina asked, taking her shoes off and leaving them on the rack in the utility room.

'It probably is,' Doris admitted, 'but it'll upset me more if I don't know.'

Georgina flicked into her phone's photo app. 'Here's the grave,' she said, putting the phone on the table so Doris could see the photograph. 'Red silk roses.'

'That's nice,' Doris said. 'Dad loved his roses.'

'I wasn't sure if you knew the church where he was buried,' Georgina said, 'so I took a photo.' She flicked to the next image.

'It's pretty. Looks as if there's nice glass.'

'I didn't go inside. I will, next time,' Georgina promised. 'And this one's the view from the churchyard.'

'Sheep. That's lovely, too. Very Thomas Hardy. We used to have sheep as well as cattle. I can remember sitting in front of the fire, bottle-feeding a lamb,' Doris said. 'Their little tails spin round when they take the milk.'

'So you enjoyed some of the farming life?' Georgina asked.

'Everyone loves newborn lambs,' Doris said. 'But, yes, I still dreamed of moving to London. Buying clothes in the King's Road. Trying things on in the Biba shop. The freedom of not living in a small village where everyone knows you and your entire family, and gossip spreads faster than the wind.'

'The city can often be a lonely place,' Georgina pointed out.

'But so can a village,' Doris said. 'I know there were a few in Little Wenborough who thought I had ideas above my station, wanting to be a teacher when I should've settled for being a housewife on a farm. And Trev, thinking he was the next big thing – when all he wanted to do was play his guitar and teach music.' She paused. 'You know you'll have to live here for thirty years before they stop calling you a foreigner and running on about how you Londoners buy up everything so the local kids will never be able to afford their own places when they grow up.'

'Everyone's been lovely to me. Cesca, Jodie, Sybbie, Young Tom and Old Tom. Times change, Doris. People change. Attitudes change,' Georgina said gently.

'Sorry. I guess I'm a bit out of sorts. Dad's like me – and yet he's not. I'm still cut off.' Doris swallowed hard.

'You're not cut off from me. And I'm trying to find things to help,' Georgina said. 'I took another photo, in the churchyard here.'

'Of my grave, you mean?' Doris paused. 'I don't think I'm ready to see it. Not yet.'

'That's completely understandable. I'll wait until you're ready. But I thought you'd like to know it's kept nicely, like your dad's but with pink silk roses.'

'That'd be Jack,' Doris said.

'And pink carnations.'

'What, real ones?' Doris sounded surprised.

'Real ones,' Georgina confirmed.

'Surely Mum can't be up to putting fresh flowers on my grave.' Doris paused. 'You could ask Jack what he knows about it.'

'I need to get in touch with him, first. And I need to take it steadily,' Georgina reminded her. 'I know you really want to speak to him and your mum again, but I can't tell them about you straight away – and they might not be able to hear you.'

'I suppose.' Doris sighed. 'Sorry. At my age I should've grown out of having teenage strops.'

'You said yourself that time blurs for you,' Georgina said. 'Don't be too hard on yourself. In some ways, you're still only eighteen – and that's not an easy age. I'm going to see if your brother's on social media, or if he's involved in any local organisations that have an email address for him or will pass a message on. And then I'll message him, tell him I'm researching the history of the house and ask if he can tell me anything about the farm or has any photos.'

* * *

Georgina was making coffee when there was a rap on the back door and it opened.

Two seconds later, she was enveloped in a bear hug, then released to receive a second tight hug.

'Will! Bea!' She beamed at them. 'It's lovely to see you both, but didn't I tell you not to rush over? Everything's fine.'

'And you really think we wouldn't want to see that for ourselves, Mum?' Will asked. 'I drove to Bea's last night.'

'In time for the best jollof rice in Camden, and bacon sandwiches for breakfast this morning,' Bea said.

'And the most uncomf—' Will stopped.

—ortable sofa in London, Georgina finished silently. Will had said that about his sister's sofa before. 'Thank you. Both of you. I know I said you didn't need to come down, but it's so good to see you. And you've got perfect timing, because the kettle's just boiled.'

Will hugged her again. 'Love you, Mum.'

'We brought flowers,' Bea said, and handed Georgina a bunch of pink and purple stocks. 'I know you've got stuff in the garden, but I also know these are your favourites. You ought to ask your gardener guy if he can grow some of these here for you.'

Young Tom, who seemed to find a good excuse and the time to do 'just a little bit more' in the garden every time Bea visited. Although Georgina suspected her daughter rather liked Young Tom, too. Though, now Ginny-or-Jenny was on the scene, if she was more than his assistant, then things might have changed. Georgina would have to find a tactful way to mention it to Bea. She breathed in the scent. 'Thank you. They're gorgeous.'

'And we know you weren't expecting us, so we went shopping on the way. We bought salmon, new potatoes and those posh greens you can shove in the microwave. I'll cook tonight. And Will insisted on cheesecake, the way he always does.' Bea rolled her eyes.

'I didn't hear any protests from you,' Will said, coming back into the kitchen with two gym bags that Georgina guessed were their overnight bags, and a tote bag full of food. 'And I'll cook us lunch tomorrow. Roast chicken, and we're so having pigs in blankets with it.'

Georgina, knowing that her children were worrying about her, didn't point out that she was perfectly capable of cooking for them. If she let them make a fuss over her, it would clearly make them both feel better. 'That'll be lovely, darling. Thank you both. Let me finish making the coffee, and we can have a proper catch-up. Go and put your stuff in your rooms, and I'll sort out the shopping.'

Bea lingered, and gave her mother another hug. 'Are you *sure* you're OK, Mum? It must've brought everything back about Dad, finding the poor man like that.'

'Yes. But your father would've told me to screw my courage to the sticking place, so that's what I did,' Georgina said.

Bea grinned. 'Ha. Just imagine Dad playing Lady M in a gender-swapped version.'

Georgina's eyes filled with unexpected tears. 'He was directing *Macbeth*, the first time I met him. Playing the lead role, too.'

'Oh, Mum.' Bea dragged in a breath. 'I miss him, too. So much. It still doesn't seem possible.'

'I'm just grateful we have films so we can still see him.' And voicemail messages, some of which Georgina listened to on days when the black hole threatened to suck her in. *Love you, Bug.*

His old nickname for her when they'd first dated, Shutterbug, had shortened over the years – and was the reason why her kitchen dresser was filled with mugs, jugs and bowls covered with ladybirds.

'Me, too.' Bea hugged her. 'But I like to think he's up there, still keeping an eye on us. Proud of Hubble doing well in his secret lab. Proud of you and your photographs. An eye on me, too, to see when I'll finally play Beatrice.'

'And you'll do it brilliantly,' Georgina said.

Bea kissed her cheek and headed out of the kitchen.

'Hubble?' Doris asked.

'Stephen's nickname for Will. As in "Hubble, bubble, toil and trouble", a scientist mixing potions,' Georgina explained softly. 'And Bea was always Queen Bee to him.'

'Your children are lovely,' Doris said wistfully. 'Trev and I hoped we'd have a boy and a girl, eventually. Once we'd settled into our teaching jobs and had our own place.'

'I'm only sorry you never got that chance,' Georgina said.

* * *

'Inspector Bradshaw.' Francesca's smile faded slightly. 'Is Georgie all right? Is there any news about Dr Garnett?'

'I haven't seen Mrs Drake since yesterday, and I can't discuss details of an active case. Could we have a private word, Mrs Walters?' he asked, the formality making it clear that this was an official visit.

'Of course. I'll just get Beth to take over from me,' she said. 'Bear with me a moment, please.' She had a quick word with her assistant, then headed back to Colin. 'Would you like to come through to my office?'

'Thank you.'

'Coffee?'

'Thank you for the offer, but I'll pass,' he said.

Francesca's office was at the far end of the farm shop. There were various charts on the pinboard in her office, a year planner with coloured stickers on various dates, a laptop and a very tidy desk. He wasn't surprised that she was the organised type. She'd struck him as someone who was full of energy. Full of brightness and colour.

'What did you want to talk to me about?' she asked.

'Your website lists ready meals, Mrs Walters,' he said.

'Call me Cesca. Everyone else does.' She smiled. 'We added pizza to the café menu on Fridays, and so many people asked us if we'd sell pizzas that people could take home and put in the oven themselves, that we gave it a trial. It went well enough that we've made it a permanent part of the farm shop stock. We've added a few dishes to the line-up since – obviously, given that my dad's Italian and we all grew up helping out in the family restaurant in London, Italian food was the way to go.' She laughed. 'I have a dish of the week, to try and persuade everyone that there's much more to Italian food than lasagne – though I have to admit that spag Bol and macaroni cheese are our big sellers, along with my Italian shepherd's pie. And my favourite customer asked me to make a green Thai chicken curry, last summer. That one was popular enough to stay.' Her eyes crinkled at the corners. 'Are you looking for a recommendation?'

'Possibly,' he said. 'Can you confirm that you live at Manor Farm?'

'Yes.'

'Would you mind showing me round the gardens?'

'The gardens?' She looked surprised. 'Mine aren't anything special. Just the herb garden, the kitchen garden – my veggies, the apple trees and the beehives – and the wildflower meadow. And then the pretty stuff that I have no idea how to manage. Old Tom, Sybbie's head gardener, looks after it for me. If you want to see a proper garden, go and have a look at Sybbie's.'

'Sybbie?' he asked.

'Lady Wyatt. Sybil. My mother-in-law,' she explained. 'She lives next door, at Little Wenborough Manor. Her gardens are open to the public every Sunday in spring and summer.'

'Right,' he said. This felt like deflection. 'I'll do that. But may I see your garden, first?'

'Sure.' She unlocked the side door and took him down a narrow path and through a gate to Manor Farm. 'There's not a lot at the front, just the roses round the door. It's a working farm,' she said.

Colin noticed the four-wheel-drive cars parked on the shingle.

'The cows are out at pasture,' she said, 'but the byre's that way, if you need to see it, and the dairy.'

'That's fine,' he said. 'Only the garden, for now.'

Just as she'd described it, the garden was divided into a kitchen garden with a greenhouse, a herb patch, a lawn, a few apple trees, three beehives, a straggly patch of what looked like weeds to him but he imagined would be full of poppies and cornflowers later in the year, and a very neat herbaceous border.

There were pots of flowers on the patio, and a climbing rose round the patio doors; but there was no oleander. He'd looked up the plant after Sammy, the pathologist, had named it, and had memorised the look of its narrow, glossy leaves; plus he'd saved a screenshot of the plant on his phone to double-check when he was out and about.

'Thank you, Cesca,' he said, remembering that she'd asked him to use her first name.

'No problem. Is there anything else I can help you with?'

'May I ask, how do you know Mrs Drake?'

'Little Wenborough's not that big. Everyone knows everyone else,' she said. 'And I'm from London, too – so of course I dropped in to say hello and welcome her when she moved to the village. We became proper friends, though, when

one of the Sunday supplements was running a feature on
Sybbie and her garden. The photographer caught Covid and
cancelled at the last minute, and I knew Georgie takes portraits
– at least, she did before she moved here – so I asked her if she'd
mind stepping in. Sybbie made her stay for tea, and discovered
that Georgie had no idea how to manage her garden, so she had
a word with Old Tom, her gardener; he sent his grandson,
Young Tom, round to see Georgie. Young Tom rescued the roses
she'd almost ruined, and now he does her garden every week.'

Colin wasn't sure whether the closeness in the village made
him wish he was part of something like this, or whether it would
make him feel claustrophobic. Probably both.

'Right. And you run the farm shop.'

She nodded. 'Sybbie converted one of the barns into the
garden centre, years ago. When I came along, we added a
tearoom and set up the farm shop. I met Giles when he was a
student in London,' she explained, 'and I was working in my
dad's trattoria and nagging him to let me start up a line in deli
meals that customers could finish cooking at home. Except I
ended up doing that here, with Giles.'

She had a faint Italian accent, although Colin wondered if
she might be ramping it up a little for his benefit. Francesca
Walters was in her late twenties, he'd guess; her dark hair was
tied back, and she was incredibly pretty. She exuded warmth
and energy; and he could imagine she'd given Roland Garnett
very short shrift when he'd tried it on with her.

'Do you make the ready meals yourself?'

'I do,' she said. 'But I also manage the shop, now that Giles
is working more closely with his dad. He'll be taking over in a
couple of years, when Bernard retires.'

'Taking over?' Colin asked.

'Running the estate,' she said. 'Though I think Sybbie will
still handle the Open Garden on Sundays. Every Sunday afternoon from March to September, one till four.'

Colin made a note. 'The garden's well-known?'

'It's famous for its collection of azaleas and rhododendrons,' Francesca said. 'Sybbie's a national expert. It's why the magazine wanted to run the feature on her.'

Azaleas and rhododendrons. From what he'd read, they were similar to oleander. 'Are there oleanders in her collection?' he asked.

'I have no idea. You'll have to ask Sybbie. If there aren't any in the Manor's gardens, she'll know where you can find them. She'll be somewhere in the garden. Find the Labradors, and you'll find her.' She smiled. 'She can be a bit fierce if you catch her when she's busy. But take her some lemon polenta cake from me and it'll put her in a good mood.' She smiled. 'In fact, you can have some, too.'

Colin thought of the talking-to he'd had from the practice nurse. And then he thought of the brownies he'd given up yesterday. Chocolate, he could just about resist. Lemon was another matter. 'Thank you,' he said.

'Which isn't a bribe – at least, your bit isn't,' Francesca said. 'Though I'd appreciate it if you could go a bit easy on Georgie. I assume you already know this, but her husband died from a heart attack, a couple of years ago. Finding Dr Garnett's dead body at Rookery Barn must've reminded her of how awful it was.' She paused. 'Was there anything else?'

'Perhaps the ingredient list for your curry,' he said.

Francesca's eyes widened as the penny dropped. 'Is that how Dr Garnett died? He was allergic to something in my curry?' Her hand covered her mouth.

It had been a casual question, because he hadn't yet established that she'd sold curry to Roland Garnett. Was she assuming from his question that *her* curry was the cause of death? Or did she know for certain that it was, and was shocked that he'd worked it out so easily?

'Oh—that's terrible,' she continued. 'But I list all the ingredients. The likely allergens are in bold in the list, and I have a separate note warning people if there's egg, nuts, wheat, soy, sesame or milk in the dish. And we always ask about allergens at the cash till, just to be on the safe side.'

'We don't think it was an allergic reaction,' Colin reassured her.

'So it wasn't my food that killed him? That's a relief. He wasn't a very nice man,' Francesca said, 'but I didn't wish him dead.'

Somebody did, though. And Colin needed to find out who. And whether it had been her food; who would've had access to it?

'Could you give me a copy of his orders from you?' he asked.

'Yes. I can't remember every order off the top of my head, but they're all on the system. Let's go back to my office.' Back at her desk, she logged in to her computer and tapped a few keys. 'He had three deliveries – the first direct to Rookery Barn, and the second two via Georgie because I didn't trust myself not to drop the stuff on his foot.' She narrowed her eyes. 'Having two X chromosomes in no way makes someone inferior. Or having one Y chromosome, for that matter.'

'I agree,' Colin said.

She printed out the three orders, plus a copy of the labelling on the curry. He glanced at them. Garnett had ordered curry the first and second week of his stay, but not the third. So it looked less likely that Francesca was the source of the poisoned curry. So much for thinking he had a solution; instead it looked as if he'd taken two steps forward and one step back. 'Thank you,' he said. 'That's helpful. Do you know any other places nearby that sell curries as ready meals or takeaways?'

'There's an Indian takeaway in Great Wenborough, the next village from here, but they don't do Thai curries. The next nearest farm shop is seven miles away, and they specialise more in traditional food. That'd leave the supermarkets,' she said.

'Right.' He made a note, and followed her back into the shop, where he accepted a slice of delicious-looking lemon polenta cake.

'You look,' she said, 'as if you need feeding up. What would you like? My treat.'

'I can't do that,' he protested. 'But I will buy something, and I'll pay for the cake.' It would take as much effort to shove something into the microwave as it would to make himself a sandwich – and he had a feeling that Francesca Walters' food would taste a lot better than said sandwich.

'Any allergies?' she asked.

'No.'

'Good.'

Though Francesca gave him a rueful smile when he chose Italian shepherd's pie and some salad. Colin certainly didn't think the green Thai curry she sold here would contain oleander – it was looking more and more as if Roland Garnett's meal was a one-off – but he couldn't quite bring himself to choose something so similar to the lecturer's last dinner.

He put the shopping in the back of his car, then drove down the long tree-lined drive to the manor house next door.

The house was beautiful. It looked like the sort that would be used in a television drama: an Elizabethan manor house, built in the shape of an E, with stepped gable ends and stone mullioned windows. Most of the bricks were red, but there was a diamond-shaped pattern on the front of the house made from darker bricks. The roof was made from red tiles, and there were two groups of four tall, barley-sugar twist chimneys on each end of the house. Wisteria grew round the doorway of the porch, which led to a studded wooden door with a large door knocker.

He knocked. What felt like an interminable wait later, a dark-haired man in his early thirties answered. 'Can I help you?'

'Detective Inspector Colin Bradshaw,' Colin introduced

himself, showing his warrant card. 'I was hoping to have a word with Lady Wyatt.'

'My mother?' He looked surprised. 'She'll be somewhere in the garden. Come through and I'll help you find her.' He led Colin into a large black-and-white-tiled reception hall with its sweeping staircase up to the next floor, ushered him through a doorway into a large kitchen which had a large wicker dog basket next to the Aga, and then through a set of French doors into the walled garden.

Colin could see exactly why people came here on Sunday afternoons to visit the gardens. The herbaceous borders were full of plants that would attract butterflies in summer, and even now were full of colour; and there was a formal knot garden in front of them, edged with yew and filled with sweet-scented plants.

Two black Labradors came bounding up to them.

'Max, Jet, sit,' he commanded.

They sat at his feet, looking hopeful that a treat might be in store.

'Find Ma,' he said. 'Take us to Ma.'

The Labradors trotted off, pausing every so often and looking back to check that they were being followed.

'It's about the only time they're useful,' he confided. 'They spend the rest of the day either pestering you to throw a tennis ball, or scavenging whatever food they can from you.'

'Dogs, eh?' Colin said as they walked through an arbour of climbing roses. Since he'd lived on his own, he'd been tempted to get a dog for company; but he knew it wouldn't be fair, not with the hours he worked.

'Sorry, I should've introduced myself. Giles Walters.'

'I guessed you might be Francesca's husband,' Colin said, shaking his hand.

'Ah, Cesca. My best beloved.' Though the words sounded

teasing, the look on Giles' face told Colin that he meant it sincerely.

Eventually the dogs brought them through the open door in the walled garden into a long stretch of lawn flanked with rhododendrons and azaleas that were underpinned by a carpet of bluebells, and which led down to what looked like a small lake.

'Ma! Visitor for you,' Giles called.

The woman at the far end, clad in faded jeans. green wellies, a green waxed jacket and a headscarf, straightened up and headed towards them, the dogs pattering along by her side.

'Ma, this is Detective Inspector Bradshaw. Detective Bradshaw, this is my mother, Lady Wyatt.' Giles smiled. 'I'll leave you to it.'

'How can I help, Inspector?' Lady Wyatt asked, turning to Colin.

She was in her mid-sixties, he'd guess, with salt-and-pepper hair in a pixie cut, crinkles at the corner of her very blue eyes that told him she laughed a lot and a generous mouth. She looked every inch an aristocrat – but the down-to-earth kind, he thought, rather than the entitled kind. 'Your daughter-in-law says you know more about rhododendrons and azaleas than anyone else, Your Ladyship,' he said.

'Dear Cesca,' Lady Wyatt said with a fond smile. 'My daughter-in-law is fabulous with herbs – utterly clueless with any other plant, mind.'

The two black Labradors nosed the paper bag he was carrying.

'Max, Jet, leave the poor man alone,' Lady Wyatt commanded, and they came to sit by her feet.

'She also sent you lemon polenta cake.' Colin handed the brown paper bag to her.

Lady Wyatt's smile broadened. 'Thank you – and for not letting Giles snaffle it.' She slid the bag into the pocket of her

waxed jacket. 'Now, what do you want to know about rhododendrons? And do call me Sybbie. Everyone does.'

Far from being fierce, the way Francesca had described her,
Lady Wyatt had the same warmth and energy as her daughter-
in-law, Colin thought. 'I believe you have a special collection of
rhododendrons here, Sybbie,' he said. 'Would that include
oleanders?'

'We have a handful of them, though oleander isn't actually a
rhododendron – it's the only species in the genus *Nerium*,' she
said. 'They're a bit susceptible to frost, so we keep them in pots
on the East Lawn for most of the year and overwinter them in
one of the greenhouses. We brought them outside last week.
Would you like to see them?'

'Yes, please,' he said.

'They're a bit dull at the moment, mind. They won't flower
until July. But come this way,' she said, and the Labradors
bounded in front of them. 'Why are you interested in our oleanders, Inspector?'

'I'm sorry. I'm afraid I can't discuss the particulars of an
active case,' he said.

She frowned. 'I can't quite imagine what on earth oleander
would have to do with a police case – unless someone's lost a
horse or a cow that's accidentally eaten a few of the leaves.'

'The plant's poisonous?' he asked, despite knowing the
answer.

'To cattle and horses, yes, which is the other reason why
we tend to keep the oleanders in pots, and well away from
where any dried leaves might fall across the fence and end up
in the silage,' she said. 'Most people are sensible enough to do
the same. But there are worse things. *Rhododendron
ponticum*, for a start – it's an invasive weed. Illegal to plant it
in the wild or let it spread from your garden,' she added,
frowning. 'And there's no need for it, with nearly nine
hundred other varieties available that don't have the same

problems. Smothers the native wildlife, hosts a fungus that kills oak trees. Dreadful stuff. I was just checking that there wasn't any regrowth of the stuff I hope we got rid of five years ago.'

But the rhododendron hadn't been responsible for the death of Roland Garnett, Colin thought. Unlike the oleander.

He duly inspected the large terracotta pots containing neat shrubs; the narrow dark green leaves looked completely innocuous. 'Can I ask, have you given anyone any cuttings of the oleanders in the past month?' he asked. 'Or do you know if anyone might have taken a cutting?'

'No to the first,' Lady Wyatt said, 'and I very much doubt it, but do give me a moment to check.' She inspected each pot in turn, and then he heard a surprised, 'Oh!'. Frowning, she beckoned him over. 'Whoever took this clearly knows plants – the stems have been cut cleanly.'

'Do you have any idea who might have taken a cutting?'

She looked blank. 'We open the garden on Sundays, but nobody takes cuttings when they visit a garden.'

'Don't they?'

'It's not the done thing.' She frowned. 'They'd buy a plant from the garden centre.'

Colin made a note. 'What about the garden centre staff? Or your gardeners – Old Tom and Young Tom, I believe?'

'And Jenny. Well, she's not officially on the team, but the poor girl's had a bit of a rough time lately and gardening is so *healing*,' Sybbie said. 'No. None of them would take cuttings without my instructions, or checking with me first. But I could ask them, if you like?'

'Perhaps I could trouble you for their details,' Colin said. For the first time, he saw a hint of the fierceness Cesca had mentioned.

'Of course. I'm not entirely sure where Jenny lives, but Young Tom can tell you that.' Sybbie dictated the addresses for the two gardeners. 'They're both Tom Nichols, but we call them Old Tom and Young Tom for obvious reasons.'

'Of course,' Colin said.

Unless Old Tom, Young Tom or Jenny had any new information, Colin thought, he was no further forward. Francesca Walters made chicken curry which she sold in the farm shop, and Garnett had bought two portions. Her mother-in-law kept oleander plants. Curry and oleander were both involved in the death of Roland Garnett. Garnett had upset Georgina, Francesca and Jodie. Between the three of them they had the means, motive and opportunity.

What was missing was the proof linking them together – or any evidence that would implicate someone else.

Any why use oleander?

This case was just plain *odd*.

'Thank you,' he said.

'That's all you wanted to know?'

'That's all,' he said.

'Well, if you think of anything else, do come back,' she said, and accompanied him back to the house.

'Thank you for your time, Sybbie,' Colin said, and headed back to his car.

Jodie was at home, but the back garden of her modern mid-terraced house was laid to lawn and had a football goal net and a trampoline rather than any kind of shrubs. Definitely no oleander, and he wanted to focus on that for now.

Old Tom was almost exactly as Colin had expected: a stocky man in his early seventies, with a weather-beaten face advertising that he'd spent most of his days outdoors for decades. He was wearing black trousers, a checked shirt, a dark green padded gilet, green wellies and a flat cap. His garden was small and perfectly tended.

Colin introduced himself and explained what he needed to know, but Old Tom couldn't shed any light on the matter. 'I've worked in the gardens at the Manor since I was a lad – when *my* grandfather was in charge of the garden,' he said. 'Lady Sybbie's made a lot of changes over the years. Opening up on a Sunday's the best thing that could have happened to the gardens. Get them seen, and it raises a packet for charity. She's a good 'un, Lady Sybbie.'

'Who takes cuttings from the garden?' Colin asked.

'Her ladyship,' Old Tom said. 'I do, and Young Tom – my grandson – if we've discussed it with her ladyship first.'

'What about people from the garden centre?'

'No,' Old Tom said. 'They don't do nothing in the Manor's gardens.' He seemed definite on the subject.

'What about visitors, when the gardens are open?'

'No,' Old Tom said. 'You want a plant of the sort you see here, you go to the plant shop and buy one. Same as you would for any garden open to the public.'

'But what if someone came with, I don't know, secateurs and a plastic bag in their pocket?' Colin asked.

'They don't,' Old Tom said confidently. 'If anyone tried it, someone'd see them and make a fuss. And the Manor's gardens are open for charity. You don't steal from a charity.'

Some people did, Colin thought, but he wasn't going to argue with the old man. 'Have you taken any oleander cuttings?'

'No. Lady Sybbie never asked me to.'

It was clear he wasn't going to learn anything new here. 'Thank you for your time, Mr Nichols,' Colin said.

Young Tom was also working in his own garden. He lived in one of the newer houses on the estate, an end-of-terrace house whose garden was bursting with bright yellow tulips and deep purple pansies, and other plants Colin couldn't name but looked incredibly pretty.

Colin introduced himself and explained what he wanted to know. Young Tom gave very similar answers to those of his grandfather, and confirmed that he hadn't taken any oleander cuttings.

'Did you have any contact with Mrs Drake's guests at the barn?'

'They're usually out when I'm working there,' Young Tom said. 'Though the last guest was having some kind of working holiday and he wasn't very happy when I mowed the lawn on the Monday, but I explained I only mow once a fortnight at this time of year and it wouldn't take me long. He grumbled a bit, but he shut up eventually.'

'Thank you, Mr Nichols. Lady Wyatt said you'd be able to give me Jenny's details.'

'Why do you need to talk to Jenny?' Young Tom asked, frowning.

'Dotting the i's and crossing the t's,' Colin said, wondering why Young Tom suddenly sounded so protective.

'Jen's had a rough time, lately,' Young Tom said. 'She's a bit fragile.'

Colin waited, knowing the power of silence.

'Her sister died a month ago,' Young Tom said eventually. 'She's taken it pretty hard.'

'Of course.' Losing a sibling when you were young would be hard for anyone to handle. 'Was this in the village?' Colin asked.

'No. In the West Country, I think. Jen grew up here, but after she went to uni, her parents moved away to be closer to her grandparents. Jen came back here last year. She got a job at the Science Park in Norwich, and there was a house-share going in the village. She's very clever, works with plant genetics,' Young Tom explained.

'Then you renewed your friendship?' Colin asked.

'Not *that* kind of friendship,' Young Tom said with a smile. 'I was in the same year as her sister at school. I asked her out a couple of times, but she only had eyes for her books and turned me down, sadly. Jen's more like the little sister I never had. That's why I've been dragging her out in the garden with me. She's been off sick ever since her sister died. Working in the garden's good for depression – fresh air and sunshine help with everything, if you ask me – so I persuaded her to come and keep me company. Even if she only twitches out the odd weed and chats to me, it's better than sitting at home alone, brooding. And I trust her to do it well.'

Colin knew how it felt to sit at home alone, brooding. 'That's kind,' he said.

'No. It's what friends do,' Young Tom said, shrugging off the compliment.

'I need to have a word with Jenny,' Colin said. 'If you could give me her details, please?'

Young Tom sighed. 'Jenny Smith, Number Four Beech View,' he said. 'It's just round the corner.'

'Thank you, Mr Nichols.'

Beech View was on the same estate as Young Tom's house – all the roads were named after trees, Colin noticed – and, like Young Tom's road, seemed to be mainly new-build terraced houses. The garden of Number Four was tidy, but it wasn't bursting with flowers the way Young Tom's was.

Colin rang the doorbell, and a young woman dressed in jeans and a hoodie answered. She wore no make-up, although her short, light-brown hair was shot through with blonde high-lights; there were shadows beneath her pale blue eyes. 'Yes?' she asked.

'My name's Colin Bradshaw – DI Bradshaw,' he said, showing her his warrant card. 'I'm looking for Jenny Smith.'

'That's me,' she said.

'Ms Smith, I'm looking into a local case, and I wonder if I could ask you a few questions?'

She shrugged. 'I can't imagine I'll be much use, but come in.'

'Thank you.'

She led him into a tidy but slightly worn kitchen, and he sat down at the pine table.

'I believe you're working with Tom Nichols?'

'Not *working*,' she corrected. 'I'm on sick leave, and I can hardly work with someone else if I can't do my own job. I'm just keeping Tom company. And making me leave the house and get some fresh air makes him feel as if he's helping.' She raised an eyebrow. 'I assume he told you about my sister.'

'Yes. My condolences.'

She gave a single nod of acknowledgement. 'So how can I help, Inspector Bradshaw?'

'What do you know about oleander?' he asked.

'It's a shrub, a bit like a rhododendron. Sybbie – Lady Wyatt – is probably the best person you can ask. Rhododendrons are her speciality,' Jenny said.

'You don't use oleander in your job?'

'I work in plant genetics,' she said. 'My team's looking at making wheat more disease resistant. We're not looking at flowering plants.'

'I see,' Colin said. 'Have you worked with Tom in Mrs Drake's garden?'

'Yes,' she said.

'Did you happen to encounter any of her guests over the last week or so?'

She frowned. 'Why would I do that?'

'Routine question,' Colin said. Was it his imagination, or did she sound defensive?

'I just hang around with Tom. Doing a bit of weeding, chatting a bit to Tom's clients – apart from Mrs Drake, most of them knew my parents.' She raked her hand through her hair. 'Everyone's been kind about my sister. Even my ex – and we fell out very badly before we got divorced.'

She was very young to be divorced, Colin thought. Though

it was none of his business and unlikely to be relevant to his case.

'The doctor gave me antidepressants. But it's just – *hard*, you know?'

He did. He'd been there. 'Talking helps,' he said. 'Right now, it's very raw for you. But you learn to live with it. You'll get days when it all comes back and it feels like a wave pushing you under, but you'll know you've got through it before and you'll get through it again, so each time it gets a tiny bit easier.'

Her eyes widened in what looked like surprise. 'It sounds like you've lost someone.'

'I have,' he said. Not a family member, but it had still been painful. Because he should've been able to save that little girl. 'And not all antidepressants work for everyone. If you've been on them for a few weeks, it's worth talking to your doctor to see if they can suggest a different one that might work better for you.'

'Maybe,' she said. 'And thanks for being kind. Sorry I haven't been any help.'

'Every bit of information at this stage is a help,' Colin said.

She grimaced. 'I should've offered you a cup of tea. Sorry.'

'It's fine,' he said gently. 'If I accepted every offer of tea or coffee, I'd need the loo every two seconds and I'd never get any work done. Thank you for your help, Ms Smith.'

* * *

Georgina's garden was his last stop. When he checked, it also contained no oleander.

Though she wasn't alone in the house, this time.

'My children, Will and Bea Drake,' she said, by way of introduction.

The chemist and the actor, Colin remembered.

'Bea, Will, this is Detective Inspector Bradshaw,' she finished.

'I'm sorry to bother you when you're clearly busy,' he said.

'Have you found out what happened?' Will asked.

Not even close, and that didn't sit well with Colin. 'We're continuing our investigations,' he said.

'And I'm still the last person to see him alive?' Georgina asked.

'I'm afraid so,' Colin said. 'As well as the one to find him. Both of which make you a person of interest.'

She stared at him, her green eyes wide.

'Hang on. You seriously think our mum would be capable of killing anyone?' Bea asked, incredulous.

'No way,' Will said. 'That's not who Mum is.'

'You'd be surprised what people can be capable of,' Colin said dryly.

'I don't think I could murder anyone,' Georgina said. She frowned. 'Unless they threatened my children. And then, actually, I think I might.'

'Exactly,' he said quietly. 'Given the right circumstances and the right motivation, most people would be capable of murder.'

'Except this Dr Garnett didn't threaten us,' Bea said. 'I've never met him, and neither has Will. Neither of us had even heard of him, until Mum said that he'd died. So that theory can be crossed off your list, can't it?'

Bea was very like her mother, Colin thought. Direct, with a sharp mind. 'I have to go by the evidence,' he said mildly.

'If he didn't die from natural causes, what killed him?' Will asked.

'I can't discuss a current case,' Colin said.

'But you've said our mother is a person of interest. If he died from natural causes, you wouldn't be interested in finding a killer,' Will said. 'And Mum told us you were asking about chemicals, so we can assume you're looking at poison.'

'Can you tell me about your job?' Colin asked.

Will smiled. 'You would've signed the Official Secrets Act as part of your own job, so I think you already know the answer to that.'

Clearly both Georgina's children had inherited her sharp mind. 'It's a fair cop,' he said with a shrug.

Will grinned. 'I'm glad you've got a sense of humour. It makes me less worried that you're going to be insensitive with my mum.'

'I know about your dad,' Colin said quietly. 'My condolences. Losing a parent is hard.'

He hadn't meant to reveal that much, but Georgina's glance told him she'd picked that up.

'We all miss Dad,' Bea said. 'But, since you've more or less admitted the death isn't from natural causes – tell me, why *do* people kill?'

'Usually, it's for love, money or revenge,' Colin said.

'You can discount all of those,' Georgina said. 'I'd never heard of Roland Garnett before he booked to stay here, so I have no reason to want revenge on him. I certainly didn't fall in love with him, even in his first couple of days here when he was still being reasonably charming. Guests at the barn pay the agency in advance, so money doesn't come into the equation, either. He'd booked for three weeks, so I only had to put up with him for a few days.'

'Noted,' Colin said dryly.

'But, because you haven't turned up anyone else who saw him alive after me, I'm still under suspicion,' Georgina said.

'I'm following several lines of enquiry,' Colin said. Just, at the moment, they all seemed to be dead ends. 'Thank you for your time. And, Mrs Drake, if I can ask you to stay local?'

SEVEN

'One hardly expects to be interviewed by the police on a Sunday,' Gabriel Soames, the Master of St Bene't's College, said, frowning.

'Unfortunately, murder doesn't seem to care about calendars,' Colin said.

Gabriel's face paled. '*Murder?* But your colleague said he died of a heart attack.'

His colleague had probably suggested that their evidence pointed that way. Softening the guy up nicely for him, Colin thought.

'Surely you don't think anyone in the college murdered him?' Gabriel asked.

It sounded as if the reputation of the institution meant more to the Master of the college than the people in it. Even though Roland Garnett had been an unpleasant man, Colin felt almost sorry for him. The atmosphere here might well have shaped the way he turned out.

'What can you tell me about Roland Garnett, Professor Soames?'

'He's – *was* – a classical scholar.' Gabriel looked thoughtful.

'He came here as an undergraduate, took a double First, and stayed to do a postgraduate masters and then his PhD.'

Those were the academic credentials, but what about the man himself? Colin wondered. He tried a slightly different tack. 'How did he get on with his students?'

'He was quite hard on them,' Gabriel admitted. 'But it served a purpose. It weeded out the ones who didn't want to do well.'

So even here, a place which Colin had expected to be the last bastion for learning, it was all about numbers and grades rather than teaching students to think and giving them a chance to explore who they were. Things had definitely changed since his day. The crippling tuition fees, for a start.

'Could I have a list of his current students?' Colin asked.

'Of course. I'll ask my assistant to collate that for you,' Gabriel said smoothly.

'How did he get on with his fellow tutors?'

Gabriel raised his eyebrows. 'You suspect one of them of killing him?'

'Not necessarily. I'm trying to build up a picture of the man,' Colin said. 'I'll need to speak to his colleagues.'

'I see.' Gabriel pondered for a moment. 'He did rather keep himself to himself.'

Why? Colin wondered. From what his ex-wife had said, Roland Garnett had grown up in care. Maybe he'd thrown himself into his studies as a way of escaping his background. Even though universities were supposedly broader in their intake nowadays, it was surely still difficult when you arrived here and realised you didn't fit in socially: hadn't gone to the same schools, didn't know the same people, weren't really part of it.

Perhaps that was what had soured Garnett and made him so unkind and demanding.

'He was Dr Garnett, rather than Professor Garnett?' Colin asked.

'Yes. Being appointed to a professorship depends on whether you meet your particular university's criteria.'

Which Roland Garnett obviously hadn't. At thirty-seven, he might have felt passed over. Had he thought he deserved the position more than one of his colleagues did, perhaps?

'Are there any academic rivalries in his department or the college?' Colin asked.

Gabriel made a dismissive motion with his hand. 'Of course not.'

Colin was pretty sure that wasn't true. In any large working environment, there would be someone who felt they'd missed out on a promotion, or resented a colleague who'd been promoted quickly. Given what he knew of Roland Garnett's behaviour, Colin thought the man had been the type to perceive slights even where there weren't any.

He tried a more oblique angle. 'Were there any colleagues he didn't get on quite so well with?'

'No. The college is very supportive.'

Maybe it was time to ask a more awkward, personal question. 'Did you like him?'

'It isn't a question of *liking* a colleague, Inspector. It's whether your colleague is an effective member of the team,' Gabriel said, suddenly prickly. 'I'm sure it's the same in your own profession.'

In other words, no, he hadn't liked Roland Garnett, but didn't want to say so.

'But I'm sorry that someone killed him,' Gabriel continued. 'Poor chap. I hope he didn't suffer.'

It was the first bit of humanity Colin had seen in Gabriel Soames. Though, given that Roland Garnett had been poisoned, Colin couldn't give him the reassurance he was clearly seeking. Instead, he said, 'Thank you, you've been very helpful.'

'If there's anything further I can do, please let me know.'

'I will,' Colin said.

'I'll let the department know what's happened and see his students myself – reassure them that their studies won't be...' Gabriel shook his head. 'Well, of course they'll be affected. But I can at least reassure them that we understand how unsettling this will be for them, and it will be taken into account.'

Was he being uncharitable in thinking that the man was thinking more about grades than the emotional welfare of the students? Perhaps. Colin was suddenly glad his student days were over. 'Actually, I'd rather talk to them myself, first. If you wouldn't mind,' he added, making it clear he wasn't being polite and he expected Gabriel Soames to comply with the official request.

'I rather think my staff would prefer to hear the news from someone senior at the university than from a stranger,' Gabriel said.

'In that case, make it very clear that they're not to discuss the situation with anyone else until I've finished talking to them all, because it will interfere with the investigation,' Colin said. The last thing he needed was people colluding and getting their stories straight.

'As you wish,' Gabriel said, though his eyes glittered with annoyance.

* * *

A few hours later, Colin realised that talking to Roland Garnett's students and colleagues hadn't got him much further on. The students all admitted that they didn't like their tutor very much – he'd been all right for the first week or two, but marked essays much harder than the other tutors, nitpicked over every single detail and wasn't the one you'd go to for help if you were stuck. His colleagues all said they wouldn't wish him ill, but then admitted sheepishly that he wasn't the sort you could relax with over a bottle of wine; he always had to be right about everything, and it was a bit wearing. A couple of them said that Roland Garnett had a bit of a chip on his shoulder, just as Colin had suspected.

The picture he was building up was of a difficult man who could be charming when he chose to and wasn't very well-liked. There was something he was missing – something important – but right at that moment he couldn't put his finger on precisely what that was.

* * *

'It's completely ridiculous that he thinks *you* would've murdered the man,' Bea said.

'I was the last person to see him alive,' Georgina pointed out. 'And the one who found him. Without witnesses.' Unless you included a ghost that nobody else could see or hear, which obviously wouldn't stand up in court.

'What about being innocent until proven guilty?' Bea demanded.

'He asked if you had oleander in the garden. So did he think the guy ate it, either by accident or deliberately?' Frowning, Will checked the internet. 'There are a lot of urban myths about oleander – there's a story about a boy scout troop who threaded their sausages onto oleander sticks and every single one of them died. And there's a similar thing about Alexander the Great's army.' He rolled his eyes. 'But there's no real factual evidence. Apparently the stuff tastes disgusting. Accidental poisoning by oleander seems to be in horses, cows and dogs, not humans.'

'You need a d—' Bea began.

'We've talked about this, Bea,' Georgina reminded her. 'My answer is still the same. No.'

Will continued to scroll the internet. 'Deliberate ingestion – suicide – all seem to involve eating a ridiculous number of seeds. Though there is something about a guy who boiled the leaves and drank the infusion.' He made a note. 'I'll have a word with someone in the lab on Monday – someone who knows more than I do about poison and tox screens. Maybe oleander behaves like something else and the police are looking at the wrong thing.'

'Thanks, Will,' Georgina said. 'And now, I propose we close the subject of Dr Garnett and Inspector Bradshaw, open a bottle of wine, have dinner, and get the cards out.'

'Oh, you are so on. Loser makes lunch,' Bea said with a grin.

* * *

After lunch on Sunday, Georgina said goodbye to Will and Bea. The house felt flat without them, so she was glad of having something to occupy her time: researching Doris.

She felt faintly guilty about not telling her children about Doris, but at the same time she knew that seeing her had made them both relax, and she didn't want them worrying about her again. How did you tell someone that you were in contact with a ghost, without them thinking that you'd gone mad?

She sat at her kitchen table, went through the information Bea had sent her and made a list of the documents she'd need to check in her search for Jack Beauchamp. She couldn't check the latest electoral roll herself until the Records Office was open again – and even then she'd need to know at least the area where he lived, because it was organised by address rather than by surname – but she could try social media, or one of the companies who indexed the electoral roll and provided records from its search results for a fee.

There were five contenders on the two social media sites she was part of. Three of them were clearly too young, but she skimmed the posts of the other two and they both seemed to be about the right age group.

She sent them both the same direct message, asking if he was the Jack Beauchamp who lived at Rookery Farm in Little Wenborough in the late 1960s, because she'd bought the house and was researching its history. If he'd be able to share any photographs or memories, she'd be thrilled to hear from him, and she could be very flexible about times. She added her email address for ease of communication.

It was entirely possible that Jack Beauchamp wasn't on social media at all, in which case she'd try the paid-for records.

Next, she followed the link Bea had given her to a local newspaper archive, signed up for a subscription, and looked up the relevant dates. The story came up immediately.

Tragic Valentine's death ruled an accident

Doris Beauchamp, 18, of Rookery Farm, Little Wenborough, was pronounced dead by doctors at home on 14 February, 1971.

The inquest heard that she was thought to have tripped on the stairs while the rest of her family were out for the evening. On their return, her parents found her in the hallway at the foot of the stairs, unresponsive. They called the emergency services, but Doris never regained consciousness.

The coroner recorded a verdict of death as the result of an accidental fall.

The popular teen, a big fan of Shakespeare, had applied to the University of London to train as an English teacher. Local headmistress Mrs Moira Shields said she was deeply saddened to hear of the death and Doris would have made an excellent and enthusiastic teacher.

Doris's mother, Mrs Lizzy Beauchamp, said that the family was devastated by their loss.

There was a grainy black-and-white photograph of Doris, standing in what looked like the back garden of Rookery Farm. Her darkish hair was long, parted in the centre, and rippled in waves over her shoulders; she was wearing jeans and a floral-patterned shirt with long sleeves. She was smiling, and she looked so happy. Georgina's breath caught as she looked at the photo. What a tragic, tragic waste. She took a screenshot of the page.

'Any news?' Doris asked.

Georgina jumped. Where was Doris standing? Had she seen the news article? Just in case she hadn't, Georgina closed the lid of her laptop. 'I've found two potential matches for your brother on social media. I've sent them both a message. So now we just have to wait for a reply.'

'You were frowning, a moment ago.'

'Yes.' Georgina drummed her fingers lightly on the table while she thought about a tactful way to explain. There wasn't one, so she'd have to go with the unvarnished truth. 'I was checking the local newspapers.'

'For the inquest report about me? Did you find it?'

'Yes.' Georgina blew out a breath. 'I'm sorry. There isn't an easy way to say any of this.'

'We both know I didn't survive,' Doris said dryly.

'The verdict was death as the result of an accidental fall. Your parents found you at the bottom of the stairs, called the ambulance, and the doctors said you were dead.'

'Did they say anything about Trev?' Doris sounded hopeful.

'Just you. They called you a popular teen, and your head-mistress said you would've made a really good teacher.'

'Can I see it?'

'Are you sure you're up to it?' How would you cope, Georgina wondered, with seeing an article about your death and not being able to have a hug from anyone?

'I need to know,' Doris said quietly.

'If I could hug you right now, I would,' Georgina said. 'And if you need music or a film afterwards, just tell me what you want.' She opened her laptop screen and waited for Doris to read the article.

'I remember Mrs Shields. She was always so supportive. She took us to see *Hamlet* at Stratford-upon-Avon in this rusty old minibus – we were all worried it would conk out and we'd miss the play, but somehow she got us there,' Doris reminisced when she'd finished reading. 'Helen Mirren was Ophelia. My first *Hamlet*. My only *Hamlet*, as it turned out.'

'My first *Hamlet* was at Stratford, too,' Georgina said. 'We could watch a production this evening, if you like.'

'Maybe,' Doris said. 'Right now, I'm not sure I'm up to a tragedy. I'm not sure I'm up to anything.'

'We've got plenty of time,' Georgina said softly. 'That's a really nice picture of you.'

'That was my favourite shirt. Cheesecloth, it was. Lilac, with purple flowers. I used to have a long string of purple beads I wore with it. And a purple velvet ribbon choker.' Doris laughed. 'We made them ourselves, narrow ribbon with a popper fastening at the back or a little hook-and-eye. I used to put brooches on mine to make it look as if I had lots of different ones – my favourite was a jewelled butterfly. And I had this massive clip-on earring I found at a jumble sale; it was so pretty. I thought I was the bee's knees.' There was a catch in her voice. 'I hope Mum kept them.'

'I'm sure she would've done,' Georgina said. Right then, she desperately wanted to hug Doris – and her own daughter. 'And your hair was amazing.'

'I used to sleep with it in plaits,' Georgina said. 'It was how we all wore our hair, back then. Long and wavy.' She sniffed. 'I think I want to be on my own for a bit, if you don't mind.'

'Sure. Come and find me if I can do anything to help,' Georgina said.

* * *

An hour or so later, her phone pinged with a text from Francesca. *Come and test the tiramisu ice cream. My kitchen, whenever you're ready xx*

Given that Doris still hadn't reappeared, and she was stuck on her research until the records office opened, Georgina said loudly, 'I'm going to Francesca's for a bit.'

There was no reply.

She walked through the village, enjoying the sunshine; at Manor Farm, Francesca ushered her into the kitchen, where Jodie and Sybbie were both already sitting at the scrubbed pine table, clutching mugs of coffee.

'Good. The test team's all here, now,' Francesca said with a smile. 'Coffee, Georgie?'

'Yes, please,' Georgina said.

'Did you have a visit from our inspector yesterday, Georgie?' Sybbie asked.

'Yes. He wanted to check my garden,' Georgina confirmed. 'For oleander. Will and Bea had come down, and Will's going to ask one of his colleagues about the chemistry of oleander.'

'Let's hope he comes up with something. The inspector came to see me, too – but I don't have any shrubs in my garden. Just a football net and a trampoline,' Jodie said.

'No shrubs in mine, either,' Francesca said, putting a mug coffee in front of Georgina and taking a seat. 'It seems that Dr Garnett died after eating chicken curry. The inspector wanted to know what I'd sold him – and, yes, that includes green Thai chicken curry – and what the ingredients were.'

'So the inspector thinks that you cooked a special curry and put oleander in it to poison the man?' Sybbie asked. 'Dearest girl, you wouldn't know an oleander bush if one danced in front of you, did jazz hands and shook a banner in your face that said, "Hello, I am an oleander bush".'

'Are you finished with the comedy routine, dearest ma-in-law? Obviously that's why I sent him to you,' Francesca said.

'Without proof, he can't claim that you cooked the poisoned curry,' Georgina said. 'But, given that he's been asking all of us similar questions, I have a feeling he thinks we're colluding. Sybbie, do you have oleander in your garden?'

'Yes,' the older woman admitted. 'And, when I checked, some cuttings had been taken.'

'Seriously? But who'd do that?' Georgina asked.

'I have no idea. It wasn't me. I asked Old Tom, later, and he said he hadn't. Neither did Young Tom. All I can think is that one of the Sunday visitors must have taken a cutting – but people don't do that sort of thing, do they?'

'What about someone from the garden centre or the farm shop?' Jodie asked.

'They would've asked me first,' Francesca said. 'Anyway, nobody in Little Wenborough knew Dr Garnett. Why would they want to poison him?'

'Which puts the suspicion back on us,' Georgina said. 'Sybbie, the oleander was yours. Cesca, he ordered curry from you.'

Francesca nodded, looking grim.

'And I delivered the order to him – in my holiday cottage,' Georgina said.

'And I had a fight with him over his grabby hands,' Jodie said.

'It's all circumstantial,' Sybbie said. 'And there's such a thing as being innocent until proven guilty. If Cesca's curry was poisoned, accidentally or otherwise, surely we would've had a few more cases of poisoning in the village?' She ticked off the points on her fingers. 'You didn't put poison in the orders you delivered, Georgie – and you stayed out of his way after that row, Jodie. I can't see the police being able to make a case out of it. What reason did any of us have to kill him?'

'The fact remains, he ate a curry that poisoned him,' Georgina said.

'And you know what village gossip is like,' Jodie added. 'He had a fight with me – and I'm no better than I ought to be, according to most of the mums and grans in Little Wenborough.'

'Dear girl, it's obvious that they're jealous. Look at you. Blonde and gorgeous,' Sybbie said. 'Like a young Debbie Harry.' She raised her eyebrows. 'Unfortunately, you have a fatal flaw: an absolutely *dreadful* taste in men.'

Jodie laughed. 'If anyone else but you had said that, Sybbie, they'd get told to mind their own business. But you're right. I do. Rob took off for Australia rather than pay child maintenance,' she admitted ruefully.

'That's a good point about gossip, though,' Francesca said, looking worried. 'As soon as people realise Dr Garnett ate a curry I sold him and died, fingers will point at the farm shop – and if that means people stop buying things from us, the business will go under.'

'You're right, Sybbie, we didn't do anything wrong. But Cesca's right, too. If the police are looking at us, then it could ruin all of our businesses,' Georgina said. 'Nobody's going to buy Cesca's food, in case they're the next one to get poisoned. Nobody's going to drink in the Red Lion if they think Jodie'll be sprinkling poison in the pints; and if any of my guests hear gossip in the pub about Dr Garnett's death and leave a review online repeating it, all my bookings will be cancelled. So we need to prove our innocence as fast as we can. And the best way to do that is to find out who actually did it.'

There was silence around the table as everyone absorbed Georgina's speech.

'If the police can't work it out, how can we?' Jodie asked.

'Some people are anxious about talking to the police. If they're talking to someone who isn't with the police – say, the woman who discovered his body and is worried that her friend is being wrongly blamed for the death,' Sybbie said, 'they might have a very different approach. What information do we have about Dr Garnett?'

'I have his home address,' Georgina said. 'So we could talk to his neighbours. We also know where he worked, so we could approach his colleagues – or even his students.'

'Students. Hmm,' Francesca said. 'Out of the four of us, you're the one who's the right age to be a student, Jodie. Someone who'd want to chat to current students and find out what the place is really like before they applied.'

'Me?' Jodie looked shocked. 'No way, Cesca. Nobody's ever going to believe I could go to university, let alone Cambridge. I scraped my four GCSEs.'

Because, Georgina knew, Jodie had gone into labour halfway through her GCSEs and hadn't taken most of her exams.

'Don't sell yourself short. You can pass as a prospective Oxbridge candidate,' Sybbie said.

'How? I don't talk like the kind of people who...' Jodie tailed off and shook her head. 'I can't.'

'Supposing you're accompanied by your rather bossy godmother,' Sybbie suggested, 'who's been charged with civilising you and is the one who does most of the talking?'

'Seriously?' Jodie looked at her, and then laughed. 'Actually, that might just work. You talk their kind of language.'

'I can definitely pass as a bossy godmother.' Sybbie smiled. 'I was at Oxford, back in the day, so my wayward goddaughter doesn't stand a chance, now I've decided she needs an education. Wear a short skirt to show you're rebelling against me, but thick tights to show you're taking some notice of what I tell you. Boots.' She looked thoughtful. 'A rebel from a posh background. Yes. It's perfect. You'll wear my diamond earrings, Cesca's pearls, black eyeliner – and very, very red lipstick. We'll call in, have a little look round the college, and maybe have a little chat with the senior tutor. What was Garnett's subject, Georgie?'

'Classics,' Georgina confirmed. 'He was writing a book about food in Ancient Greece.'

'I've never been to Greece,' Jodie said, 'and I was never any good at languages at school. They're never going to believe I can do Latin.'

'They won't have to. Just do the sulky teenager bit, as Sybbie suggested,' Georgina said, 'and mumble your answers to any questions.'

'You can hardly go in and ask if you can speak to Dr Garnett. Surely the police will have already told them he's dead,' Francesca pointed out.

'But his death won't be public knowledge for a while longer so, if they tell us he's dead, it'll look natural that we're shocked by the news,' Sybbie said. 'Now, we've heard how good he is as a lecturer and young Jojo here wanted to go to St Bene't's because of him. I happened to have the day off so I was taking her to have a look around the city and thought we'd pop into the college. We express our condolences, and then I'm brisk and say, well, we're here now, so perhaps we can speak to one of his colleagues instead. And maybe one of the other students can show us round.'

'Don't you usually have to make an appointment, though?' Georgina asked.

'Who's going to say no to Lady Wyatt?' Francesca asked.

'Good point,' Georgina said. 'All right. While you two are doing that, maybe Cesca and I can tackle the neighbours. And talk to his ex-wife, though we need to get her contact details. All I know is she's his next of kin.'

'We'll see what we can get from the college,' Sybbie said. 'It's about an hour and a half to Cambridge from here. I suggest we leave as soon as you've dropped Harry at school, Jodie.'

'That works for me. I'll drive,' Georgina said.

'Hang on. I'm supposed to be working here tomorrow,' Jodie pointed out.

'You're still working,' Francesca said, 'just not in the farm shop. I'll get someone to cover us both tomorrow.'

'But –' Jodie began.

'This counts as work,' Francesca said gently. 'Just in a slightly different area.'

'We need to clear our names,' Georgina said.

'It's going to be a road trip,' Sybbie said. 'We're going to have fun, as well as get some answers. We can be the female equivalent of the Three Musketeers and D'Artagnan.'

'Even *I've* heard of them,' Jodie said with a wan smile.

'Don't do yourself down, child. Everyone's good at something. You don't have to be academic to do well in life,' Sybbie said. 'You have street smarts, which are probably more useful.'

'Agreed,' Georgina said. 'You're great at talking to people, either at the farm shop or in the pub, or to my guests at the barn. That's a skill not to be underrated.'

'Thirded,' Francesca said. 'No more arguments, Jodie. Besides, you lot are meant to be taste-testing the tiramisu ice cream.' She served up three bowls, each garnished with a long stripy wafer biscuit.

'I like these,' Georgina said, after the first taste.

'*Cannoli lunghi bicolore*,' Francesca said. 'When I told Dad last week I was thinking of branching out into ice cream, he sent me these.'

'Delicious,' Sybbie said.

'I think I'll need a second one before I can give you a verdict,' Jodie said. 'Or perhaps a third.'

Francesca laughed. 'Good. So that's a hit.'

The verdict on the tiramisu ice cream was a definite yes.

'Oh, and I have some news about your house research, Georgie,' Francesca said. 'Billy the butcher knows someone who went to school with the family who lived at Rookery Farm in the 1960s. It's a really sad story. Their teenage daughter died.'

'Doris, her name was,' Jodie said. 'I talked to Gran. She told me the same thing. She was five years above Doris at school, so she didn't know her that well, but Doris was a nice kid, it seemed. Apparently she slipped and fell down the stairs and hit her head in the wrong place. A year or so after she died, her family moved away.'

Which was exactly the story Doris had told her. 'I get that,' Georgina said. 'It's hard living somewhere, coming back and expecting to see someone there – and they're not. Moving house stops you feeling as if you've lost them all over again, every time you walk in the front door.'

Francesca squeezed her hand. 'Sorry. I know that's why you...' She wrinkled her nose awkwardly.

'My great-gran was friends with Doris's mum and they stayed in contact for a while, but eventually they lost touch. Gran isn't sure where the family moved to, just that it was the other side of Norwich,' Jodie said. 'The people who moved in after Doris's family had small kids, so Gran didn't have much in common with them.' She glanced at her watch. 'Sorry. Mum's looking after Harry and I promised I wouldn't be long. I need to go.'

'Me, too,' Georgina said. 'But, before I do – I was going to ask you all about ghosts.'

'In Little Wenborough?' Francesca asked. 'Well, there's a story about the Grey Lady at the Manor, and she haunts... Is it the drawing room, Sybbie?'

Sybbie nodded. 'Apparently, a couple of hundred years ago, the daughter of the house died in childbirth. The story goes that if you're in the house and you're expecting a girl, then she watches over you to make sure you're safe. I've never seen her, but Bernard's grandmother claimed she did, when she was pregnant with Bernard's aunt, Anna,' Sybbie added. 'And there's the story of the grey lady who haunts the grounds – apparently there was a priory attached to the house, in Henry VIII's time, though there's nothing left of it now. I'm not sure what the story's supposed to be, there.'

'I'm not sure I believe in ghosts,' Jodie said. 'They're just stories to frighten kids, aren't they?'

'Go to bed when I tell you to, or the ghost will get you, you mean?' Francesca asked.

'I've never seen a ghost,' Sybbie said thoughtfully, 'but there's an area in the garden where the dogs absolutely refuse to go. Throw a tennis ball into it, and they'll run round it in a wide circle and whine until you fetch it. I've always wondered if that was something to do with the old priory.'

Francesca shivered. 'So why are you asking about ghosts, Georgie? Do you think Rookery Farm's haunted?'

Georgina didn't just think it was, she *knew* it was. But, given the obvious scepticism of her friends, maybe now wasn't the right time to mention it. 'It's an old building. I wondered if there were any stories I should check out while I'm researching the history of the house.'

'Fair enough,' Francesca said. 'I'll ask Billy to ask the local history boffins.'

EIGHT

When Georgina got back to the farmhouse, she found no message waiting from either of the two Jack Beauchamps she'd contacted, though there was a message from Bea to say that Will had dropped her safely at her flat. She made herself a sandwich, filled Doris in with what she'd learned, and together they watched *Hamlet*. Halfway through, Will texted to say that he was home, adding, *Still think you should get a dog.*

No. Love you xx she texted back, smiling.

If Dad lived there, you'd have a dog.

If your father was here, she typed back, *he'd be too busy building an experimental Shakespeare theatre.*

A minute or so later, a text came in from Bea. *Yes, but he'd have a little dog. Tray. Or Blanch. Or Sweetheart.*

Georgina groaned. 'They're tag-teaming me.'

'Think yourself lucky. They could've suggested Crab,' Doris said, laughing. 'The most badly-behaved dog in Shakespeare...'

No little dogs, the pair of you! xx Georgina typed back, but she was laughing, too.

'So you're actually planning to investigate a murder?' Doris asked.

'Yes – but I'm not going to tell Bea or Will,' Georgina said. 'I don't want to worry them. Besides, I'm not doing this on my own. Sybbie, Cesca and Jodie are helping.'

'What would Stephen have said?' Doris asked.

'When he'd finished the "murder most foul" speech?' Georgina thought about it. 'I think he would've encouraged me. *Truth will come to sight; murder cannot be hid long... at the length, truth will out.*' She could almost hear his voice whispering the words to her.

'*The Merchant of Venice?*' Doris asked.

'Yes. We need to clear our names, Doris. Finding out who really did it is the best way.'

* * *

The next morning, Georgina picked up Jodie, Sybbie and Francesca at Little Wenborough Manor and drove to the Cambridge park-and-ride to catch the bus into the city centre. They split up, as arranged: Georgina and Francesca to see Roland Garnett's neighbours, and Sybbie and Jodie – who'd followed Sybbie's wardrobe instructions to the letter and looked like a sulky teenager – to St Bene't's College.

'If we all message the group chat when we're done, we can meet up in the centre of town,' Georgina said.

Sybbie nudged Jodie. 'Which means having lunch somewhere nice,' she said in a stage whisper. 'Good luck with the neighbours,' she said to Georgina and Francesca. 'And we' – she gave Jodie a conspiratorial smile – 'will have some fun. I haven't acted since my student days, but we'll give it a good go.'

Georgina and Francesca walked through the narrow streets flanked by the high walls and elaborate gatehouses of the colleges, heading towards the residential part of the city. She'd put Roland Garnett's home address into the map on her phone and used the app to navigate their way. They ended up in a road full of pale yellow-brick townhouses with bay windows on the ground floor and ironwork railings between the street and the front garden, some with bicycles padlocked to the railings.

Roland Garnett's house had a solitary bay tree in a terracotta pot next to the front door; the rest of the front garden was pea shingle. By contrast, his neighbours either side had borders of late spring flowers, tulips and forget-me-nots and lily of the valley; one had a camellia climbing up a trellis, the waxy white petals contrasting with the glossy dark-green leaves.

'Let's try that one first,' Georgina suggested, indicating the camellia. She and Francesca walked up to the front door. She rang the doorbell and they waited. They were on the point of deciding that nobody was there when the door opened and a woman stood there, rocking a crying baby in her arms.

'Sorry, I don't buy at the door,' she said. 'And I'm afraid I don't want to discuss religion or politics. Have a nice day.'

Her eyes had dark smudges underneath them, and Georgina guessed that she'd had a few broken nights recently.

'We're not here to try and sell you something, or talk religion or politics at you,' Georgina said hastily, before the woman could shut the door. 'I just wondered if we could have a word about your neighbour.' She indicated Dr Garnett's house.

'Are you from the police?' the woman asked.

Georgina and Francesca exchanged a glance. 'No. Dr Garnett's been staying in my holiday cottage for the last three weeks,' Georgina said.

'Oh. Well, I've already told the police everything I know. I can't think of anything else that would help.'

'I'm really sorry to bother you, but could we have a chat, please?' Georgina asked. 'Though it's something I'd rather not discuss on the street, if you don't mind.'

The woman hesitated.

'We really don't want to be any trouble,' Francesca added.

'We can see you're busy with the baby. All we're asking for is five minutes. And then you can throw us out.'

The woman sighed. 'Maya's teething; that's why she's grumpy. And why *I'm* grumpy.'

'I remember those years,' Georgina said. 'Days when it felt as if nothing was ever going to help. The more tired and cranky my daughter got, the more panicky I felt, and she used to pick up on it. I tried everything: teething gel, those teething rings you kept in the fridge, the powders and the gels. The only thing that actually stopped her crying was being danced and sung to.'

'Yeah. You'd think, as a GP, I'd know all the tricks,' the woman said wryly. 'But I've learned the hard way there's a big gap between how babies behave in textbooks and how they behave when they're with you twenty-four hours a day. It's like being a medical student all over again, except this time I'm convinced that Maya has every rare complication under the sun.'

'You poor thing. My nephew had a hard time teething,' Francesca said. 'Though my sister swears I'm a baby-whisperer, because he always used to calm down with me. Do you want me to see if I can distract Maya while you talk to my friend Georgie?'

'I...' The young woman closed her eyes for a moment, then seemed to come to a decision and stepped back from the door. 'All right.' She closed the door behind them and ushered them into the living room.

Francesca scooped the baby into her arms and began singing quietly, rocking the baby in the rhythm of a lullaby.

'So what's this all about?' the young woman asked.

'My name's Georgina Drake, and this is Francesca Walters,' Georgina said. 'We're from a village in Norfolk called Little Wenborough. Dr Garnett has been staying in the holiday cottage next door to my house, so he can finish writing his book.'

'We did wonder if he'd gone on holiday, when it first went

quiet,' his neighbour said. 'I was hoping it was a six-month sabbatical so we wouldn't have to put up with him for a while, but we wouldn't be that lucky.' She bit her lip. 'And I feel guilty saying that, now. You shouldn't speak ill of the dead.'

'He didn't let you know before he left that he was going to be away, or give you his spare key in case of emergency?' Francesca asked, raising an eyebrow.

'No. As you've probably guessed, we weren't exactly on great terms with him.' She grimaced. 'I'm Rebecca Brown, by the way. Sorry. I should've introduced myself earlier.'

'How long did you know him?' Georgina asked.

'Mark – my husband – and I moved here three years ago. Garnett was fine when we first came here. Nice, even. A bit of a charmer.' She winced. 'And then there was some stupid disagreement – I can't even remember what it was about, now. After that, he turned into the neighbour from hell.' She shook her head. 'I know what I just said about not speaking ill of the dead, but he really was a nightmare. He played the most awful classical music really loudly at night, just when I was trying to get the baby to sleep, or during the day when Mark was on nights. Mark's a doctor in the emergency department,' she added. 'And Garnett complained about *everything*.'

'That sounds like the man we knew,' Georgina said wryly. 'The dawn chorus is too loud in the country.'

Rebecca rolled her eyes. 'God, I can imagine him saying that.' She paused. 'When I told the policewoman that Mark and I are medics, she asked whether I knew if he had a heart condition or anything like that.' She shrugged. 'You know how it is. If you're a medic, everyone wants to talk to you about their health. Though he never did, not even in the days when we got on with him.'

'We might get into trouble for telling you this,' Georgina said, 'but the police don't seem to think it's from natural causes. It was my holiday cottage where he died, and as far as we know

I was the last person to see him alive. I was also the one who found the body, so it makes me a suspect. They haven't come out and actually said it, but we've worked out from what they've asked us that he was poisoned.'

'By a chicken curry. Coincidentally, he bought chicken curry from my farm shop, made by me,' Francesca said. 'Which makes me a suspect, too.'

'He really *was* poisoned?' Rebecca's eyes widened.

'Don't worry,' Francesca said, handing the now-sleeping baby back. 'Apart from the fact that Georgie didn't kill him, and I definitely didn't poison his curry' – she nodded at the baby – 'your little one was perfectly safe with me.'

'That wasn't what I was worried about – and thank you for the baby-whispering,' Rebecca said. 'You just said he was poisoned.' She bit her lip. 'The thing is, the Ropers – they're the neighbours on his other side – think he poisoned their cat, a year or so back. He was always on about their cat pooing in his garden. But what were they supposed to do about it? It isn't as if you can train a cat, the way you can train a dog. And it isn't even as if he has a nice garden he was proud of – just that bay tree he doesn't bother pruning or feeding.'

'Your front garden's stunning,' Francesca said.

'Thank you. Gardening's how I decompress after work,' Rebecca said. 'I'm still on maternity leave, but I'm glad the garden practically looks after itself at the moment, because otherwise it'd be overgrown with weeds – madam here takes up all my time.' She stroked the baby's cheek tenderly. 'I used to prune the bay tree for Garnett and keep it nice, when we first moved here – but not since he started driving us mad with his bloody music.'

'What happened with the Ropers' cat?' Georgina asked.

'Honestly, you wouldn't believe a grown man would act like this. But he kept putting cat poo through their letter box, saying it was their cat so it was their mess and they could have it back.

Naturally, there was a hell of a row. A week later, the cat died. The Ropers couldn't prove anything, but everyone round here knew he'd threatened to poison the cat if it pooed in his garden again.'

'Didn't the police do anything?' Georgina asked.

'Without proof, what can they do? And there wasn't any.' Rebecca looked at them. 'Was he nasty with you?'

'Complaining about the barn, mostly,' Georgina said. 'With a lot of Latin sprinkled in.'

Rebecca rolled her eyes. 'He was like that with us. Then he realised we knew a lot of medical Latin terms, so he stopped trying to impress us.'

'I didn't get the complaints, but he didn't seem to understand about personal space,' Francesca said drily. 'Did he try that with you?'

Rebecca nodded. 'A couple of times, when Mark was on duty and I was here on my own – I'd just fallen pregnant and I was sleeping all the time. I didn't dare tell Mark about it. Not because I didn't think he'd believe me,' she added, 'but I didn't want him to charge round and punch the guy, because then Garnett would've sued him for assault.'

'What did you do?' Francesca asked.

'I told him we had one of those video doorbells, it was recording what he said and, if he ever tried it again, I'd take the footage to the police. And I reminded him that, as a GP, I knew exactly where the places to inflict the most pain were.'

'Nice,' Francesca said approvingly.

Rebecca shrugged. 'He left me alone after that.'

Georgina blew out a breath. 'How can someone so vile get away with behaving like that?'

'It sounds as if he didn't, since someone poisoned him,' Rebecca said. 'Unless he'd taken the poison with him, in case you had a cat that annoyed him, and he managed to get it mixed up with whatever meds he was on.' She shook her head. 'Except we had mice about a year ago, and the stuff the guy from the council brought round was like wheat, dyed blue. You couldn't possibly confuse it with anything else. Maybe I'm talking nonsense. Even though the neighbour from hell's been away, Maya's had me up most nights, so I'm still a zombie.'

'Lack of sleep's a nightmare,' Georgina agreed sympathetically. 'But I promise it gets better.'

'Good.' Rebecca gave her a wan smile.

'Was he on medication?' Georgina asked.

'He wasn't one of my patients – and I'd have to cite medical confidentiality if he was,' Rebecca said. 'But, as I said, when people know you're a doctor, they tend to talk to you about their health. He never did.'

'Would you mind telling the police what you told us?' Francesca asked. 'About his behaviour with next door's cat, and his threat to poison it?'

'Are you going to speak to the Ropers, too?'

'Yes, if they're in. And we'll leave them a note if they're not,' Georgina said. She took a business card from her bag. 'My mobile's on this. I'd really appreciate if you or Mark would call me if you hear anything. And please talk to the police.'

'All right,' Rebecca said.

The neighbours the other side were in. Betty Roper was short, plump and bustling, with iron-grey hair cut in a bob that framed her face; Geoff was lean and bald, and had lines at the corners of his mouth to suggest that he laughed a lot. Georgina took to them immediately; they struck her as the kind of neighbours who'd chat over the fence for a few minutes if you saw them in the garden, or drop a slice of cake round after a baking session. As soon as she explained their business, Betty invited them in, furnished them with tea and homemade biscuits, and confirmed Rebecca's story.

'I swear he killed our Freddie,' Betty said. 'But we don't have any proof. The police said it would be his word against ours, and they logged it as a domestic. Even though we'd lived here years before he moved next door.'

Geoff took her hand and squeezed it, as if to comfort her.

'And he's so horrible to those poor youngsters on the other side. He plays heavy classical music at full volume just when Becca's trying to get the baby to sleep, or when Mark's come back from a night shift. I know they've complained to the council, but nothing ever gets done about it. We've complained, too. He knows the law and he's careful not to do it after eleven at night or before seven in the morning, and every time someone from the council tackles him he says he plays music to help himself think when he's working.'

'If that's true, why couldn't he play it on noise-cancelling headphones?' Francesca asked.

Geoff Roper rolled his eyes. 'No doubt he gave them some pathetic excuse.'

'And he didn't give you his key or tell you he'd be away before he left?' Georgina asked.

'He probably thought we'd shove it down his throat,' Geoff said. He sighed. 'I can't believe he's gone. I know you shouldn't speak ill of the dead, but he really was a nasty piece of work.'

'He was,' Betty agreed. 'His wife completely changed in the year she lived here with him. Hayley was lovely and bright, when she moved in; she always had a smile on her face. But it got to the point where she was walking about with hunched shoulders, looking at the ground, and avoided catching your eye in case you wanted to talk to her. I did go round there a couple of times when he was out, asked her if she was all right or if we could do anything, but she just said no and closed the door on us. Well, except the last time. I could see how upset she was, so I persuaded her to give me her mum's phone number. I told her mum what was going on, and she came straight away and collected Hayley.'

'And the poor lass didn't come back again,' Geoff said.

'Though she sent us some lovely flowers to say thank you for helping her,' Betty said.

'Garnett kind of had it in for us, after that – he blamed us for interfering,' Geoff said.

'It sounds as if someone needed to interfere,' Francesca said.

'She did drop us a note to say she'd married again, a man called Ryan Summers. She sounded happy, which was good to know after *him*,' Betty said.

'You don't happen to have her number or address, do you?' Georgina asked.

'Sorry, love,' Betty said. 'I know she stayed local-ish because she said she still had the same job. She worked in the county archives.' She smiled. 'Or you could always ask the police.'

'They probably won't be able to tell you, because of data protection and that,' Geoff said. 'Besides, they should be the ones looking for her. We told them everything. They said they might need to come back to us, but so far they haven't.'

'Well, thank you for your time,' Georgina said.

'Do you think he took the poison accidentally, or on purpose?' Betty asked.

'There wasn't a note, so I have no idea,' Georgina said. 'I just want to clear our names.'

'Best of luck, love,' Geoff said.

Back in the street, Georgina and Francesca looked at each other. 'Now what do we do?' Georgina asked.

'Hope that Sybbie and Jodie manage to get some information,' Francesca said. 'I'll text Sybbie to let her know that we're done. And while we're waiting, I could do with some coffee.'

* * *

The college porter – a burly man in his thirties dressed formally in a dark suit, white shirt and college tie – glanced up as Sybbie and Jodie walked into the reception area. 'Good morning,' he said cheerfully. 'Can I help you?'

'We'd like to take a look around the college, please,' Sybbie said.

'Do you have an appointment?' Though he smiled to make it clear he was asking to be helpful rather than obstructive.

'No,' Sybbie said. 'But we were having a look round the city, and thought we'd drop in on the off-chance. My goddaughter was thinking of applying here in September, you see,' she said, indicating Jodie, who'd hung back.

'We're always happy to let prospective students look round the grounds, outside exam season,' the porter said, 'and we have a self-guided tour. We only ask that you keep your voices down, because people will be working and studying, even though teaching doesn't officially start until tomorrow.'

'Of course – with finals coming up,' Sybbie said with a smile. 'But we were hoping we might be able to have just a tiny peek into the college library.'

'I'm afraid we don't allow access to the buildings,' the porter said, shaking his head regretfully.

'How terribly disappointing.' Sybbie gave a heartfelt sigh.

'There are some student-led tours – they're usually booked up well in advance, but I can see if anyone's dropped out of today's, if you like.'

'That would be lovely,' Sybbie said.

The porter checked his computer. 'I'm sorry. It looks like they're all full.'

'There's no chance you can just squeeze the two of us in?' Sybbie asked. 'Jojo was terribly keen to come here – St Bene't's has such an amazing reputation for classics. Dr Garnett's your main teacher here, isn't he?' She crossed her fingers that the police hadn't yet been in touch with the college, or at least hadn't spoken to the porter.

An expression of dislike flickered across the porter's face, quickly hidden. 'Yes.'

'Oh. Is he a bit... difficult?' Sybbie asked.

'He was an academic,' the porter said.

Meaning, Sybbie guessed, that Garnett ignored anyone at the college who didn't teach or wasn't a student. He'd been the sort who'd snap his fingers at someone in the college buttery; and no doubt he treated the porters as if they were a lower form of life instead of being the people who were the first contact point for visitors, acting as the face of the college. 'Thank you for the warning,' she said. 'If we could do the self-guided tour, then that would be wonderful. Is there anything in particular we should look out for?'

'This time of year, definitely check out the Fellows' Garden. It's full of gorgeous spring flowers,' the porter said. 'If you wanted to see where Garnett's rooms are – where your goddaughter might have tutorials – they're in Middle Court.' He gave her a laminated card. 'If you could let us have this back, when you've had your look-round?'

'We will. Thank you.' Sybbie smiled. 'And if you could recommend somewhere nearby with good coffee, I'd be very grateful.'

'I shouldn't *really* do this,' the porter said. 'But if you head for the main court and go into the Buttery, tell Alice at the counter that Lenny said you'd be all right to have coffee there. At least then you'll get a bit of a peek inside one of the buildings.'

'That's *so* kind of you, Lenny.' Sylvia held her hand out to him. 'And it's been terribly rude of me not to introduce myself. I'm Lady Wyatt – *do* call me Sybbie – and this is my goddaughter, Jojo.'

'Pleased to meet you, Your Ladysh—Sybbie,' he corrected himself, taking her hand and shaking it warmly. 'Jodie.' He shook her hand, too. 'Enjoy your visit to St Bene't's. Come and see me if you have any questions, and I'll do my best to answer them – or find out for you if I don't know.'

'I can't believe you did that,' Jodie whispered as they headed through the quadrangle.

'If you don't ask, you don't get – and you're more likely to get what you want if you ask nicely,' Sybbie said. 'Now, I'm hoping there might be a bedder about.'

'Bedder?' Jodie asked.

'Cleaner. Specifically of student rooms,' Sybbie said. 'It's short for "bedmaker".'

'You mean the students here are too lazy to make their own beds?' Jodie's eyes widened in outrage.

'Shh. We're supposed to talk quietly,' Sybbie reminded her. 'We don't want to get thrown out before we can ask a few questions.'

'I thought we were going to talk to Garnett's colleagues?'

'Unless any of them are in the Buttery, that's not going to happen. But, actually, I think we might get more help from the non-academic staff,' Sybbie said. 'They're less likely to close ranks.'

They strolled through the gardens, taking in the honey-coloured stone buildings with their mullioned windows and walls covered in wisteria that would look and smell amazing in a couple of weeks, the perfectly striped lawns and the bright splashes of spring flowers underneath the trees.

'This looks like something out of Harry Potter,' Jodie whispered.

'They used Oxford for the films,' Sybbie said. 'But I know what you mean.' She glanced round. 'No oleander bushes here. Let's check the rest of the gardens.' When she couldn't see any oleander in the rest of the gardens, she sighed. 'Whoever poisoned him didn't get their oleander from here. It looks as if *my* oleander was the one the killer used.' She pursed her lips, not sure whether she was more annoyed that someone had thrown unfounded suspicion on her, or that they'd interfered in her garden. 'Right. We're looking for Middle Court.'

They'd just found it when a woman came out of the building, carrying a cleaning caddy.

'Let's go and have a chat,' Sybbie said. She walked swiftly over to the cleaner. 'Excuse me – could you tell me where Dr Garnett's rooms are, please?'

'Staircase B, first floor,' the cleaner said. 'Though I don't think he's in today. At least, I haven't seen him.'

The police definitely hadn't spoken to the cleaning staff yet, then – and maybe the university hadn't got round to telling everyone.

'My goddaughter is thinking of reading Classics here,' Sybbie confided, with a glance at Jodie, who took the hint and dipped her head, avoiding eye contact. 'I know I'm being an old fusspot, but I want to be sure she'll be happy here. It's why I insisted on coming for a look-round with her. My best friend, her mother—' She blew out an exasperated breath. '*Clueless.* She's more bothered about the research expertise and how many people get a First. But if you're not happy in a place, you can't study properly and do well in your exams, can you?'

'No, you can't,' the cleaner agreed.

'Sybbie Walters,' Sybbie said, holding her hand out. 'Nice to meet you.'

'And you. Carol Taylor.' The cleaner shook her hand. 'You're right. They've got to be happy to study. Most of the kids here are OK, though some of them can be a bit snooty if the mood takes them.'

'What are the teachers like? Jojo's mum said this Professor Garnett's the main man.'

'Him.' Carol rolled her eyes. 'He's not a professor. That's half his problem. No, if your Jojo comes here, tell her to try and make sure Professor Bradley teaches her. She's all right.'

'What's so bad about Prof—Doctor, is it? Garnett?'

'Very charming, until he decides that you're not any use to his career. Then he ignores you, if you're lucky, or he's an arse who puts in complaints just because he can. Though I think they know enough now to file his complaints in the bin. And he shouts at his students, though none of them dare complain about him,' Carol added. 'One of them, poor love, ended up leaving, last term. She just couldn't take any more of him. I did hear she ended up in hospital, having her stomach pumped, and her parents cleared her stuff out and took her home. All that hard work, just wasted – not to mention how much it costs to study, nowadays.'

'Poor girl. What a shame. Couldn't her parents do anything?' Sybbie asked.

Carol shrugged. 'I doubt it. He's had a few run-ins with the other dons, over the years, but he's the sort nothing ever sticks to. He's been investigated, and every time he's cleared. I wouldn't want any of my kids mixed up with him, put it that way.'

'Perhaps,' Sybbie said, 'I'd better talk Jojo into looking at a few more places before she makes her choices.'

'Good idea,' Carol said.

'I'm sorry. I can see you're busy and we really shouldn't be keeping you.'

'That's all right. We're here to help,' Carol said. 'Good luck,' she said to Jojo.

Jodie gave her a shy smile. 'Thanks.'

Once Carol was out of earshot, Jodie said, 'How the hell has that bloody man managed to keep his job? If he's bullying his students, having fights with his colleagues, trying to get the support staff into trouble...'

'I don't know. But we need to find out more about the girl who left, and see if we can have a word with her,' Sybbie said. 'First, we get coffee – and I think we should buy Lenny a slice of his favourite cake to say thank you.'

'Yeah. He didn't have to be so nice to us,' Jodie agreed. 'And then we'll text Georgie and Cesca.'

* * *

An hour later, the four of them met up in a little café on one of the tiny back streets. 'The coffee's meant to be really good here,' Francesca said.

'Right. Time to report,' Georgina said, after they'd ordered coffee and sandwiches. 'Do you mind if I record this on my phone? It'll be quicker than me trying to scribble down what everyone said.'

The others agreed and Georgina filled them in on their meetings with the neighbours, then Sybbie reported on their visit to the college.

'I ended up chatting to the server in the Buttery, too,' Sybbie said. 'They'd heard the rumours about the girl who left last term. Apparently Garnett had her in tears regularly. She'd finally had enough of his bullying and left – and it's possible she took an overdose, first.'

'The mean old bastard,' Jodie said. 'She spent years study-ing, paid all that money for him to teach her – and he just bullied her instead and made her miserable. And if she tried to do herself in... Why is the college letting him get away with it?'

'They can't, any longer,' Francesca reminded her.

'I think,' Jodie said, 'I'm glad he's dead. He was horrible to his students, didn't get on with his colleagues, was vile to his neighbours, made his ex-wife miserable... That sort of person's just a waste of skin.'

'Agreed,' Georgina said, 'but it's not our place to be judge and jury.'

'Then whose is it?' Jodie asked. 'And why didn't they do their job and stop him behaving like that?'

'Good question. Though I don't think any of us has the answer,' Sybbie said.

'His neighbours agreed to talk to the police,' Georgina said. 'So now we need to track down his ex-wife and the student. I don't suppose you got a name?'

'Jill,' Sybbie said. 'I couldn't get a surname.'

'If there are any student forums,' Francesca said, 'maybe we can ask about Jill in there.'

'Good idea. She might have some friends who have her home address,' Georgina said. 'If not, then there's social media.'

'How are we going to find Garnett's ex-wife? She might've gone back to using her maiden name after the divorce, or married someone else,' Jodie said.

'She did marry someone else. Betty Roper told us. She's Hayley Summers,' Francesca said.

'The police said she was his next of kin,' Sybbie said thoughtfully. 'We could try ringing the college and ask if they can give us her details.'

'But he's dead, so his records are probably closed and they won't be able to tell us,' Georgina said.

'So how are we going to find her? There must be hundreds of women called Hayley Summers,' Jodie said.

'But we know where she used to work, at least at one point,' Georgina said. 'The county archives.'

She checked the website, but it didn't list staff. 'I'll have to call reception,' she said.

'Hang on. She might be on one of those business networking sites. Let me have a look,' Francesca said, tapping into an app in her phone. 'We're in luck,' she said with a smile, and took a screenshot which she sent to Georgina. 'Here you go. Her mobile.'

Georgina glanced at her watch and took a swig of her coffee. 'If I catch her now, she might be having a lunch break and be able to talk to me – or, if not, at least maybe she'll agree to talk to me later.'

She headed outside and found a quiet spot overlooking the river.

Hayley Summers answered her phone within five rings. 'Hello?'

'Is that Hayley Summers?'

'Who's calling?'

'My name's Georgina Drake. It's about Dr Roland Garnett, and I wondered if you had time now to answer a few questions?'

'Inspector Bradshaw said there might be more questions.' She sounded tense. 'Do I have to come in to see you at the station or anything?'

'No, no. We can do this on the phone.' Georgina crossed her fingers. She hadn't actually *said* she was from the police, though Hayley had clearly inferred it.

There was a sigh on the other end of the line. 'He's dead, so it shouldn't really matter. All right, what do you need to know? I suppose he wanted me to finish the story.'

'If you could, Hayley. You were married to Dr Garnett and lived at Nineteen Trinity Way, Cambridge?'

'Yes. I left there nine years ago.'

'And you divorced Dr Garnett...?'

'Seven years ago, after I lost the baby. It was too awful to talk about the other day, and I'm grateful to the inspector for being so patient, but I've calmed down a bit now. So, when I was with Roland, I got pregnant, and I was so sick. He made me utterly miserable. He made it clear he didn't want me to have the baby and it was all my fault – but then, when I lost the baby, he switched completely, said he'd been desperate for a baby and blamed me for doing something to make me lose it.'

Georgina swallowed hard, aware that she'd stumbled onto sensitive ground. Her heart bled for this woman, who had gone through so much pain. 'I'm so sorry for your loss, Hayley,' was all she could say.

Hayley continued almost without hearing, as if it was cathartic to get the story out. 'I was at my lowest ebb when Betty Roper came round to see me. She gave me a cuddle and I cried all over her. And then she persuaded me to let her talk to my mum.' Hayley paused. 'My mum came and got me. She and Dad were brilliant. They supported me until I could get a divorce. Even when Roland came round and kicked up a fuss, they kept him away from me.' She dragged in a breath. 'I divorced him on grounds of unreasonable behaviour. The judge was a bit difficult, especially because Roland – well, he lied in court. But I think the fact I wanted absolutely nothing from Roland convinced the judge that I was telling the truth. I didn't want anything except my freedom.'

'I'm glad you got out,' Georgina said. 'I met the Ropers earlier. They're lovely, and they appreciated your flowers.'

There was silence, then, as Hayley Summers clearly worked out how much the Ropers had told her.

'They think Dr Garnett might have poisoned their cat,' Georgina added.

'Oh, no.' Hayley sighed. 'That's awful. I know he didn't like their cat, but I never thought he'd go that far.'

'And he plays classical music very loudly when his neighbours need to get their baby to sleep or when the father is trying to get some sleep after a night shift in the emergency department.'

'Oh, God.' Hayley groaned. 'Bloody Schoenberg.'

'Apparently, he said it helped him think.'

'No. It just annoyed everyone who heard it. Though that in itself would've made him happy.' Hayley coughed. 'Sorry. Obviously the end of my marriage was a bit rough.'

'Don't apologise. And I'm sorry for bringing the bad memo-

ries back,' Georgina said. 'Can I ask, do you know anyone called
Jill?'

'No,' Hayley said. 'I'm sorry.'

'Did Dr Garnett usually get on well with his students?'

'Too well, with some of them,' Hayley said. 'I wasn't actually his student, but I was doing my MA when I met him. I
wasn't the first student he'd dated when he was a tutor, and I
definitely wasn't the last.'

So he'd cheated on Hayley as well as making her miserable?
'I'm so sorry,' Georgina said.

'Not as sorry as I am, believe me,' Hayley said dryly. 'He
was so charming – and it wasn't until I'd married him that I
found out what he was really like. What they say about
marrying in haste and repenting at leisure – that's so true. He
swept me off my feet. Mum and Dad weren't happy about us
getting married while I was still a student, but they came round
to the idea. As I told the inspector, they gave us the deposit for
our house as a wedding present.'

The house, Georgina thought, that Roland Garnett had still
lived in and Hayley had clearly walked away from. 'I didn't
notice at first that we saw less and less of my friends. Less of my
family,' Hayley said. 'There was always an excuse, and it always
sounded so reasonable.'

'What about his family?'

'He didn't have any – or so he told me. He said his parents
died when he was about seven and there wasn't anyone to take
him in, so he grew up in a children's home.'

Then why hadn't he embraced his wife's family?
Georgina wondered. Unless he'd wanted Hayley all to
himself.

'And then I fell pregnant and – well, you know that bit.'
Hayley huffed out a breath. 'When the police called me, I
couldn't believe he still had me down as his next of kin. It felt
almost like his last... I don't know, a way of shoving things in my

face. I'm just glad he's dead, so he can't inflict himself on anyone else.'

'It sounds as if it was a horrible situation,' Georgina said.

'It was. And I'm so glad I'm out of it now,' Hayley said. 'Do you need anything else?'

'I don't think so.' Though Colin Bradshaw might. 'Thank you for talking to me, and I'm sorry I dredged up all the bad memories for you,' Georgina said.

'Now I'm out of the situation, I can talk about it,' Hayley said. 'It took me years before I was ready to trust anyone again, and it took Ryan three years to convince me to marry him. But we've got a little boy, now, and we're happy. It's what it should've been like with Roland.'

'I'm really glad you're happy now,' Georgina said, meaning it. She ended the call, then went back into the café to join the others and fill them in on her conversation.

'We already know he didn't respect personal space and looked down on anyone who didn't have a degree,' Francesca said. 'He probably poisoned his neighbour's cat; he played music loudly at times when he knew either a baby or a junior doctor needed to sleep; he bullied his students – and had affairs with them; and he tormented his wife and was horrible when she was pregnant and when she lost the baby.' She ticked the points off on her fingers. 'It's like a heads-I-win, tails-you-lose thing. He's the kind of weasel who always manages to get away with doing whatever he likes.'

'Until someone killed him,' Georgina said. 'It seems there are a lot of people who have a motive to want him dead, or at least to make him ill enough to stop the way he was behaving. We know he was poisoned by a curry, using oleander – probably from Sybbie's garden, though we don't know who took the cutting or where the food came from. He made it very clear he didn't cook, so he must have bought it from somewhere.'

'Or someone cooked it for him,' Sybbie said. 'But who knew

where he was staying and would have the opportunity to give him the curry?'

'If someone used the kitchen at Rookery Barn,' Georgina said, 'they left it absolutely spotless – unlike the rest of the place.'

'Surely that's suspicious?' Francesca asked.

'I don't have any answers,' Jodie said, glancing at her watch, 'but if I'm late to pick Harry up from school, I'll be in trouble.'

They finished their lunch, and Georgina paid the bill.

'Hang on. We should split this,' Francesca protested.

'I'm treating you. No arguments,' Georgina said firmly. 'You're all here to help me clear my name.'

'And ours,' Francesca reminded her.

'We just need to work out who wanted to kill him, who visited the barn – I definitely didn't see anyone there – and where they got the food and the poison,' Georgina said.

But it was starting to feel like a hopeless task.

NINE

Once Georgina had dropped Jodie at the school – in time to pick up her son – and Francesca and Sybbie back at the manor, she headed for home.

The house felt echoey and empty. Maybe Will and Bea *were* right about her needing a dog. It would be company. Georgina had spent more time with other people this week than she had in the previous month put together, and right now she felt a bit lost without people round her. Maybe at last she was starting to move on with her life.

Though she still missed Stephen. Bone-achingly so.

Before she set out to type up what they'd found in Cambridge, she made herself a mug of tea and checked for new emails.

'Any news?' Doris asked.

Georgina jumped slightly.

'Sorry. I didn't mean to creep up on you,' Doris said.

'Not your fault. I can't see you,' Georgina said.

'So how did you get on in Cambridge?' Doris asked.

'We tracked down a few—Oh!' Georgina broke off when she saw the name at the top of the email.

'What?'

'Keep your fingers crossed,' Georgina said. 'This might be *your* Jack Beauchamp.' She quickly opened the message.

Dear Mrs Drake – or may I call you Georgina?

Thank you for getting in touch. It's nice to hear that Rookery Farm is in good hands, and how fascinating that you're researching the history of the house. I'd love to know what you discover.

My family moved from the farm just over fifty years ago, when I was sixteen. You may be aware that my older sister, Doris, died in an accident and is buried in the churchyard. My father passed away ten years ago, but my mother's still here. She lives in sheltered accommodation in the next village to me, but is still as bright as a button mentally, and I'm sure she'd love to share some of her memories with you at some point.

I'd be delighted to talk to you about the farm. Perhaps you'd like to come over to visit me and my wife? Do give me a call when you're free and we can arrange something, and I'll dig out the old photos.

I look forward to hearing from you.

Kind regards,

Jack Beauchamp

His phone number was at the bottom of the email.

'Oh, my God. That's amazing,' Doris said. 'And Mum's still alive! That's wonderful.'

'I'm going to call him now,' Georgina said. 'I'll switch the audio on my phone so it goes to speaker rather than my hearing aids, so you can hear both sides of the conversation.'

'That's—' Doris sounded close to tears.

'Are you all right, Doris?' Georgina asked.

'Yes – and no. Both at the same time,' Doris admitted. 'I can't wait to hear my brother's voice again, after all these years! But, at the same time...'

The ringing tone felt as if it echoed in the room, and Georgina could feel her heartbeat speeding up. Then an answering machine clicked in, and she sagged with disappointment. She listened to the message, then waited for the long beep to end.

'Hello, Mr Beauchamp. It's Georgina Dra—'

The phone was picked up in the middle of the word. 'Georgina? It's Jack. Sorry about that. We've had a lot of those stupid calls where a computer dials you and puts you through to a scammer who offers you cheap insulation or new windows or says you need to press a number to cancel a subscription you never had in the first place. The answering machine screens them out.'

She smiled. 'Good idea.'

'I always pick up if it's a real human leaving a message,' Jack said. 'You live at my old home, then?'

'Yes. I moved here a couple of years ago, from London.'

'You've settled in all right?' he asked.

'Yes, thank you. I was really pleased to get your message. I'd love to come over and see your photographs – and I can bring photos with me to show you how the house and garden are now,' she offered.

'I'd like that,' he said. 'You said that you can be flexible with time?'

'I'm a freelance photographer,' she said. 'I work for myself, so I can meet you whenever it suits you best.'

'Right. Well, I've got an allotment meeting tomorrow; it

always ends up as a long lunch. Are you free in the evening?'

'That'd be lovely. What sort of time?'

'About seven?'

'Perfect,' Georgia said.

'Good. Got a pen?' At her affirmative, he rattled off an address. 'The satnav should find us easily enough. We're at the end of the close – the bungalow with the blue door.'

'Lovely. I'll look forward to seeing you on Tuesday,' she said, and rang off.

Doris gulped. 'That's the first time I've heard my brother's voice for half a century. Well, obviously I could hear him while he still lived here, but he couldn't hear me – and then my family moved away. I can't believe... My little brother,' she said softly.

'What do you want me to ask him?' Georgina asked.

'I don't know. I need to think about that. But I do want to know if he's happy.'

'Is there anything you want me to tell him from you?'

'I'd have to think about that, too.' Doris dragged in a breath. 'Do you think he might come here?'

'I can ask. But, Doris, if you want me to tell him that I can hear you and answer for you, I'm going to need to prove that I'm not trying to be a confidence trickster,' Georgina warned. 'I'll need to tell him something that isn't public record – something that only you would know.'

'I'll try and remember something,' Doris said. 'But, in the meantime, tell me what you found out in Cambridge.'

'You can read it as I'm typing it up, but the quick version is that Cesca and I talked to Garnett's neighbours while Sybbie and Jodie went to his college and talked to some of the staff. Then I talked to his ex-wife. He wasn't a very nice man,' Georgina said. 'And it sounds as if an awful lot of people fell out with him. He cheated on his wife and treated her really badly, he keeps his neighbour's baby awake – and his neighbour, when he's on nights – and the neighbours on his other side think he poisoned their cat. He bullies his students, and has affairs with others.'

'How on earth does he get away with it?' Doris sounded shocked. 'Surely the way he behaves with his students alone would get him sacked from his job?'

'Only if there was evidence. The students would have to talk to someone and admit what happened,' Georgina said. 'Maybe he scared them to the point that they wouldn't tell.'

'What a creep. More than a creep,' Doris said. 'I don't normally swear, but he's a bastard.'

'Sybbie got the impression he doesn't get on with most of his colleagues. It sounds as if he's jealous of the ones who are professors, and he's scared that anyone his junior will be promoted over him,' Georgina said thoughtfully.

'Could any of the people he'd fallen out with have come here?' Doris asked.

'Apart from the fact that he might not have told anyone where he was – he definitely didn't tell his neighbours – I didn't hear or see any visitors,' Georgina said. 'Did you?'

'No,' Doris said. 'To be fair, I wasn't really looking out for anything. You were out, so there was no chance of music or a film. When you're not around, I tend to sit at the end of the garden, listening to the birds.' She paused. 'What about that thing Will set up for you on the computer? The CCTV?'

Georgina felt her eyes widen. 'I never even thought about that. And I'm surprised Will didn't mention it. Or maybe he thinks it wasn't worth it because I never use it.' She rolled her eyes. 'I mean, in a way, he'd be right – I never look at it. I thought he was making too much of a fuss over nothing when he installed it. Little Wenborough's much safer than London.'

'If we don't count the dead body in the barn,' Doris reminded her.

'How did you know about that, anyway?' Georgina asked.

'I was there when the taxi came. Or, rather, I heard the horn beeping, and I went to see what was happening. When the taxi left – without a passenger – I looked through the windows. He hadn't closed the curtains. That's when I saw the body lying on the bed. He wasn't moving, and he'd been sick everywhere.'

'So you didn't see who killed him?'

'No,' Doris said.

'And I didn't tell the police about the CCTV,' Georgina said, guilt flooding through her. 'I've wasted so much of their time; I'd better sort it out now.'

It took a while before Georgina could find the app – which turned out to be on her phone rather than her computer – but she duly logged in and found the link to the footage from Thursday night. A bit of fiddling with the app meant that anything without motion would be played at high speed, and then the playback would return to normal speed when there was something to see. 'Right. Let's start from three o'clock,' she said.

There were three birds and a cat on camera between three o'clock and her car leaving the driveway at half past five. Nothing for another two hours; and then there was a car she didn't recognise. A light-coloured car.

She paused the film, rewound it slightly, and played it at slow speed. The car number plate was mainly obscured by mud and, because the footage was of the rear of the car, she had no idea who was driving.

'I don't know whose car this is,' she said, 'or why they'd be driving through my gate. It can't be a delivery service, because I didn't have anything delivered on Thursday.'

'Could they have delivered the curry to Roland Garnett?' Doris suggested.

'It's seven o'clock. That's a possibility,' Georgina said.

'So you're in the clear,' Doris said.

'Not unless they can trace the car and it ties in with an order,' Georgina said. 'But it's progress.' She continued reviewing the footage, and frowned. 'There's no sign of the car's return journey. If it was a delivery, I'd expect the car to show up on the CCTV again a couple of minutes later.' She carried on watching. 'Another cat. And then my car, at half past eight.' There was still no sign of the light-coloured car. 'So it looks as if Roland Garnett had a guest on his final evening.'

A fox padded across the shingle; finally, the light-coloured car drove back through the gates and onto the main road through the village, just before ten o'clock. Georgina was still none the wiser as to the driver's identity because, as well as the fact that it was dark, they were wearing a hoodie and a cap that obscured their face.

'I think maybe you ought to call the inspector and show him what you've found,' Doris said.

'I agree.' Georgina found the card Colin Bradshaw had given her earlier, and called his number.

He answered after the first ring. 'Bradshaw.'

'It's Georgina Drake,' she said. 'I think I have some information that might help you.'

* * *

Colin listened to her, his frown deepening. 'You're telling me you've only just remembered that you have CCTV – *three days* after someone was killed in your holiday cottage?'

Georgina sounded guilty. 'I know it sounds bad, but...'

'Sounds? It *is* bad,' he said.

'My son installed a CCTV camera on my gate, last summer, and I completely forgot about the thing. I've never even looked at the feed because Little Wenborough's so safe.'

'It wasn't safe for Roland Garnett,' he pointed out dryly.

'I'm sorry I didn't tell you about it before. I really did only just remember it.' She sighed. 'Look, do you want to see this footage, or not?'

'I do,' he said. 'And I'll want a copy.'

'I'm not entirely sure how to get a copy,' she said, 'but I'll ask Will.'

'Right. Is there anything else you want to tell me?' Colin had been planning to talk to her about her trip to Cambridge, but he wanted her to tell him what she'd done before he grilled her.

'Such as?'

She clearly wasn't going to confess upfront. Disappointment made his shoulders sag. 'A little jaunt of, ooh, sixty-odd miles and back?'

'Oh. You know about Cambridge.' She sounded more guilty still.

'Mrs Drake, you're not Miss Marple. Interfering with a case can get you slapped with a charge of perverting the course of justice. Not to mention the charge of impersonating a police officer.'

'I didn't impersonate a police officer,' she said crisply.

'But you didn't say you *weren't* with the police, did you?' Even though, strictly speaking, Colin knew he should be furious with her, he found himself enjoying this. It was the most pleasure he'd had from his job in months, though he wasn't going to dig too deeply into why that might be.

'I'm hardly perverting the course of justice. We've—I've,' she corrected herself swiftly, 'been trying to find out who killed Roland Garnett, because it wasn't me.'

'We,' he said, pouncing on her slip. 'So who abetted you?'

'I haven't done anything wrong,' she said, neatly evading the question.

'Actually, you have,' he said. 'You've interfered with witnesses.'

'You'd already spoken to most of them, and I've found you some new information,' she said.

'Oh?'

She filled him in on Hayley's story; he knew most of it, but the details about the baby and divorce were new.

Colin listened, appalled. He'd been thrilled to bits when Marianne fell pregnant. Cosseted her, went out at ridiculous times to the supermarket to get something when she had a craving, rubbed her back and went to all the antenatal classes with her. Holding his newborn daughter in his arms had been one of the best moments of his life. He knew Marianne had had more than enough grounds to divorce him for unreasonable behaviour, but she'd been kind.

Though, even when his drinking had been at its worst, he knew he would never, ever have treated his wife the way that Roland Garnett had treated Hayley Summers.

'You also need to find out what Dr Garnett used to kill their cat,' Georgina continued.

Her words steered his mind away from maudlin thoughts. 'If you mean the Ropers, we can't be totally sure that he killed the cat. It might not be connected. Even if the vet's records show the cat was poisoned, it might not say what kind of poison, and it won't be evidence that Garnett was the one who administered the poison.'

She sighed. 'But it might be connected. And the records might show what the poison was. What if the killer gave the cat the poison, knowing that the neighbours would blame Garnett?'

'And then wait for more than a year before poisoning him? I don't think it's anything to do with his murder,' Colin said.

'It's still something to think about, isn't it? Look, you can't blame me for wanting to clear my name. I found Roland Garnett in my holiday cottage, and I'm the last person you know of who saw him alive, but I definitely didn't kill the man. Think about it. Killing my clients isn't going to be good for business, is it? I need to clear my name so I can rent the cottage out. And I have potential leads for you.'

'Given the one you've already told me about, I'm not sure

the rest will be that helpful – or admissible in court, because it's hearsay,' he said. 'We'll talk about it after you've shown me the CCTV. Until then, no more of the Miss Marple act, OK?'

She muttered something he didn't catch. Even though he was annoyed with her for interfering, he understood her logic. It sounded as if she was as cross with him as he was with her. 'I'm on my way,' he said.

Half an hour later, he drove through the gate of Rookery Farm and stopped. The CCTV camera was very subtly placed, on the rear of the gatepost. But his team should still have noticed it, and checked for any other CCTV. Not close neighbouring houses, in this case – Rookery Farm had fields to the rear, and there was quite a gap between the farm and the houses either side – but the village, at least.

He got back in his car and parked on the shingle at the front of the house, and rapped the doorknocker. Georgina had clearly been looking out for him, because she answered the front door immediately.

'Inspector,' she said, giving him a tight little nod. The Miss Marple comment had clearly rankled.

'Mrs Drake,' he said.

'The kettle's on,' she said. 'Can I get you some coffee?'

'Thank you.' He followed her through the hallway, but this time he lingered by one of the photographs. 'Is this one of yours?' he asked, gesturing to the monochrome picture of a pale lightning-struck tree against what he assumed had been a bright blue sky.

'Yes.'

'It's good,' he said, and paused to look at the other framed photographs. There was a portrait of a dark-haired man who looked enough like Will Drake for Colin to guess that this was his father. Georgina's husband – who seemed to be concentrating on something, completely unaware that he was being photographed. There was a slight smile on his lips, as if whatever he was looking at pleased him; his dark eyes were intense, and there were crinkles at the corners to show that his smile was genuine.

'Your late husband?' he asked, just to be sure.

'Yes, at a dress rehearsal of *The Winter's Tale*. He was completely immersed in what the actors were doing, and didn't realise I was photographing him as well as the actors,' she said. 'This was Stephen in his happy place. The theatre, when all the hard work had been put in and the actors were ready to go and shine, transport the audience to a different world.'

Had Stephen Drake's happy place not been with his family? Colin wondered.

Then again, he had no room to talk. He'd been consumed by his work, too.

'One of his happy places, I should've said,' Georgina corrected herself. 'The other main one was home – whether he was curled on the sofa listening to music with me, or arguing metaphysics with friends over dinner, or playing cards with the children.'

It sounded as if that had been her happy place, too, and she clearly missed him very much.

He knew how that felt. It had taken him a couple of years to stop missing Marianne, but you couldn't go back and start over.

This time, when she walked on, Colin followed her into the kitchen.

She opened an app on her phone and set it running. 'It's high speed when there's no movement, and normal speed when there's something on camera. Though that includes wildlife,' she warned. 'Watch out for the cat.' She gave him a wry smile. 'And the pigeons, though the cat isn't among them.'

He couldn't help smiling back, liking her sense of humour; he'd always enjoyed plays on words.

By the time she'd finished making coffee, he'd paused the footage on the light-coloured car. 'The number plate's half-

obscured by mud,' he observed. 'Though we have no way of
knowing if it was done deliberately or happened because the car
had been driven on a dirt track.'

'I'd say it was deliberate,' Georgina mused, 'because otherwise the spatter would've gone further up.'

He looked at her. 'Are you quite sure that's not police
training talking?'

She coughed. 'And who was it who accused me of impersonating a police officer?'

'Mrs Drake.' He frowned at her.

'You might as well call me Georgina,' she said, rolling her
eyes. 'It's not police training. It's from taking photographs and
noticing how different substances move, to give different
effects.'

'Right. So you trained as a photographer?' he asked, curious.

'Not originally. My degree's in English literature. I was
going to be a journalist. I probably spent more time at the
university newspaper than I did studying English.' She gave a
wry smile. 'Stephen was directing his first Shakespeare. I was
going to interview him, but our snapper was ill so they asked me
to take his photograph as well as do the interview. That's when I
discovered I liked taking photographs and I was good at it.'

A bit like the way he'd fallen into police work instead of
being the corporate lawyer his parents had expected him to be.
He'd enjoyed it, at least in the early days. Though he'd been
very aware of his father's disappointment. 'Did you specialise in
portraits – weddings, and that sort of thing?'

'I only did three weddings, as an assistant, and that was
more than enough for me,' she said. 'I take mainly portraits,
sometimes for magazines and sometimes for theatre companies
or other businesses who need headshots. I enjoy talking to
people, getting a sense of who they are, and persuading them to
relax so I can capture who they really are in the photographs.'

'So you have good interviewing skills?' he asked.

'I like to think so. I don't think Cambridge was a disaster, Inspector. We have some useful, valid information.'

'All right,' he said with a sigh. 'Let's do the CCTV first, and then we'll talk about what you did today.'

'OK. But, just so you know, Roland Garnett really wasn't a very nice man,' she said.

'That's not up to me to judge. The man was murdered, and he deserves justice for that. The law's meant to serve everyone equally,' he reminded her.

'It doesn't, though, does it?' she asked. 'There are always people who are above the law.'

'Or who think they are,' he corrected. 'And that shouldn't happen.'

'I agree, though it's been the same in every civilisation,' she said. 'Look at Julius Caesar.'

'I thought you said you studied English, not Classics?'

'I was thinking Shakespeare,' she explained. '*Julius Caesar*, where the mob kills Cinna the poet because he has the same name as one of the conspirators. They think they've served justice to someone they thought was a murderer, but they committed murder, too.'

'The death sentence,' Colin said, 'doesn't work. It's not just about who did something – it's *why* they did it that matters. That's where you can look to change things for the future.'

She smiled, and he was shocked to feel his heart flip.

'I didn't expect to be discussing philosophy with you,' she said quietly.

'Because I'm a copper?'

'No. Because when I first met you it was a bad day, when you were in a bad mood and I was still in shock from finding a dead body, and we rubbed each other up the wrong way.' Her lips twitched. 'Not to mention the fact that you've clearly decided my friends and I colluded.'

'It's one line of investigation,' he said. 'I'm looking for

answers. I want to know who killed Roland Garnett, and why. This is a murder investigation, Georgina. It doesn't matter where the victim comes from, or who they are; they deserve justice. And that's my job. The living can still push and ask questions; they can look after themselves. The dead can't.'

'What if the dead could ask questions?' she asked.

'If the dead could talk,' he said, 'there'd be no need for me to investigate. Apart from needing to find the evidence to prove what I was told, I suppose. But the dead can't talk.'

There was a very strange expression on her face, one he couldn't read. 'Can't they?'

'In my experience, there's no such thing as ghosts,' he said. 'Memories, yes – regrets and guilty consciences. There's evidence I can't see that a pathologist can uncover for me in a lab. But not ghosts. So I need to find out what happened to Roland Garnett.'

'The CCTV shows that someone else visited him before he died,' she said.

'After you left the farmhouse.'

'For my Pilates class,' she said. 'Which was after I saw Garnett.'

'If the person in the car saw him, then you weren't the last one to see him alive,' Colin said. 'But what if they didn't see him?'

'Then they were somewhere in my grounds for a very long time, and I have no idea what else they might have been doing – and that's worth investigating,' she said. 'Look, here's my car on my return from the Red Lion. That's where a group of us goes after class. I was the designated driver, so I was on sparkling mineral water, before you ask.'

He gave her a sidelong look. 'I'm not looking for evidence to charge you for drink-driving.'

'Good. Because I'd never be that reckless.'

'I didn't,' he pointed out mildly, 'suggest you would be.'

Though she was definitely antsy about something. But what?

'Here's the other car again.'

He stopped the video and scrutinised it. 'The driver's face in is shadow. And it's dark. With a hoodie and a peaked cap, they weren't taking any chances of being recognised, were they? And the front number plate's also partly obscured.' He made a note of the bits that were visible. 'Did you see or hear the other vehicle when it left?'

'You've driven to the barn yourself, so you know that the driveway to Rookery Barn forks off to the right, away from the farm. You've also seen for yourself that Rookery Barn and the courtyard where visitors' cars tend to park isn't visible from here. And I didn't hear anything.' She frowned at him. 'Hearing aids aren't perfect. Even with my new ones, good as they are, I still have trouble with the direction of sound. And your brain also gets used to some sounds and filters them out – it's why, when you change your hearing aids, it takes a couple of days to get used to all the new sounds, because your brain can't tell what to ignore.'

'I should've realised from what you told me when we first met. I apologise,' he said.

She gave him a smile of acknowledgment. 'So, the car. I thought at first it might've been from a delivery service or a taxi, but then surely the car would've left within a couple of minutes. It was here for a few hours. That suggests to me it belonged to a visitor,' she continued. 'Maybe they brought the curry with them. Did you find any takeaway cartons in the rubbish you took the other day?'

'I can't discuss details of an open case,' he said.

'I know you can't, but I can tell you what I think about the situation and you can stay poker-faced,' she said.

This was absurd, but he was still enjoying himself. And he was curious to know what her take was on the Garnett case.

'Maybe the visitor took the cartons away,' she said, 'to make sure there was no evidence left behind. I'm assuming they washed the cutlery and plates.'

And used bleach. Not that he was able to tell her that. 'It's a theory,' he said. 'Strictly speaking, I shouldn't be discussing any aspect of this case with you at all, let alone theories.'

'Because I'm a suspect?'

'Because I have to do this by the book.' The words slid out before he could stop them.

'Why?' she asked.

He scrabbled for a plausible excuse. 'Because otherwise the evidence won't hold up in court.'

But the pause had been too long – and she'd clearly noticed. He could see in in her face. He sighed. 'And because I messed up, in London. A case that went bad.'

Her expression didn't seem judgemental; if anything, she looked concerned.

'If you want to talk about it,' she said, 'it won't go any further than me.'

This was ridiculous. Colin had met the woman only a couple of times and he'd known her for a handful of days. How did he know he could trust her word? But his instincts about people were usually spot on, and he liked Georgina Drake. He liked the way she thought. Maybe, just maybe, he could tell her.

* * *

Georgina hadn't realised that Colin Bradshaw was married with children. He didn't wear a wedding ring, but that meant nothing. It was more that she didn't have the impression he had a partner to take care of him and be taken care of in turn; to share the good and the bad the way she and Stephen had.

'The case messed with my head,' he said, 'because a young girl was killed, in a very nasty way, and I couldn't solve it. My daughter was about the same age at the time, and I couldn't stop thinking about it and worrying about her. I became the biggest cliché in the book. You know how it goes: middle-aged cop tries to blot it out with booze. I learned the hard way that there aren't any answers in the bottom of a vodka bottle.' He shrugged. 'I ended up divorced and in rehab. I could've been kicked out of the force, but I had a good record and they gave me another chance at work. I get to see my daughter, but I don't have joint custody. I know how much I let her and my wife down, and I hate the fact someone else is being a better dad to Cathy than I am, but it's not about me. It's about my daughter being settled and happy. I'm not going to do anything to rock that.'

She liked the fact that he was putting his daughter first, or at least trying to. 'That's still hard. Does she live near?'

'In London,' he said. 'Two hours away.'

'That's where my daughter lives, too. And my boy's more than four hours away. Video calls,' she said, 'are the absolute best thing about smartphones.'

'Yeah. I think I've learned that.' He looked at her. 'I'm still not discussing the case with you – but I'd like to know what happened in Cambridge.'

'No repercussions?'

He narrowed his eyes.

She sighed. 'It wasn't done to wreck your investigation. Anyway, your colleagues had already talked to the people we talked to, so we weren't really interfering.'

'Go on,' he said.

'I was over at Cesca's yesterday, with Sybbie and Jodie. We talked about it.' She looked at him. 'As you said, you can't discuss this with me, but we'll do this the way my best friend got round discussing her mother-in-law's dementia with the GP: there are no rules saying I can't say things to you, or that you can't act on what I tell you.'

He gave her an approving nod.

'Our theory is that you believe Cesca cooked the poisoned

curry, with oleander she got from Sybbie, and I gave the food to Garnett. Then I "found" the body, which I thought would prove that I couldn't have committed the murder.'

'It's a theory,' he said. 'Though, if you're going to "find" a body –' he added the speech marks with his fingers '– then it's a good idea to have a witness to corroborate it.'

Georgina had had a witness, all right, but not one who could corroborate the fact for her. She was the only one who could hear Doris.

'I'll bear that in mind,' she said. 'But this isn't just about me. Little Wenborough's a small place. People talk. I'm an incomer. So what they say about me probably isn't going to make any difference to me. I won't even know about most of the gossip. But it does worry me that I might be tainting people by association. Jodie, for a start. All it takes is some busybody deciding that she's not a fit mother and talking to social services. She'd then have to fight to clear her name and could even lose her son, which isn't fair. Then there's Cesca; if people decide she put poison in the food she sells, they'll stop buying anything from her and her business will go under. As for Sybbie...' She smiled. 'Actually, I think people might think twice before they dare spread any rumours about her.'

'Lady Wyatt can look after herself,' Colin agreed.

She liked the flicker of humour in his gaze. But she also needed him to understand the full situation. 'Cesca and Jodie are vulnerable, and they've been good to me,' she said. 'I was a wreck when I came to the village. They persuaded me to go to Pilates, and to do a talk on photography for the WI. Without them, I'd still be sunk in misery. They've helped me so much.'

'Protecting people is a motive for murder,' Colin said mildly.

'None of us murdered anyone. But we need to clear our names,' Georgina said. 'We thought it'd be useful to talk to people who knew Roland Garnett, so we could find out more about him. What made him tick? What would make someone want to poison him?'

'I'm listening,' Colin said.

'He doesn't treat people well. He married his ex-wife when she was a student. I could give him the benefit of the doubt, here, but my impression is that he realised her family was well off and would give them the deposit for a house. Which they did,' Georgina said. 'Then he made her life a misery, cutting her off from her family and friends. One of their neighbours intervened, so she ended up reunited with her family – and he bore a grudge against the neighbours after that. He fell out with the neighbours on his other side, too, and they've complained about the noise he creates.'

'So you think the neighbours might have murdered him?'

'No. They've talked to the council about him. But nothing ever gets done,' she said. 'He didn't get on with people in his personal life. He doesn't seem to have got on with any of the support staff at the college. He had affairs with students – how he got away with that, I really don't understand – and last term one of his students dropped out of her course because he made her so miserable. It's possible that she took an overdose, first.'

Colin blinked. 'His student dropped out? And took an overdose?'

'Didn't you know about that bit? I thought you'd talked to his colleagues.'

'I did,' Colin said.

'Just the academics? Because the bedder and the woman serving in the Buttery told Sybbie.'

'So far, what you've told me is hearsay and circumstantial evidence,' Colin said.

'Not all of it, and you know it. The council has documented complaints about the noise. The local police will have witness statements from the Ropers about their cat. If it's on record, then that's actual evidence, surely?'

'Georgina—'

'And you need to talk to Jill, the girl who dropped out,' Georgina continued, undeterred.

'What's her surname?'

'We didn't get that, and we could hardly go back and ask someone in the college without it looking suspicious. But *you* can ask that sort of question.' She gave him a pointed look. 'If you're careful how you approach her, there's a good chance she'll give you evidence that might lead to more information.'

'Are you telling me how to do my job now?' he asked, sounding faintly exasperated.

'No. Well, maybe a bit,' she admitted. 'But I want to clear my name, and those of my friends. It's obvious that Roland Garnett had a lot of people who didn't get on with him. His neighbours. His ex's family. His students. His colleagues. They're all lines of enquiry that I think will be a lot more useful than interviewing and re-interviewing anyone here in Little Wenborough. In Cambridge, you have people who had to put up with him every day. They're the ones with the real motives.'

He sighed. 'All right. I'll do the follow-up interviews myself. But no more interfering, OK?'

She winced.

'What else have you done?' he asked.

'Talked to my son,' she said. 'As a chemist, he has friends and colleagues who have a great deal of knowledge about poison and tox screens. It might be that oleander mimics the effects of a different chemical agent.'

Colin's grey eyes crinkled at the corners. 'You talk like a scientist.'

'That's Will's influence,' she said. 'But the thing that really strikes me as odd is that Garnett left a mess everywhere in the barn except the kitchen. I know he wasn't a cook, because he made a fuss about the oven not working – the instruction manual was in the file but, if he'd been a cook, he would've worked it out for himself anyway. Plus he wanted to know about takeaway delivery services. And although there were crockery and cutlery in the sink when I cleaned the barn, the second week he was there, it wasn't like that on the day I found his body. The kitchen was spotless when I walked in, as if someone had already cleaned it, and I can't see him doing it.'

'Go on,' Colin said.

'So who did clean it? His visitor? If you went to visit someone who was on a work retreat or a holiday, and you brought a takeaway with you – or one of you cooked dinner from scratch – how likely is it that you'd clear up the kitchen afterward? With bleach, to the point that whatever you did in the kitchen was untraceable?' She paused. 'I know you can't tell me this, but I'm willing to bet that the only prints in that kitchen were mine. I don't think Garnett was the sort to clean meticulously, given the state of the place the first time I cleaned it, and the way the living room and the bathroom were at the end. And that makes me think that whoever cleaned the kitchen wanted to be quite sure they'd got rid of any evidence of poison, to make it look like a natural death. And their DNA,' she said. 'Because if you visited someone and you were wearing gloves, they'd notice and ask questions. So they'd want to get rid of their DNA as well.'

* * *

She was right. It was highly probable that the driver of the car had given Garnett the curry and then cleaned their DNA from the scene. He'd had the team check the sink, in the hope that there might be some evidence, but all that was in the U-bend was bleach.

'It's a theory,' he said.

Georgina narrowed her eyes at him.

'The problem is,' he said, 'if he did have a visitor, we don't have an identity for that visitor. Unless we can find out who drove that car, and unless we can find forensic evidence linking them to the Rookery Barn, we can't prove their presence.'

'I hope,' she said, 'I've given you enough to think about so you'll realise that Cesca, Sybbie, Jodie and I had nothing to do with it.'

'You've given me plenty to think about,' he said.

She sighed. 'I was hoping you'd agree that the four of us are innocent.'

'I can't comment on that,' he said.

She looked deflated. 'I suppose not. Well, I can give you a copy of my notes,' she said. 'And I'll pass on whatever Will sends me about oleander and what else mimics its effects.'

'Thank you,' he said.

He almost – almost – asked her if she'd like to have dinner with him. Because, the more time he spent with her, the more he enjoyed her company and he wanted it to continue. She was refreshing; she made him see things in a slightly different way.

But, until one of the other lines of enquiry ruled her out, she was still a suspect on this case. Even talking to her here, instead of making her go to the station and sit in an interview room where they'd have another member of his team in attendance, and the entire conversation was recorded on tape, was skirting the boundaries of what was acceptable.

So he squashed the impulse, accepted the emailed copy of her notes and took screenshots and timing notes from the CCTV. 'I'll get one the tech team to come and see you, so we can get a copy of the footage,' he said.

'All right,' she said. 'Thank you, Inspector Bradshaw.'

She'd asked him to call her Georgina.

And, even though he knew it was probably a bad idea, he said, 'My name's Colin.'

'Colin.' And that little glint in her eyes made him feel warm all the way back to Norwich.

TEN

On Tuesday evening, Georgina drove over to meet Jack Beauchamp and his wife, Tracey. She took flowers and a box of Cesca's brownies, and Doris had given her some information to tell Jack that nobody else would know.

'You really didn't need to do that, love. But thank you,' Jack said, shaking her hand. 'Come and sit down. Can I get you a glass of wine?'

'I'm driving, so I'd better stick to something soft, if you don't mind,' Georgina said.

'Then let's have a pot of tea to go with those brownies,' he said. 'This is my wife, Tracey. Tracey, this is Georgina, who lives in the house where I grew up.'

Tracey gave her a hug. 'Lovely to meet you. Though I saw the news this morning about the man dying in the barn. You must've had a tough few days.'

'It's been a bit difficult,' Georgina said wryly.

'And it's not the first death at the farm,' Jack said.

Tracey squeezed his hand. 'Love, I know. Try not to upset yourself.'

'Sorry.' He shook himself. 'It's been more than half a century, but I still miss my big sister.'

'Of course you do,' Georgina said, feeling a lump in her throat. And she knew how much Doris missed him, too.

'I've got all the old photographs out,' he said. 'Come and see.'

There was a pile of albums that had clearly been cherished. Georgina sat at the dining-room table next to Jack and looked at the photographs as he leafed through the pages and talked her through what she was seeing.

Rookery Farm in the 1960s still had roses round the door, but the place was clearly a working farm. 'Rookery Barn looks very different,' she said.

'It was the dairy, back then,' he said. 'This is my mum making butter and cheese. Everything was done by hand, in those days. We used to put the milk in churns and send the excess to the Milk Marketing Board – there weren't any bulk tanks, not back then.'

Tracey came in with a tray bearing a floral-patterned china teapot, matching milk jug and sugar bowl, and cups and saucers. 'Help yourself to milk and sugar, love,' she said, pouring the tea and passing a cup and saucer to Georgina.

'Thank you.' Georgina smiled and added milk to her cup.

Tracey had put the brownies on a plate, and made sure everyone had a brownie as well as tea.

Georgina was fascinated by the pictures inside the house. 'You're using the fireplaces with proper fires,' she said. 'Now, there are wood burners, not open grates, and I tend to rely on the central heating.'

Jack nodded. 'We didn't have central heating, just the Rayburn in the kitchen and the fireplaces in the living room and dining room. The coalman used to come round on a Wednesday and tipped a couple of sacks of coal into the outhouse. My job used to be raking out the ashes in the morning before school.'

'And the fires heat the whole house?' Georgina asked.

'Not very well,' he admitted. 'We always had ice on the inside of the windows in the mornings.'

'Same for us,' Tracey said. 'I left home before my parents got central heating. If you sat too close to the coal fire, your legs would be too hot and burn; if you didn't get close enough, you'd shiver.'

'I don't miss that bit of the past,' Jack said. 'We always wore at least two jumpers in the winter. Though you kept warm by keeping busy, because a lot of the work was manual.'

'My parents used to talk about the bad winter of 1963,' Georgina said. 'I can't even imagine it. Months and months of being snowed in.'

'We had a foot of snow on Boxing Day,' Jack reminisced. 'Even the sea froze. The village was cut off – but Dad had reckoned on it being a bad winter and managed to get all our livestock close enough so we could feed them. We thought winter would never end, that year.'

'Still went to school, though,' Tracey said. 'I remember the little bottles of milk we used to have at morning playtime – they froze and burst their way through the foil cap.'

'I think they'd stopped doing milk by the time I went to school,' Georgina said.

Jack turned over the page. 'That's my big sister, Doris.'

Georgina swallowed hard. It was a colour version of the photograph used in the paper; Doris's hair was gloriously red, and her smile was warm. 'I'm so sorry you lost her. She looks lovely.'

'She was.' Jack had tears in his eyes. 'I've never been able to handle Valentine's Day, not since she died. It's not romantic, for me – it's the day that took my sister away. And I know I should give my wife flowers and a card, but I just...'

'I know you love me, you daft ha'porth,' Tracey said,

squeezing his hand. 'You don't need to buy me cards and what have you on the day the shops want you to.'

'It must've been very hard for you,' Georgina said.

Jack nodded. 'Mum and Dad couldn't cope with it. They sold the farm and moved this side of the city. It was easier not to have to look at the place where she died every day.' He bit his lips. 'It's more than half a century ago now, and I've been without her for much, much longer than I had her, but I still miss her.'

'Of course you do.' Part of her really wanted to tell Jack that Doris was still here, and missed him just as much; but she knew that now wasn't the right time.

'I printed out some pictures for you, of how Rookery Farm looks now,' she said.

'We were going to have a look-round, when we saw the old house come up for sale,' he said. 'Weren't we, Tracey? But then I got Covid and, by the time I was up to going out again, the place had been sold and it was too late.'

'You're both welcome to come and have a look-round, any time,' she said. 'You've got my number. Friday morning is changeover if I have anyone staying in the barn so, if you want to see that as well, then Friday morning around eleven is good.'

'We'll ring you, first, to make sure you're there. Thank you, love.' He smiled. 'It'd be nice to see it.'

She gave him the envelope of photographs, and Jack leafed through them. 'It's much lighter and brighter than it was in my day,' he said. 'I remember it being a bit gloomy, or maybe that was the terrible curtains.'

'Orange and brown, my parents had,' Tracey said, laughing. 'All those swirls that never matched anything else. Oh, and that awful grungy yellow!'

'Dad's office must've been where the study is now. He had a big old table, and shelving with all the farm books on them. And

we had a boot room where we kept the wellies, the jackets and
what have you.'

'I think the boot room probably became the utility room,
along with a bit of space pinched from the study,' Georgina said.
'The previous owners said they used a mix of original and
reclaimed flooring. They had them cleaned professionally, then
sealed.'

'Pamment tiles,' he said. 'I remember Mum had these tins of
wax floor polish that smelled of lavender. You'd put it on with a
rag, and then buff it.' He pointed out her darkroom. 'Is that a
walk-in pantry?'

'It's my darkroom,' Georgina explained. 'That's the only
change I've made, to have that built. I wanted the door to look
like the rest of the doors on the outside, but the inside of the
door seals out the light properly so it doesn't ruin my paper or
damage my films before I've processed them.'

'Did you print these in your darkroom?' he asked.

She smiled. 'Off the computer, I'm afraid. The ones I do in
my darkroom are black and white.'

Jack looked at the photo of the kitchen. 'That's lovely. Back
in my day, it was all shelving and free-standing cupboards, and
the Rayburn – it was cheaper than an Aga. We had a fridge, but
no freezer. There was just a tiny icebox at the top of the fridge,
with enough space for a packet of frozen peas and a little metal
grid thing you put on a tray to make ice cubes, except it never
really worked.' He continued leafing through the pictures. 'The
front bedroom was Mum and Dad's. Mum would've loved an
en suite,' he said. 'They had one in their last place. My room
was next door, looking over the front. Doris's looked over the
garden, and there were two spare rooms in case family came to
stay.'

'My son and daughter have a room each,' Georgina said,
'and there are still two spare rooms for family and friends.'

'I love what you've done to the garden,' he said.

'Again, that was the last owners,' Georgina admitted. 'I'm not very green-fingered. I have a lot of help from my gardener. I guess you might've known his grandad, Tom Nichols, at school?'

'Yes, I did. His dad used to get first prize every year for his carrots at the village show,' Jack said. 'Mum and Dad had a vegetable plot, but we ate everything.' He smiled. 'Doris used to have to help in the house, and I had to do the garden. Dad did the heavy stuff, but my job was the weeding. I used to hoe between the rows of carrots, potatoes, cabbages and onions, and moaned about it, too!'

'Ironic that you hated it, back then, but now you're on the committee for the allotment,' Tracey said with a smile.

'So what have you found in your research into the farm's history, so far?' Jack asked.

'I've worked back using the deeds and some of the census records. My daughter works for a probate genealogist when she doesn't have an acting role,' Georgina explained. 'So I know the names of the people who had the farm after you, and before you were your grandparents and great-grandparents.'

'My mum would be interested in what you find,' he said. 'She's still as bright as a button, at ninety-four, but she's not as mobile as she was. It was hard to get her agree to accept help, but now she's glad she's in sheltered accommodation.'

'I know what you mean; my mum's heading for eighty,' Georgina said. 'I don't want to take her independence away, but I do worry about her. She's still in London, so my daughter pops in to see her and keep an eye on her.'

'That's good,' Tracey said. 'Our kids are good, too – Matthew and Lucy. They take their gran flowers.'

Jack looked sad. 'We lost Dad, ten years ago. I try and keep his grave nice, with silk flowers. We do the same with Doris.'

'I hope this doesn't sound inappropriate, and I'm sorry if I'm intruding,' she said, 'but when I found out what happened, I visited the churchyard. I wanted to put some flowers from the garden on your sister's grave. I thought the carnations you'd left there were lovely.'

'I didn't put carnations on,' he said. 'I put silk roses.'

'The carnations weren't silk. They were fresh,' Georgina said.

'That's odd. I wonder who put them there,' Jack said, frowning.

'Do you think it might it have been her boyfriend, Trev?'

Jack's eyes narrowed. 'I didn't tell you about him.'

'I know,' Georgina said quickly. 'Billy at the butcher's is the head of the village historical society. One of them had a chat with me about her memories. She mentioned that everyone thought Doris was going to marry Trev, after she trained as a teacher.'

Jack relaxed. 'Oh. Yes. We all thought that, too.'

'Are you still in touch with him?' Georgina asked.

'No,' Jack said. 'When we moved away from the farm, we lost touch with a lot of people. It wasn't like it is now, with mobile phones and the internet. You had to write to people, or go to a phone box when you'd prearranged to call. If someone else was using the box, you'd have to wait and hope that the person you wanted to call would wait, too.'

'It's a lot easier now,' she agreed.

'I often wonder what happened to him. There was talk of him being in hospital, after Doris died. His nerves, you know? But back in the seventies people hushed that sort of thing up.' Jack shook himself. 'Ignore me. I'm being a maudlin old man. I just wish things had been different.'

Tracey said nothing, but squeezed his hand again and topped up his tea.

'I understand how you feel,' Georgina said. 'I lost my husband two years ago. He died from a heart attack while I was away on a job, and I've never forgiven myself for not being there – if I hadn't been away, I could've saved him.'

'That's how Mum felt, I think,' Jack said. 'I always wondered – if I hadn't gone to my best friend's, that night, I might've heard her fall and got help in time.' He bit his lip. 'Or maybe it would've been too late anyway. I hope she didn't suffer.'

Georgina wondered for a moment if Doris was still stuck because her family blamed themselves for her death; maybe this was the unfinished business that Doris needed to settle. 'My counsellor,' she said, 'told me not to think like that, because it would probably still have happened. It wasn't anyone's fault.'

'It's hard,' Jack said.

'It must've been awful for all of you,' she said. 'I'm sorry to bring it all back.'

Jack wiped away a tear. 'Maudlin old man,' he said again, giving her a watery smile.

She couldn't leave here without at least trying to tell him what she knew.

'Jack, do you believe in ghosts?' she asked.

'Everyone's heard stories, whether it's Black Shuck the devil dog on the coast, or Anne Boleyn's dad driving a carriage with headless horses over bridges,' he said with a shrug. 'But I've never seen one myself.' His eyes narrowed. 'Why do you ask?'

'My late husband was a theatre director,' Georgina said. 'Actors are superstitious – there are all the stories of a grey lady, and you can't speak the name of the Scottish Play out loud.' She took a deep breath. 'Until last week, I always thought it was just stories. But something strange happened to me, last week.'

'Go on,' he said.

'I got new hearing aids on Friday,' she said. 'And since then I've been able to hear someone.'

'Hear someone?' Tracey asked.

Georgina nodded. 'I thought at first I'd accidentally tuned into the radio – you know, similar to when you accidentally call someone when your phones in your pocket. But then I realised I hadn't.'

Jack blinked. 'So what was it?'

Georgina took a deep breath. 'A person. I didn't believe it, at first. I thought it was someone cold reading me or repeating things that were on public record – things my husband had said about me or the children in interviews.'

'Who?' Tracey asked.

This was the big one. Georgina knitted her fingers together. Please, please let him believe her. 'There isn't an easy way to say this, Jack. I can't see her, just hear her.' She paused. 'It's Doris.'

He went pale. 'No,' he said. 'No. You're lying.'

'I promise you, I'm not,' Georgina said. 'I was born on Valentine's Day in 1971. I don't know if that's got anything to do with –'

'Get out,' he said, cutting her off.

'Jack—Mr Beauchamp,' she said. 'Please.'

'I don't want to hear any more of your rubbish,' he snapped. 'Mum paid God knows how much to some woman who claimed to be a medium and told her a load of mumbo-jumbo about our Doris. I'm not paying you a penny.'

'I don't want any money. That's not why—'

'Get out,' he said, pressing his hands over his face; his shoulders shook as if he were sobbing. 'Just get *out*.'

And the weariness and despair in his voice tore at Georgina's heart.

'I'm sorry,' she said. 'I never meant to hurt you. Look, I can prove it. She told me about the m—'

'Don't you tell me any more of your lies! Get *out*!' Jack shouted.

He clearly wasn't going to listen to her.

Right now, there was nothing else she could do. Leaving the photographs where they were, she walked out of the room.

Tracey Beauchamp escorted her to the door, looking shocked and hurt and angry. 'What the hell were you thinking?'

'I'm sorry,' Georgina whispered. 'I wanted to help, not...'

'Well, you didn't help, did you?' Tracey asked. 'You made it worse.'

'I'm not a con artist. I don't want money or anything like that. I came to tell him what really happened that night.'

'I don't care what you think you're doing. He's been hurt enough,' Tracey said. 'Just go, please.'

Making one last-ditch attempt to bat for Doris, Georgina said, 'Can you at least tell him she loves him? When he spoke to me at the farm, she heard his voice for the first time in more than half a century. She's missed him so much.'

'Just *go*,' Tracey repeated.

Defeated, Georgina left.

By the time she got back to Rookery Farm, she was crying. It took her three goes to unlock the back door.

'How did—?' Doris stopped, clearly realising that Georgina was upset. 'It was bad?'

'Really bad. I'm so sorry, Doris. I messed it up,' Georgina said. 'It was fine when we were talking about the house. But then I told him about you. And...' She dragged in a hoarse breath. 'He didn't believe me. He was so hurt and upset. He told me to leave.'

'Oh, no. *No*.' Doris's voice sounded as shaky as Georgina felt.

'I'm so sorry. I'll try again. I'll write to Tracey,' Georgina said. 'Maybe I can make her realise I'm not trying to play some cruel trick on them. But, for now... I'm just so sorry.'

'You tried,' Doris said. 'I can't ask more of you than that.'

But, despite her attempt at bravery, Doris's despair sounded in her voice.

Georgina needed to fix this. But, if Tracey Beauchamp also refused to speak to her, what then?

* * *

The pieces of the puzzle were shifting, but they weren't falling into place.

'We need a different angle,' Colin said to Mo and Larissa, his team. 'We know Dr Garnett ate a chicken curry laced with oleander. But we don't know where the curry came from. It's highly probable it was brought by the driver of the car we saw on the CCTV from Rookery Farm. It looks like a Ford Fiesta, a pale colour; but we still don't know who owns it, let alone whether the owner was driving it or whether it was stolen.'

'Is there anyone who'd want him dead?' Mo asked. 'Family, colleagues, neighbours?'

'His neighbours on both sides hate him. One side thinks he poisoned their cat, and the other's fed up with him playing loud music to wake their baby – or the doctor when he's on night shift,' Colin said. 'He mentally abused his ex-wife and cheated on her, but she's steered clear of him ever since she left him and divorced him. One of his students dropped out last term, and the hearsay is that he drove her to take an overdose. He was grabby and mouthy with Jodie Fulcher and Francesca Walters, so Jodie refused to clean the barn and Francesca wouldn't deliver his orders. But is any of that enough of a motive to kill him? Plus we'd need to know if any of them had the opportunity.' He frowned. 'I'd clear the ex because we know that she was driving back to Cambridge from York when he was killed.' He drummed his fingers on the table. 'We need to find out who owns the car, and whether it was reported stolen. Chase up the progress on getting his email and phone records, and then we can see if they bring up anyone in particular.'

'It's worth checking out the hearsay about the student, too,' Larissa said. 'Everything seems to point back to Cambridge.'

'It does. I think we should pay a visit – if nothing else, it'll help us rule out potential suspects,' Colin agreed. 'Which of you wants to come?'

'Toss you for it,' Mo said, taking a coin from his pocket.

'Heads,' Larissa said.

Mo tossed the coin and revealed it on the back of his hand. 'Tails. So that'll be me escaping the office, today.'

* * *

In Cambridge, Colin parked in the space outside the Porter's Lodge at St Bene't's College.

'We normally ask visitors to book a space in advance,' the porter said. 'Mr...?'

'Detective Inspector Bradshaw,' Colin said, showing his warrant card, 'and this is Sergeant Mo Tesfaye.'

'Ah. That's different. Let me sort out your permit, and then I'll find whoever it is you need to see.'

'Actually,' Colin said, 'you're the first point of call for visitors, aren't you?'

'And college members, yes,' the porter said. 'I'm Lenny Peters.'

'Perhaps,' Colin said, 'we can have a chat, Mr Peters. Somewhere a little quieter.'

'There's an office in the back. Come through.' After checking the registration number of Colin's car and putting it into the computer, Lenny logged out of the system and took Colin into the office. 'Can I get you both a tea or coffee?'

'Thanks, but I'm fine,' Colin said.

'Not for me, thanks,' Mo said with a smile.

'We're working a murder enquiry,' Colin explained. 'You're not under caution, but we'd like to talk to you to get some background information. We might need you to sign a witness statement afterwards.'

'Murder?' Lenny blew out a breath. 'I don't know of any

murder, certainly not here at St Bene't's, but I'll do what I can to help.'

'How long have you worked here, Mr Peters?' Colin asked.

'Lenny. I've been here for fifteen years,' he said.

'Can you take us through what your role is, Mr Peters?' Mo asked.

'The porter is the first point of call for college members, visitors and tourists,' Lenny said. 'I book people onto tours, deal with enquiries, handle room bookings and parking spaces, and sort out the mail into pigeonholes. I'm a first aider and a fire warden, and I'm responsible for security. With old buildings like this, we need to be very conscious of the fire risks, so we have CCTV plus fire and intruder alarms.' He smiled. 'Everyone's got this idea that the porter's the one in a bowler hat who yells at you and tells you to keep off the grass. We don't have bowler hats, nowadays, but I do tell people to get off their bike and wheel it through the college, and issue parking notices.'

Colin made a note. 'Would you say you know everyone in college?'

'All the staff, yes, and you get to know the new students pretty quickly. It doesn't take long to work out if they're likely to be trouble, and you try to defuse situations before they get nasty,' Lenny said.

'Sensible,' Mo commented.

'You said you're responsible for security. I take it you'd know if any of the rooms in the college were empty?' Colin asked.

'And a fire risk. Yes,' Lenny confirmed.

'Have any students moved out in the last term?' Colin asked.

Lenny looked awkward. 'Yes. It's a bit of a sad business. One of the postgrads was struggling with her workload and the stress got too much for her, so she took an overdose. Luckily the girl in the next room raised the alarm, and she was taken to hospital.'

So the overdose story wasn't just hearsay, Colin thought. 'Was she all right?'

'I think so. Her parents cleared her things out of her room and took her home,' Lenny said. 'Hopefully she'll get some support and can sort out what she wants to do once her head's back in the right place, poor kid.'

'Can you give me her details, please? Home address, mobile number?'

'You'll need to ask Admin for those,' Lenny said. 'I don't have access to that information. But I can tell you her name was Jill Cassidy.'

Colin glanced at Mo, who nodded. 'Where can I find Admin, please?' he asked.

'Old Court,' Lenny said, and gave him a college map.

'Thanks. I'll go and see them,' Mo said.

'Just a few more questions,' Colin said as Mo left. 'What can you tell me about Roland Garnett?'

'He's one of our Classics lecturers. His rooms are in Middle Court. Well, they *were*, I should say. He died over the Easter break. We were told he'd had a heart attack.' He frowned. 'Are you telling me it was murder?'

'We're investigating his death,' Colin said.

Lenny's frown deepened. 'Funny, someone was asking about him, the other day. I don't know if it's relevant, but it was a Lady Wyatt. Her goddaughter's applying here in September and they wanted a look round the college. We didn't have space on a tour, so I gave them the laminated cards for the self-guided tour. The girl didn't say a word – I'm not sure if she was shy or sulking – but the godmother was nice. Very polite.'

Colin knew exactly who Lady Wyatt was, and forbore to tell the porter that Sybbie Walters was the source of his information about Jill. 'Thank you. That's helpful.' He paused. 'Was Dr Garnett popular?'

Lenny wrinkled his nose. 'I'm not sure I can answer that.'

'It might be relevant,' Colin said. He didn't think Lenny Peters was the sort to take part in a cover-up, but he did think that Lenny might be wary of speaking ill of the dead.

'It feels a bit bad to talk about someone who can't speak up for themselves anymore,' Lenny said, confirming Colin's instinct. 'He's—*was*, I mean,' Lenny corrected himself, 'quite hard on his students. You never saw him having a drink or lunch with the other dons, and they didn't seem to like him. To be honest, he ignored anyone he thought was beneath his notice or wouldn't be useful.'

In other words, Garnett was a snob and a user, Colin thought. 'Any rumours?'

'There are always rumours in a place like this,' Lenny said wryly. 'And I don't tend to spread them.'

'Gossip is sometimes what helps us break a case,' Colin said.

Lenny paused. 'There was a bit of a fuss when he got married, quite a few years back. The girl wasn't his student, though, so he wasn't in a position of trust and got away without any disciplinary. The marriage didn't last long, though.'

Corroborating what Hayley Summers had said, Colin thought. 'Did he live in or out of college?'

'In, until he got married. Then he moved out very quickly. As far as I know, he uses his rooms for tutorials and supervisions.'

Colin inclined his head. 'You said the marriage didn't last. Any reason why?'

'He has an eye for a pretty girl.' Lenny compressed his lips. 'But there's never been any complaints or evidence. If he did date them, that's not professional, mind.' Lenny shrugged. 'He's Teflon, though. Nothing sticks.'

'Thank you,' Colin said, 'that's very helpful. He was Jill Cassidy's tutor, wasn't he?'

'Yes.'

'Was he dating her?'

'I don't know. I didn't hear any rumours,' Lenny said.

'You said you got to know the students. What can you tell me about Jill?' Colin asked.

'Quiet lass, always had her nose in a book. She came here in September the year before last to do her postgraduate MA, and stayed on to do her PhD.' Lenny frowned. 'Poor kid. I hope she's doing all right. If she comes back, I'll make sure her pastoral tutor's aware of what happened.'

'That wasn't Garnett?'

'No. We tend to have separate pastoral and academic tutors. It can be useful if a student doesn't really gel with their academic tutor,' Lenny said.

Lenny Peters, Colin thought, cared an awful lot more about the students than the master of the college did. They were lucky to have him. 'Thank you for your time,' he said.

'No problem. If you need anything else, you know where I am,' Lenny said.

Colin nodded. 'Thank you. And if you remember anything that you think might be useful, please get in touch.' He gave Lenny his business card.

Mo was walking back to the porter's lodge just as Colin left. 'All done, guv,' he said. 'Though I had to reinforce that this is a murder investigation and that, if we have to, we can put someone on a charge of obstruction of justice.'

'Do they think we're going to give the information to some pet journalist?' Colin rolled his eyes. 'For pity's sake. Their students should be more important than their academic dignity, or whatever they want to call it.'

'We've got a mobile, a landline and a home address for Jill Cassidy,' Mo said.

Colin smiled. 'Good work.'

Her mobile number went straight through to voicemail; the landline also went through to an answering machine. He sighed inwardly. 'This is Detective Inspector Colin Bradshaw, calling to talk to Jill Ca—'

The phone was snatched up abruptly. 'Hello?'

'Hello. Am I speaking to Jill Cassidy?' he asked.

'No. I'm her mother. What do you want with Jill?'

'I'd like to talk to her in connection with a case. She's not in any trouble,' he added, wanting to reassure her mother. 'I just need some background information.'

'I'm afraid you can't talk to her.' Her voice was clipped.

Colin reminded himself to be kind. Understanding. 'Mrs Cassidy, I appreciate that you—'

'No, you don't understand,' Jill's mother said. 'You can't talk to her, because we buried her last month.'

It was the last thing he'd expected to hear, and it caught him off balance.

'I'm sorry to hear that,' he said. Why the hell hadn't the college admins told Mo about that? Were they trying to cover up something, or were they so unbothered about their students that they didn't even know Jill had died?

And, if she'd died last month, then she definitely had nothing to do with Roland Garnett's death.

Asking about whether she'd taken the overdose because of her tutor seemed cruel and pointless.

'It must be difficult for you,' Colin said. 'My condolences. Clearly she doesn't have a connection to my case. I apologise for disturbing you.'

He put the phone down. He was no further forward.

ELEVEN

On Wednesday morning, Georgina sat in the kitchen, her eyes gritty from lack of sleep.

A week ago, she'd been relatively happy. Life had been normal. She hadn't found a dead body in her barn, discovered that the house was resident to a ghost, or messed everything up.

Today, she felt miserable. A failure.

But wallowing in misery wasn't going to make things better with Jack Beauchamp. She needed to write a letter: longhand, rather than typed, because it felt more personal and more sincere.

When she'd screwed up the fourth sheet of paper with half a paragraph on it, she made herself a strong coffee and opened her laptop. Maybe she needed time for the right words to form in the back of her head. In the meantime, she could talk to Cesca and Sybbie about the CCTV.

'Perfect timing,' Francesca said when Georgina turned up at the farm shop. 'I took a batch of choc-chip cookies out of the oven ten minutes ago, and I'm due a break. Let's grab some coffee and sit in Sybbie's garden. It'll be quieter there and I can concentrate.'

Sybbie was in the greenhouse, talking to Old Tom, Young Tom and Jenny. 'If you wouldn't mind pricking out these trays, that would be wonderful,' she said.

'Come and grab a cookie, while they're still warm,' Francesca said. 'I brought a plateful because Giles and Bernard are bound to appear.'

'Thanks,' said Sybbie and the gardeners, all happily accepting a cookie.

'You said you wanted to show us some CCTV?' Francesca asked.

'From last Thursday night,' Georgina said. 'It shows a car going to the barn at about seven. You can only see a bit of the number plate, but I wondered if you might recognise it – if it belongs to someone local. I know it's a bit of a long shot but...'

'I didn't know you had CCTV, Georgie. This is a break-through; let's get some drinks to go with these cookies and you can show it to us,' Sybbie said.

'It was Will's idea. I forgot about it,' Georgina said.

* * *

Five minutes later, settled on the terrace, Georgina held her breath while Cesca and Sybbie watched her phone screen.

'Oh, my God,' Francesca said softly. 'I recognise that car.'

'You do?' Georgina brightened. 'That's fantastic.'

'No, it isn't.' Francesca lowered her voice. 'It's Young Tom's.'

'It can't be. He's not a murderer,' Sybbie said, her own voice low. 'I've known him since he was a toddler, coming here with his little trowel to help his grandad in the garden. I can't believe it.' She peered at the screen of Georgina's phone. 'Oh, God, Cesca. You're right. It does look like Young Tom's car.'

'I didn't think he had a car. He always comes to Rookery Farm in a van,' Georgina said.

'That's his work van. But he can hardly use that for going out with friends or taking his grandmother somewhere,' Francesca said.

'There must be some other reason,' Georgina said. 'Maybe he was doing some late planting or something.'

'It's too dark to do any gardening at that time of night,' Sybbie said. 'When does the car leave?'

'About ten,' Georgina said. She didn't want to believe that Tom was the murderer. She liked him. Sybbie trusted him. Bea *like* liked him. How could he be the murderer? He didn't even know Roland Garnett, did he? 'What are we going to do?' She glanced over at Young Tom, now back at work in the greenhouse. Sweet, kind Young Tom – a murderer?

'We're going to have to tell the police,' Sybbie said.

'But *Young Tom*...' Francesca shook her head. 'He's the most unlikely murderer ever. He even hand-reared a baby blackbird, last summer! He'd never kill anyone.'

Stephen's voice floated into Georgina's head. *One may smile, and smile, and be a villain...* 'I don't want to believe it, either.' She bit her lip. 'But think about it. He has access to your garden, Sybbie – and the oleander. And the CCTV shows his car. Just... why would he want to kill Roland Garnett?'

'That's something for the police to find out,' Sybbie said.

'I hate this,' Georgina said. 'You're absolutely sure it's his car?'

'He has a white Ford Fiesta – and that's a light-coloured Ford Fiesta. The only letters you can see on the number plate are the last two, BK,' Francesca said. 'I'm pretty sure those are the last two letters on his number plate.'

Georgina swallowed hard. 'I'll go home and call Inspector Bradshaw. It doesn't feel right to ring from here.'

'Do you want one of us to come with you?' Sybbie asked.

'No. But it feels horrible, accusing someone I've come to

think of as a friend. Accusing him of...' She tailed off, not wanting to say the word.

'I know, but it has to be done. Call us if you need us,' Sybbie said.

Georgina called out a vague, 'Bye,' in the direction of the greenhouse – she couldn't bring herself to face the man she was about to report to the police – and headed back to the farmhouse.

By the time she got home, she was feeling distinctly queasy. Probably nerves, she thought, but as she unlocked the kitchen door, she had to clamp a hand over her mouth. She just made it to the kitchen sink in time.

'Georgina? Are you all right?' Doris asked as Georgina was violently sick.

'Nerves,' Georgina said, and threw up again.

'Why are you nervous?'

'I need to call the police.' Georgina said. 'I know whose car is on the CCTV. It's Young Tom's.'

'Young Tom – the gardener – murdered Dr Garnett?'

'I don't want to believe it, but it's looking that way,' Georgina said. She splashed cold water onto her face. 'I feel terrible.'

'Maybe you should lie down before you ring the police,' Doris suggested.

Georgina sighed. 'No, I need to get this over with.'

* * *

'Bradshaw,' Colin said.

'It's Georgina Drake,' the voice said at the end of the line. 'I know who the car belongs to. I showed Cesca and Sybbie the CCTV, and—oh, God. Excuse me.'

Colin could hear the sound of something that sounded like vomiting.

'Georgina? Are you all right?'

'I must be coming down with something,' she said. 'I keep being sick, and I feel a bit dizzy. Maybe I ate something that didn't agree with me.'

He went cold. Possibly he was making a bit too much of this, but Sybbie had the oleander bush and Francesca was a cook. Even though he'd liked the women when he'd met them, what if they *were* collaborating and Georgina was their latest target?

'Hang on. I'll get help,' he said.

He called the emergency service and got through to ambulance control. 'I'm a police office and there's a possible case of non-accidental poisoning. How long would it take an ambulance to get to Little Wenborough?'

'All our ambulances are out at the moment,' the controller said. 'There's been a big RTA involving a bus, the other side of Norwich, and several people are hurt. It might be a while. Is the patient conscious?'

'She was, when I spoke to her a couple of minutes ago.' He spoke his fear out loud. 'If it's what I think it is, she might not be conscious for much longer.' He glanced at his watch and did a quick calculation. It would be quicker to fetch Georgina and drive her to hospital himself than to wait for an ambulance. 'I'm going to get her and take her to hospital. Can you tell the emergency department that Inspector Bradshaw will be coming in with a poisoned patient, please?'

He called Sammy on his car phone on the way to Little Wenborough. 'Sammy, sorry, I know you're busy, but what's the treatment for oleander poisoning?'

'Have you got another case?' she asked.

'Possibly, and you said it doesn't show on standard tox screens. Can you text me with what the emergency department should be looking for, please?'

'Of course,' she said.

He'd just passed the village sign for Little Wenborough when his phone pinged to signal an incoming text, which he hoped was Sammy. He took the shingled drive to Georgina's farmhouse and hit the brakes, ignoring the shower of stones. He glanced at his phone's screen and was relieved to see that Sammy had sent him the details he needed.

Leaving the car door open, he ran to the back of the house. Even though it was technically a security risk, he was glad that Georgina didn't lock her kitchen door when she was here alone.

He found her retching over the sink.

'It's OK,' he said. 'I've got you. I think you might have been poisoned.'

She stared at him, her eyes unfocused. 'I couldn't have been.'

'You said it came on suddenly after you'd seen Sybbie and Cesca.'

'Yes, but they wouldn't poison me. They're my friends,' she protested.

'We'll argue later. I'm taking you to hospital.' He just about had the presence of mind to scoop up some of the vomit from the bowl in the sink into two of the evidence bags he usually kept in his pocket, as a sample for the hospital techs to check for oleandrin so they could treat Georgina, and the forensic team so they could compare it to the contents of Garnett's stomach. 'Where are your house keys?'

'Handbag,' she said weakly.

He saw her phone on the worktop, next to her handbag, and stuffed it into her bag while he fished out her house keys, and looped the strap of her bag over his shoulder. He led her outside, noting how wobbly her legs were, locked the door and shoved her keys back in her bag, then scooped her up and carried her to his car.

'You can't. What If I'm sick in your car?'

'It'll clean,' he said. 'And I've got a bottle of water in the car so you can rinse your mouth if you *are* sick.'

'My head hurts,' she complained as he put her in the car seat, fastened her seatbelt and handed her a plastic evidence bag 'in case you need it'. 'You're making a fuss about nothing. It's probably just a bug.'

'A bug wouldn't come on that quickly,' he said. And he needed information now, in case she fell unconscious. 'What have you eaten and drunk?'

'One of Cesca's cookies and some coffee – but Cesca and Sybbie ate the cookies, too,' she said.

'And drank the same coffee?'

'Sybbie drinks tea. But we took it from the farm shop café.'

'Were you at the farm shop, or Sybbie's?'

'We sat on Sybbie's terrace and I showed them the CCTV. That's what I was trying to tell you – I was calling about Young Tom.'

He frowned. 'What about him?'

'It's his car on the CCTV. Cesca recognised it.'

'How come you didn't recognise it, when he's your gardener?'

'Because he always brings his van when he does my garden. I didn't even know he had a car,' Georgina said.

'I thought that everyone knew everything about everyone else, in a small village.'

She flapped a dismissive hand. 'That's ridiculous. But something's not right. Young Tom's not a murderer. He's a total sweetheart. Anyway, he only met Roland Garnett once, when he was mowing the lawn and Dr Garnett wasn't very happy about the interruption to his work. But that's not a reason to kill someone, is it?'

'I'll look into it,' he said. 'Give me two minutes – and don't go to sleep. If you feel your eyes closing, open the window.'

He called the station on his hands-free car phone, very aware that Georgina was being sick into the bag he'd given her.

'Yes, guv?' Larissa said.

'I need you to check on some things for me, please. It's urgent,' he said. 'I need you to go to Little Wenborough Manor and take samples of the choc-chip cookies from the farm shop – but first, I need you to go to Lady Wyatt's garden. If there are coffee cups and cookies still on the terrace, bag the lot up for testing. Tell the lab you need an urgent tox screen and you're looking for traces of oleander.'

'I'm on it, guv.'

'I also want you to arrest Tom Nichols – as in Young Tom – on suspicion of murder and the attempt to commit grievous bodily harm. Keep him at the station for me, please.' This was one interview he definitely wanted to do.

'Will do, guv,' she said.

'And in the meantime, I want someone to run a check on his vehicles. There should be a van and a white Ford Fiesta.'

'Got it,' she said. 'I'll keep you posted.'

'Thanks, Larissa.'

'I'm sure Tom's not a murderer,' Georgina said. 'Besides, how could he have poisoned me? He didn't come anywhere near us on the terrace.'

'At all?' Colin asked.

'Only to grab a cookie,' she said. 'Sybbie was in the greenhouse with the garden team, potting up stuff, when we got there. I'm not sure what.' She frowned, looking close to tears. 'If he poisoned me, then he must've have poisoned Cesca and Sybbie, too. You need to check on them.'

'Don't worry,' he said. 'We'll sort everything out. I'm going to call your son and daughter.'

'No – please don't do that. I don't want them worrying about me. I'm sure it's just a bug.'

For a bright woman, she could be exceedingly dense, Colin thought.

She retched miserably into the bag. 'I don't think there's anything left in my stomach to come up,' she said, sounding wan.

'We'll get you to hospital. If they admit you, then I'll ring your son and daughter,' he said. 'Even *you* have to admit that's reasonable.'

'I suppose,' she said.

He kept her talking about completely inconsequential things for the rest of the journey, mainly to keep himself reassured that she was conscious. At the hospital, he checked her in with the triage nurse and explained that he had information to give to the doctors about the possible poisoning.

The medics, once they'd established that he wasn't Georgina's next of kin, made him wait in the waiting room while they examined Georgina, but did at least take the information that Sammy had given him.

Time passed more slowly than Colin would've believed possible. Every time he glanced at his watch, it seemed that only a minute or two had gone by.

Patience had never been his strong suit.

He was drumming his fingers on his knee, which itself was jiggling up and down, when Larissa called. 'I've got the cookies and they're with the lab. Sorry, I couldn't get the cups because they'd all been washed.'

'Thanks for trying. Were Lady Wyatt and Mrs Walters all right?'

'Yes. They asked if you'd call them and let them know how Georgina is, and they'll look after her when she's back home.'

That was one of the things he was afraid of. Until he was sure they weren't involved, he didn't want to put Georgina at risk. 'I'll see what I can do,' he said.

'Tom Nichols is here in custody. He's been cautioned,' she added.

'Thanks. I'll touch base with you shortly,' he said.

The clock would be ticking down on how long they could keep Young Tom at the station. And waiting was driving him crackers. He went to find the nursing staff.

'I'm really sorry to be a nuisance,' he said, 'but I'm needed back at the station. Can I ask if you're planning to admit Georgina Drake?'

'We're still stabilising her,' the nurse said, 'but we're likely to keep her in for observation overnight. Do you know how the poison got into her system?'

'At the moment, we're thinking coffee or cookies,' he said. 'I'll be back as soon as I can.' He gave her his business card. 'If her condition changes, please would you get in touch?'

Back at the station, he took Larissa with him into the interview room because it would be good experience for her. He named all the people in the room and repeated the grounds for the arrest for the tape, then repeated the caution. Tom had waived his right to a solicitor.

'Can you tell me the registration plate of your car, please, Mr Nichols?' he asked.

Tom recited it.

'And can you confirm for me that this is your car? For the tape, I'm showing exhibit A to Mr Nichols. It's a still from CCTV film, showing a light-coloured Ford Fiesta with the last two letters of the registration plate visible. BK.'

'It looks like my car, though my car's never that dirty,' Tom said with a frown. 'Where was that taken?'

Colin ignored the question. 'Can I ask what you were doing on Thursday the twentieth of April from 6pm onwards?'

'Thursday last week? Yes. I was at the Feathers – the pub in Great Wenborough,' Tom said. 'I got there at half past six for something to eat.'

'Do you have anyone who can confirm this?' Larissa asked.

'Everyone in the pub,' Tom said. 'The Feathers has a pub quiz on the third Thursday of the month. I was there with my team, the Young Ones, and we won.'

'Can I have the names and phone numbers of your team members?' Colin asked.

Tom recited them, and Larissa wrote them down.

'Did you drive to the Feathers?'

'No. My mate Spike picked me up at around quarter past six, and dropped me off after the quiz. We finished somewhere around half past ten, so I would've got home at about quarter to eleven,' Tom said.

If this could all be corroborated by the pub staff and Tom's quiz team members, then that put him out of the running for Roland Garnett's murder. The CCTV had shown Tom's car going up the driveway at seven and back at ten.

'Does anyone else have a key to your car?' Colin asked.

'No,' Tom said.

'Is there anyone who could've used it without asking you?' Colin asked.

He frowned. 'I don't see how. The key's in the same bunch with my house key and my van key, and they were in my pocket at the Feathers. I don't have a spare set.'

Tom might have a good alibi for Roland Garnett's murder, Colin thought, but there was still the issue of Georgina.

'Interview suspended,' Colin said for the benefit of the tape. Outside the interview room, he asked Larissa to give her list to Mo so he could check out Tom's alibi, and get the forensic team to check the car for any evidence or signs of hot-wiring. While she was doing that, he checked his phone and was relieved to find nothing from the hospital. No change was a good thing, wasn't it?

Back in the interview room, he restarted the tape for further questioning, and asked Tom, 'Did you know Roland Garnett?'

Interestingly, there was a sudden flush on Tom's cheeks.

'I already told you about that, the last time you spoke to me,' Tom said. 'I only met him the once, when I was mowing Georgina Drake's lawn and he objected to the noise, I apologised and said I wouldn't be long.'

'You didn't know him – or of him – before you met him at Rookery Barn?'

'No.'

But there was a slight flare of the nostrils that made Colin sure that Tom wasn't telling the truth. But what reason did he have to lie?

'What were you doing at Little Wenborough Manor today?' he asked.

'Helping my grandad. We were putting summer bedding plants into trays, ready to start hardening them off for planting out in the borders next month.'

'Do you prune the shrubs or take cuttings?' Colin asked.

Tom shrugged. 'If I'm asked to.'

'Has anyone asked you to prune the oleander or take cuttings?'

'No.'

Colin pushed a bit further. 'Have you ever taken cuttings from the oleander, now or in the past?'

'No. Lady Wyatt usually deals with those herself.'

This really wasn't getting him anywhere. 'What's your relationship with Georgina Drake?' he asked.

'She's my client,' Tom said. 'I do her garden twice a week. She's a nice woman. I guess I'd count her as a friend.'

'What contact have you had with her today?'

'I said hello,' Tom said, 'when she was sitting on the terrace with Lady Wyatt and Cesca. You can ask them, or my grandad or Jenny – they were in the greenhouse with me when Cesca offered us cookies.'

Which was pretty much what Georgina had told him.

'Thank you, Mr Nichols. That's all for now.'

The lab came back to say there was no trace of poison on the cookies.

Mo reported that Tom's alibi was unshakeable. 'Spike picked him up before the quiz at quarter past six, and dropped him home after the quiz at quarter to eleven. The barman says Tom was sitting on a table in view of the bar, and he was there all night except for a very brief visit to the gents'. And I can even tell you what Tom had for his dinner, because the chef is apparently a bit sweet on him and gave him extra crispy mushrooms with his chicken.'

'He's definitely not telling us the whole truth,' Colin said. 'But we're going to have to let him go. For now.'

When Colin called the hospital, he learned that Georgina had just been admitted to the ward for observation, and visitors were allowed. 'Just going to check on Mrs Drake,' he told Mo and Larissa.

* * *

Georgina was pale, but at least she wasn't being sick anymore.

'I wasn't sure if flowers or grapes were allowed,' he said. 'But I just wanted to see you – to see how you were doing,' he added swiftly.

'You saved my life, Colin,' she said. 'Thank you.'

He brushed it aside, partly because he didn't want to entertain the idea that she could have died, and partly because he didn't want to deal with the way she made him feel. She was part of his investigation and he needed to keep impartial. 'Just doing my job,' he said. 'Besides, the nurse said you hadn't ingested enough poison to kill you.'

'If they hadn't treated me when they did, I would've felt much sicker for much longer,' she said.

'Yeah, yeah.' He sighed. 'Do you remember having an agreement with me that I'd call your kids if you were admitted?'

She winced. 'I'll be out tomorrow.'

'Even so. In your shoes, I'd want my daughter to know, not least to reassure her that I was OK. Your phone, Mrs Drake?' He held out his hand.

'In my bag. Which is in the cupboard next to my bed.'

He guessed she didn't have the energy to retrieve the bag herself, but he handed her the bag rather than rummaging in it. She unlocked the phone and gave it to him. 'They're listed under their first names.'

He called Bea first.

'Oh, my God! I'll get the next train to Norwich,' Bea said.

'Your mum's in for observation tonight, so you won't be able to do anything,' he said. 'She needs to rest. They're probably letting her out tomorrow, and I'll collect her and drive her home.' He paused, 'And I could collect you from the train station, if you let me know when your train gets in.'

'That's kind,' Bea said. 'But you're a policeman, not a taxi service.' She paused. 'Are you and my mum...?'

'Friends,' he said, looking at Georgina. 'I think.'

'Right. Can I talk to her?'

He gestured to Georgina, who nodded and accepted the phone.

From her end of the conversation, he deduced that Bea had asked Georgina the same question she'd just asked him about their relationship. Georgina reassured her daughter that she was going to be fine, then hung up. 'Bea's going to tell Will and my mum. And that's very kind of you to offer her a lift.'

He shrugged. 'It's what I hope someone would do for my Cathy.'

'If your daughter ever needs a lift around here,' Georgina said, 'then get her to call me.' She looked at him. 'And as we've moved to "friends", I guess you should call me Georgie.'

Colin felt himself blush.

'Did you arrest Tom?'

'Yes,' he said.

'Was he the one who poisoned me?'

He grimaced. 'I can't prove it was him – or anyone else.'

'You're surely not still suspecting Sybbie and Cesca?' she asked, sounding shocked.

'There were no traces of oleander on the cookies – but, without the evidence to back it up, I can't say with certainty that they *weren't* involved,' he said.

She closed her eyes and lay back against the pillow. 'They're my *friends*. Do they know I'm here?'

'Yes. My constable told them when she went to see them to collect samples,' he said.

She was still holding her phone. 'I'll call them.' Her eyes narrowed at him. 'And don't suggest it's a bad idea because they'll rush up here and stick a pillow over my head to finish the job.'

'I wasn't going to,' he said mildly.

She grimaced. 'Sorry. That was unforgivably rude. I'm feeling rubbish and I shouldn't take it out on you, especially because you're the one who got me here in the first place. It's just...'

'...nobody wants to think their friends are the ones who deliberately made them ill,' he finished. 'I'll let you rest. Do you need me to bring you anything from home for tonight? A phone charger or anything?'

'I'll manage,' she said.

'OK. I'll call the hospital tomorrow morning to find out when I can take you home. Let me know what time Bea's train gets in.'

'That's definitely above and beyond the call of duty,' she said. 'But thank you, Colin.'

The look in her eyes flummoxed him, particularly as he

wasn't sure what to do next. If you visited a female friend in hospital, did you kiss her goodbye on the cheek when you left? Or would she take it the wrong way? Oh, God. All the vodka he'd drunk during his difficult months had obviously killed off most of his social skills along with some of his brain cells.

In the end, he took refuge in mumbling, 'You're welcome,' and rushed out of the ward.

* * *

Georgina could hardly have asked Colin to walk into her kitchen and say out loud that she was in hospital but was making a good recovery. He would've thought she was mad, and if she explained that she wanted a ghost to know what was happening, he'd definitely question her sanity. But Doris would no doubt be worried sick.

There was only one way Georgina could think of to let her know.

Feeling slightly foolish, she called her own landline and waited for the beep for the answering machine. 'It's Georgina. Someone poisoned me, but Colin got me to the hospital in time. I'm recovering and I'll be home tomorrow,' she said.

Hopefully Doris wasn't in the garden and would hear the message, and hopefully when Georgina got home she could delete the message before anyone else heard it and asked awkward questions.

* * *

The case was stalled, Colin thought. The only thing that had come in during his absence was

a note from Garnett's solicitor, about the will. Garnett had left his entire estate to St Bene't's College, provided the bequest was used to fund a student bursary in his name for the student who gets top marks in the year. That tallied with the impression Colin had of Garnett: that the lecturer had wanted to be associated with the best.

Who had driven Tom Nichols's car to Rookery Barn, and why had they wanted to kill Garnett? Until Colin could pin that down, he'd have to follow other lines of enquiry. But right at that moment he wasn't sure where to start.

TWELVE

'Guv, the hospital just called,' Larissa said.

Colin went cold. Please don't let anything have happened to Georgina. He strove to sound calm. 'What did they want?'

'There's been another poisoning in Little Wenborough,' she said.

A third poisoning; if it was deliberate rather than accidental, that would mean he potentially had one case of murder and two attempted murders.

'Who is it? And are they going to be OK?' Colin asked.

'Tom Nichols. The younger one,' Larissa clarified. 'They're still working to help him. One of the nurses on the emergency ward remembered Georgina Drake's case, and she made the connection so they knew what to check for.'

'Do we have any details?' Colin asked.

'Mr Larke – the elderly gentleman whose garden it was – asked his assistant, Jen, if they wanted a cup of tea. She went to ask Tom and found him at the bottom of the garden where he'd been digging, collapsed next to his spade and throwing up. Mr Larke called the ambulance.'

'Did his assistant go to hospital with him?' Colin asked.

'I'm not sure,' Larissa said. 'I'll ring back and check.'

'It could be a double bluff,' Mo said. 'We thought Young Tom was the poisoner; maybe this was his way of diverting suspicion from himself.'

'Would someone really poison themselves?' Colin asked. 'If it's oleandrin, it's nasty stuff. And remember Young Tom's got a cast-iron alibi for Garnett's murder.'

Though he didn't necessarily have an alibi for Georgina's poisoning.

Colin frowned. 'Who would want to kill Young Tom? And if it's the same person who poisoned Roland Garnett and tried to kill Georgina Drake, what's the connection between them?'

'The obvious one – apart from poison – is Rookery Barn,' Larissa said. 'Dr Garnett rented it, Mrs Drake owned it, and Young Tom did the garden.'

'Why would someone want to kill all three of them?' Colin asked.

'Maybe there's something at the barn that someone wants to keep hidden,' Mo suggested. 'Though obviously we don't know who or what.'

'Plus,' Colin said, 'the poisonings didn't start until Garnett arrived. Mrs Drake bought the farm a year ago, and Young Tom's been doing the garden for months. Why wait until now before poisoning them?'

Their new hypothesis seemed to be generating more questions than answers, which wasn't helpful.

'What else connects them?' Colin asked.

'The CCTV,' Larissa said. 'But, again, why only now? Anyone going to the farm would've been on CCTV ever since Mrs Drake had it installed.'

'What about a professional or personal connection?' Colin said.

'Nothing that we've found,' Larissa said. 'I'll go through the notes again.'

'I'm going to the hospital,' Colin said. 'If Young Tom's well enough to talk to me, he might be able to tell me more. If he can't, then I'll try Jenny, his assistant.'

At the hospital, Young Tom had just been admitted to a ward for observation.

'He's tired and needs to rest,' the nurse warned.

'I know,' Colin said. 'I won't stay for very long. And I could do with a quick chat with the team who treated him in the emergency department. Just to clarify events,' he said.

'I'll find out who treated him and I'll be back in five minutes,' the nurse said. 'And then Mr Nichols rests.'

'Got it,' Colin said.

Young Tom was lying in the hospital bed, his face ashen.

'How are you doing?' Colin asked.

'I hurt all over,' Young Tom said. 'What are you doing here?'

'I wanted to ask you a couple of questions,' Colin said. 'Can you run me through what you did this morning? What you ate or drank?'

'I had a bowl of granola with a banana and a mug of tea for breakfast, like I normally do. I made a flask of tea so I could have another cup when I got to Mr Larke's – his tea's horrible, like dishwater, so I always take my own,' Young Tom explained with a grimace. 'I picked Jen up early because I was going out to see Spike's band tonight and wanted to finish early today, and I was digging over a patch Mr Larke wanted replanting when my guts suddenly felt as if they were on fire. I've never been so sick in my life. I thought I was going to die.'

'You might've done, if they hadn't called the ambulance,' the nurse said, coming back into the room. 'That's enough, now. He needs to rest.'

'Just one more question, please,' Colin said, giving her his best smile. 'Mr Nichols, do you have any idea why anyone might want to poison you – or who might've done it?'

'Not a clue,' Young Tom said. 'But I wish you'd hurry up and catch them, before they poison someone else.'

That made two of them. 'I'll leave you to rest,' Colin said, mindful of the nurse's folded arms and her fingers tapping on it. 'But if you can think of who might be responsible, or how they gave you the poison, please get in touch. I'll leave my business card here on your bedside table.'

The nurse gave Colin the details of the emergency team who'd treated Young Tom, and shooed him out of the ward.

The emergency team confirmed what Colin had already found out from Young Tom: Jenny found him, Mr Larke called the ambulance and Young Tom came to hospital on his own. Fortunately, the triage nurse had remembered Georgina's case and suggested checking for oleandrin, and they were able to treat him effectively.

Georgina was horrified to learn the news. 'Is he going to be all right?'

'The ambulance brought him to hospital in time, so he should be OK,' Colin reassured her.

'Good.' Georgina looked relieved. 'But that also blows your theory about him being the poisoner out of the water.'

'How do you work that out?'

'Why would he poison himself? Whoever poisoned him must've poisoned me.'

'Unless it's a double bluff,' Colin said, using Mo's hypothesis.

'That's so cynical.'

'I have to question everything, so I'm satisfied that what I know is the truth,' Colin pointed out. 'It goes with the job. If you're ready, we'll go and collect Bea from the station.'

'Thank you. It's really kind of you,' Georgina said. 'I could've got a taxi home, or asked Sybbie or Cesca to pick me up.' She narrowed her eyes at him. 'Unless you still suspect them of being the poisoners.'

'No comment,' Colin said. 'Actually, you're still officially on the suspect list because we haven't eliminated you yet. I shouldn't be talking to you about the case at all, let alone without a witness.'

She coughed. 'I'm a victim, so I expect to be kept informed about my case. Plus there's the small matter of clearing my name, and those of my friends. Colin, we both know you shouldn't be talking to me. You shouldn't be discussing the case with anyone outside the police, let alone with someone who's on your suspect list. But I can assure you that I have no intention of calling your superior and telling him that you're bending or even breaking the rules.'

That was a relief. 'I don't know who poisoned you,' he said. 'But it's highly likely that whoever did also poisoned Tom Nichols and Roland Garnett. What I can't work out is why. What's the connection between the three of you?'

Georgina was bright. A photographer, who noticed small details. And, with her student journalist training, Colin thought she'd be good at putting information together and analysing it. She might be the one to help him see his way through the puzzle.

'Maybe,' he said, 'we can discuss things hypothetically.'

She smiled. 'Perhaps in my garden, with a cup of tea.'

It was the English answer to everything, he thought: a nice cup of tea.

'Especially,' she added, 'as you don't have a garden.'

'How did you know that?' he asked.

She tapped the side of her nose and grinned. 'Call me Jane.'

As in Marple, he realised. She'd investigated him?

His surprise must've shown on his face, because she smiled. 'If you were a gardener, you would've remarked on something in my garden. But you didn't, so I'm guessing you either have a tiny square at the back of your house, or a window box.'

'It's a flat. Not even a window box,' he admitted. 'All right. You're sharp. But, much as I'd like to, I don't have time to sit in your garden – at least, not today. Can we talk in the car on the way to the train station?'

'All right,' she said.

Once they were driving, he said, 'I've thrown a few ideas around with Mo and Larissa – my team. But none of it makes sense and we're coming up blank.'

'Someone said to me,' she said, batting her eyelashes outrageously at him, 'now, what was it...? Ah, yes. No more Miss Marple.' She exaggerated the quote with her fingers.

He coughed. 'All right, Georgina. I apologise. You're good at working things out.'

'I want to clear my name – and, more importantly, as I said, I want to clear my friends' names,' she said. 'So what's your hypothesis?'

'Someone gave Roland Garnett a poisoned curry.'

'Not Cesca,' she said immediately.

'Probably not Cesca,' he agreed, 'though do bear in mind you were with her when you were poisoned, and she saw Young Tom yesterday as well – and today *he's* in hospital recovering from poisoning.'

'Not Cesca,' Georgina said firmly.

'He hadn't ordered a curry from her recently, so it's more probable that he got it somewhere else – though we don't know where,' Colin said. 'Our investigations so far show that Garnett didn't order anything from a local takeaway. He made it obvious to you he doesn't cook. So I'm thinking the person in the car on your CCTV either brought the meal with them, or they cooked it at the barn.'

'The kitchen was spotless,' she said. 'If anyone cooked there, they cleaned up afterwards. How well did they clean? Did they leave any prints?'

'There's no trace evidence,' he admitted. 'They knew enough to use bleach and gloves.'

'Which they probably picked up from watching a TV drama,' she mused, 'so we can't say the poisoner has to be a chef or a scientist. At the moment, you know what happened, where, when and how. You just don't know who did it or why.'

He raised an eyebrow at her. 'I know we've had this conversation before, but are you quite sure you're not police trained?'

'All part of rookie student newspaper journalism training. Kipling's six honest serving men,' she said.

As he'd thought, too.

'So, in theory, who would want to kill Roland Garnett?' she asked.

'The owner of the holiday cottage,' he said promptly. As he'd hoped, she laughed, and it felt as if the sunshine had grown that little bit brighter.

'*Touché*. And her friend who cleans the barn, and her other friend who runs the farm shop. Except none of them has a real motive. They all thought he was an annoying little man, and they had better things to do with their time than worry about him.'

'OK. So let's take them off the list. Who else?' he asked.

'Both sets of neighbours had a motive. He got on badly with them, possibly poisoned the cat belonging to one set – which means that murder by poison could seem like poetic justice,' she pointed out, 'and he played music really loudly to make life difficult for the other set. In their shoes, surely anyone would want to murder him.'

It was clear she didn't think they did it, either. 'But?'

'The neighbours who owned the cat are elderly, and a lot of elderly people prefer not to drive at night,' she said. 'Especially as it'd be an hour and a half's drive each way, and they would've been stuck in rush-hour traffic as well on the way out of Cambridge, in order to get here at the time the light-coloured car arrived.'

'What about the other side?' he asked.

'They're young and sleep-deprived. I think they were more likely to snap with frustration and bash him over the head with something when he woke the baby or the doctor who'd just come back from a night shift. To drive here, administer the poison, clean up and drive back again... that feels planned.'

'Premeditation,' he said, 'would make it cold-blooded murder.'

'They say that revenge is a dish best served cold, and I'm not sure the neighbours are at that stage – at least, they weren't when Cesca and I talked to them, and neither of them knew he'd even gone away, let alone where he'd gone,' Georgina said. 'But, even if we assume that they found out somehow, if any of them came to Rookery Barn, given that Garnett clearly loathed them, why would he invite them in? Surely he would've said something offensive and shut the door in their faces, instead? And, in that case, unless they battered the door down or smashed a window to get in – which we know didn't happen – why would they hang around for a couple of hours? It doesn't make sense.'

Exactly Colin's thoughts. 'Agreed,' he said.

'What about his ex-wife? He was awful to her,' Georgina pointed out.

'She had more of a motive, but not the opportunity. Her alibi checks out,' Colin explained.

Georgina thought about it. 'Would I be right in saying that most murders are committed by someone the victim knows?'

'Murders by random strangers are rare,' he said.

'Someone he knew. That means family, neighbours, colleagues and students,' she mused. 'What about his family? Apart from his ex, I mean?'

'Apparently his parents died when he was quite young and he grew up in care,' Colin said. 'His ex-wife said he'd lost touch with other family members, other than his parents. But that's a good point. We need to check his family. Can you text me a note to say that?'

'Sure.'

He heard his phone ping with a text notification. 'Cheers.'

'What about his colleagues?' Georgina asked.

'The academics are closing ranks, and saying he was a hard marker who pushed his students to do better,' Colin said.

'Or smashed their confidence to smithereens,' Georgina added dryly. 'What about the non-academic colleagues? Sybbie got the impression they didn't like him.'

'As you said yourself, dislike isn't quite enough of a motive for murder.'

She drummed her fingers on her knee. 'Not family, not neighbours, not colleagues. Friends?' she suggested.

'None that we can find,' Colin said.

'Which is odd. Most people have at least one person they're friendly with.' She frowned. 'Who was the best man at his wedding?'

'That's a good point,' he said. 'I'll check it out.'

His phone pinged with another text. He hadn't even needed to ask her to send him a note, this time.

'Thank you for the note,' he said. 'What if Garnett lost touch with his best man, too?'

'He seems to make rather a habit of losing touch with people,' she said. 'What about his students, past or present? I'm guessing, from what Hayley said, he had several affairs with his students. Was it someone he dumped?'

'We don't have any evidence,' Colin said.

'What about the girl who took an overdose and left the college – the one the cleaner and the Buttery staff told Sybbie about?' Georgina asked. 'Could she have poisoned him, to get revenge on him for ruining her academic career?'

'No.' Colin winced. 'I talked to her mum. She died.'

'Oh, no. Poor girl. And her poor family.' Georgina said. 'That's so sad.'

'Yeah.'

Georgina paused. 'If she couldn't get revenge on him herself, what about someone close to her? You said to my children that anyone could commit murder if the motive was strong enough. What about this girl's mum?'

'She lives on the other side of the country. Though I'll check the details of her car,' he said.

'Or a sibling, maybe?'

It was an angle he hadn't considered. He hadn't asked Jill's mother whether she had other children. 'Send me another note, please,' he said. 'And I'll need to check if there's medical or scientific knowledge in the family, too.'

'Except we still need a reason for Roland Garnett to let that person into the barn,' she said.

'And work out where you and Tom come into it,' Colin said. 'I was hoping you might be able to help me see it.'

'I can see why you're going round in circles. You're looking for someone who knew Roland Garnett, who drove a light-coloured car or had access to one which had a similar number plate to Young Tom's car.'

'The working theory was that his car was stolen – and there was no evidence of hot-wiring – or there was another Fiesta with a similar number plate. The database didn't bring up anything,' Colin said.

'OK. But whoever it was must have been someone that Garnett was happy to see. That last condition would rule out just about everyone.' She drummed her fingers on her knee again. 'I think the answer has to lie in Cambridge. Had he dumped someone who wanted to get revenge on him? Or the poor girl who died – someone in her family.' She spread her hands. 'That's the best I can come up with.'

'And where do you and Young Tom fit in?'

'I was poisoned after I found the CCTV,' Georgina said. 'And Tom – it looks like his car on the CCTV, but what motive would he have to poison Garnett?'

'He wasn't driving it – at least, not that evening. He has an alibi,' Colin said. 'And I don't think he poisoned himself to draw suspicion off him. If someone tried to kill you to stop you telling me about the CCTV, did that person also try to poison Young Tom because he'd seen something or maybe knows something?'

'Like what?' Georgina asked.

'If I knew *that*, I wouldn't be struggling with the case,' he pointed out. 'I need to find out who was driving that car.'

'And maybe find out more about the student who died,' she said. 'The best thing you could do now is to let it sit in the back of your mind. Marinate a little. That's what Stephen used to do when he hit a brick wall with the way he wanted to direct a play. And then, when you take the pressure off, maybe the pieces will slot into place.'

Lots of mixed metaphors for an English graduate, he thought. 'You're probably right. Thank you. I owe you one. Maybe I can buy you dinner, or lunch, or something.'

He regretted the words the moment they left his mouth, because her expression suddenly became neutral.

'As friends,' he said, knowing it was already too late.

'Maybe,' she said.

Thankfully they were almost at the train station. He parked in the little drop-off car park and went with Georgina to the concourse. The London train had just come in, and Bea rushed over towards them.

'Oh, Mum! We've all been worried sick,' she said, hugging Georgina hard. 'You don't know how glad I am to see you.'

To Colin's shock, she gave him a hug, too. He couldn't

remember the last time someone had hugged him, and it made him feel odd.

'Thank you for rescuing Mum – and for collecting me,' she said. She handed him a paper carrier bag with a logo he recognised as being from an expensive chocolatier. 'Just a small token from me and Will to say thanks. It's possibly sexist of me,' she added with a grin, 'but it doesn't feel quite right to give a bloke flowers.'

'You really didn't have to, but thank you,' he said.

Georgina sat in the back of the car with Bea, and the two of them chatted all the way back to Little Wenborough. Colin took the opportunity to use the hands-free car phone to have a quick word with his team, to get them to check the medical records for the student who'd overdosed and how she died.

Georgina had clearly let Francesca know that she was coming home because, almost as soon as she'd unlocked the back door, Francesca arrived with fresh sourdough bread, a quiche and assorted salads.

'So you can rest and not rush around in the kitchen,' Francesca said. She gave Colin a narrow look. 'Do you want to check it all for poison, first?'

'It's my job to be suspicious,' he said mildly. 'Though you might like to consider that if you're not the poisoner, you might be at risk. Even if you discount Roland Garnett because he wasn't local and he wasn't a friend or acquaintance, Georgina and Young Tom were both poisoned. Who's next?'

She had the grace to flush. 'Sorry. But it's not very nice, being accused of poisoning your friend.'

'I didn't accuse you. You're merely on the suspect list until I've ruled you out,' he said.

'That's splitting hairs.'

He shrugged.

Francesca sighed. 'I don't want to fight with you, Inspector. Are you staying for lunch?'

'No. Thank you for asking, and I'm not refusing because I think it'll make me the next victim – I have a killer to catch, so I need to be back in the office,' he said. 'Rest up, Georgina.'

'I'll make sure she does,' Bea said.

'Thanks for all you've done, Colin,' Georgina said. She was still mulling over what he'd said just before they arrived at the station. He'd recovered quickly, but it had definitely sounded at first as if he was asking her out on a date.

Was she even ready to date again?

And now wasn't the right time to think about it. Not when she was recovering from being poisoned – by someone who was still at large.

There was also something else she really needed to deal with. 'I'm just going upstairs to change,' she said.

She slipped into the living room and quickly deleted the message on her answering machine.

'I appreciated you letting me know,' Doris said softly. 'That was a good idea, talking to the answering machine so I could hear you. If I could work buttons and what have you, I would've deleted the message for you. But I'm glad you're all right. Don't talk now – we'll talk when you're alone.'

'All right,' Georgina whispered.

* * *

'Guv, the hospital's emailed over the treatment notes,' Larissa said when Colin walked back into the office. 'I rang to see if I could have a quick chat with the doctor who treated Jill. Luckily he was on duty, and he called me back as soon as he'd finished seeing his current patient.'

'It looks as if you have news,' Colin said.

'I do. Jill Cassidy was pregnant,' Larissa told him. 'The doctor who treated her said that the overdose was a cry for help.

Her boyfriend told her to get rid of the baby, but she didn't want to. She didn't know what to do.'

'Poor kid,' Colin said. Roland had wanted Hayley to get rid of their baby, too, and then blamed her when she'd had a miscarriage. 'Maybe I'm seeing connections where there aren't any – but we know that Roland Garnett had dated students in the past. Jill Cassidy was his student. Is it possible that Roland Garnett had been dating her, and then treated her the same way he'd treated Hayley?'

'It's a workable theory,' Mo said. 'How can we find out if he was her boyfriend?'

'The two people who could confirm or deny it for definite are both dead,' Colin said. 'I'd rather not ask Jill Cassidy's family something so sensitive if there's another way of getting the information. We could try Jill's friends or classmates, first. There could be something in the phone records. How are we doing with those?'

'Still chasing them,' Larissa said. 'I'll get on their case again.'

'Did you manage to get any more information about her death?' Colin asked.

'I checked with the team at Bristol,' Mo said, 'so we didn't have to bother her family – like you, I didn't want to be insensitive.'

'Good call,' Colin said.

'I'm really glad I did, when they told me.' Mo blew out a breath. 'She drowned, poor kid.'

'Accidental or intentional?' Colin asked.

'Intentional, they think,' Mo confirmed, grim-faced.

Colin winced. 'Her family must be devastated. We'll definitely have to wait and see if the phone records show anything before we ask questions.'

Georgina had good instincts, he thought. Knowing he was bending the rules again, but also knowing that she wouldn't go to the press with the details because she had kids of her own and would handle the news sensitively, he texted her. *Checked into the student. Poor kid was pregnant. Boyfriend wanted her to have a termination.*

* * *

Later that evening, Bea was having a bath and Georgina was curled up on the sofa, listening to music.

'Hi,' Doris said. 'How are you feeling?'

'My throat's a bit sore from throwing up, and my ribs hurt, but otherwise I'm OK,' Georgina said, keeping her voice low. 'How are you?'

'Same as ever,' Doris said. 'Do you know who the poisoner is?'

'Not yet,' Georgina said. 'But there's been some updates. Young Tom was poisoned, this morning. He's going to be fine, but it looks as if whoever went after me went after him as well.'

'And dishy Colin thinks that Cesca did it?' Doris asked. 'I heard them bickering in the kitchen.'

'Cesca didn't poison me,' Georgina said firmly.

'For what it's worth, I agree with you,' Doris said.

'And Colin looked into the student who took the overdose in Cambridge. Everyone thought it was because Garnett had been harsh with her and she gave up her course. Except it turns out she was pregnant and her boyfriend wanted her to have a termination.'

'Pregnant?' Doris gasped. 'Oh, my God.'

'I know I'm from a different time, but I was more shocked by her boyfriend thinking it was his choice what to do with her body, than by the fact she was pregnant,' Georgina said dryly.

'No, it's not that. Though I agree with you, too,' Doris said. 'Pregnant. That's—that's what happened to me.'

A prickle of unease ran down Georgina's spine. 'You were pregnant when you died?'

'You saying about that poor girl being pregnant... that's brought some more of my memories back.'

'What happened?' Georgina asked gently.

'I... I'm just sorting it through in my mind. I knew I would've been planning to see Trev on Valentine's Day,' Doris said. 'I remember talking Mum and Dad into going to a Valentine Night dinner-dance at the Red Lion with their friends, and Jack was going to stay at his best friend's. Sundays usually meant a roast at one o'clock, but because they were going out that night Mum just made us a sandwich instead.'

'What were you and Trev planning to do?' Georgina asked. 'Go out for dinner?'

'I was going to cook him a proper posh dinner at our place,' Doris said. 'Prawns with Marie Rose sauce, coq au vin and Black Forest gâteau.'

A real 1970s menu, Georgina thought, remembering things her mum had told her in the past.

'That was Trev's favourite. Mum even helped me make the gâteau. We were going to have the leftovers the next night.' There was a slight crack in Doris's voice when she continued, 'Mum told me not to do anything I shouldn't. She didn't realise it was a bit too late for the lecture.'

'How far gone were you?' Georgina asked gently.

'About ten weeks. But Trev and I knew it was the wrong time for us to have a baby. We were in the middle of doing our A levels, and I couldn't go to university with a baby – back then, it wasn't like it is now. The plan was, that night, we'd have dinner, and then I'd drink a lot of gin and have a very hot bath.'

Georgina winced, realising exactly what Doris meant. 'Couldn't you have seen a doctor?'

'I did, and at least I was able to do that without it getting back to my parents. He gave me the standard advice,' Doris said grimly. 'Gin and a hot bath, then fall down the stairs a few times.'

'Right now,' Georgina said, feeling her eyes fill with tears of sympathy for the teenager in trouble that Doris had been, 'I really want to give you a hug.'

'Just like I want to hug *you*, because all that stuff with that horrible little man must've brought back too many memories of losing your husband.'

'It has.' Georgina scrubbed at her eyes. 'Why didn't you tell your mum and dad about the baby? Surely they would've helped you?' If Bea had come to her, the first thing she would've done was hug her and say she loved her, and then that she'd support whatever choice Bea made; and she knew Stephen would've done the same.

'My parents would've been horrified. Ashamed that I was no better than I should be, and disappointed in me because I was meant to be one of the clever girls in my year and I should've had more sense,' Doris said. 'Dad would've gone over to see Trev's parents and made them give consent to a wedding before I showed too much.'

'Consent?'

'Trev was four months younger than me. You had to have your parents' consent to get married if you were under eighteen,' Georgina explained. 'Though I think Trev's mum would've said I was just trying to trap him. I remember it so clearly now. I was so scared of her, sure that she would've told my parents to send me to a mother-and-baby home six weeks before the baby was due, then give the baby up for adoption.'

'But – that sounds like something from the nineteen fifties,' Georgina said, genuinely shocked.

'Believe me, it was still happening in the seventies,' Doris said drily. 'It's not like how things are now, with nursery places and help. Trev's dad would've probably made him get a job instead of going to university. And, stuck here, our dreams all gone, Trev and I would've ended up resenting each other. We talked about it. Gin, hot baths and the stairs – just like the doctor said – seemed our only way out. It was a horrible thing to do, and it being Valentine's night made it feel even worse, but it was the only choice we had.'

'How awful for you. I'm so sorry,' Georgina said. 'Forgive me for asking, but is that how you died, when you fell down the stairs?'

Doris was silent.

'Doris?'

'I suppose it must be,' Doris said eventually. 'I can't remember what actually happened, that night. I remember buying the orange squash – it was horrible stuff and I never usually drank it because it made my throat hurt – and Trev was going to borrow his brother's motorbike and get the gin in Norwich. If we'd bought it locally, someone would've surely seen him and put two and two together and told our parents. I don't remember Trev coming round, but maybe we did the gin and hot bath thing, and it went wrong with the stairs. Maybe I tripped. That bit's still hazy.'

'I'm so sorry,' Georgina said. 'I don't know what to say. I wish it had been different for you.'

Doris sniffed. 'Thank you. It's strange that you were born the day I died, but you kind of feel like my aunt. And you kind of feel like my daughter as well, because the baby would only have been six months younger than you.'

'It's weird,' Georgina said. 'that's how I feel. In some ways you're younger than my daughter, but in others you sound like my mum – even though you're a few years younger than her.'

'Yeah,' Doris whispered, and Georgina could hear the catch in her voice.

When Bea came downstairs, a few minutes later, Georgina held her very tightly. 'I love you. And I'll always, *always* have your back,' she said fiercely. 'You do know that, don't you?'

'Of course I do, Mum.' Bea hugged her back. 'What's happened?'

Her daughter was open-minded, but Georgina wasn't sure how Bea would react to the idea of her mother talking to a ghost. Probably not as harshly as Jack Beauchamp had, but with at least the scepticism Jodie and Francesca had shown when Georgina had casually mentioned ghosts. And Georgina herself had thought ghosts were just superstition, until she'd met Doris. 'Just thinking about the might-have-beens,' she said lightly.

And she was sure she could hear Doris crying softly.

THIRTEEN

'I've got the phone and email records back, guv,' Larissa, Colin's DC, said when he walked in the next morning. 'The emails aren't that interesting, but I think you're going to want to see the texts.'

'Thank you.' Colin sat at his desk and leafed through the records. As Larissa had said, the emails shed no light on the case – but the texts were another matter. It was clear from the texts he'd sent to her before Christmas that Roland Garnett was having an affair with Jill. It corroborated what he'd learned from both Hayley Summers and Lenny Peters.

Then, after Christmas, there were furious texts from Jill about Garnett using her work in his book without permission, with Garnett sneering and putting her down and saying nobody would believe her.

On February the twenty-seventh, there was a desperate-sounding text from Jill. *I need to see you. We need to talk.*

Was that, Colin wondered, when she'd discovered she was pregnant?

Garnett's reply was cool. *I'm in tutorials until 5.*

I'll come at 5.15, she responded. *If anyone asks, I'm checking something from my diss with you.*

Clearly whatever Jill wanted to see him about wasn't academic at all, and clearly it wasn't the first time she'd had to make an excuse for seeing him.

On February the twenty-eighth, there was another text from her. *I can't do it. I just can't. Please don't make me.*

His reply was short. *You have to. No choice.*

The tone of Jill's next text changed completely. Frowning, Colin looked at the dates of the two texts. There was more than a month between them. And something about one of the dates rang a bell.

He logged in to his computer and pulled up the timeline notes from his case file.

The text begging Garnett not to make her do something had been sent on the same day that Jill had taken an overdose. The doctor who'd treated her had told Larissa that Jill was pregnant and the boyfriend had been pushing her to have a termination. In that context, the wording of the text fitted with the hypothesis that Garnett was Jill's boyfriend.

The following text was dated the seventeenth of April – three days before Garnett's death. *I miss you. I just want to go back to how we were. Can we start again? xxx*

The back of Colin's neck tingled. What the hell? No way could Jill have sent that text. She'd died in March. He checked the file with the timeline again. Jill had died on March the fifth. She couldn't possibly have sent those last texts, asking to start their relationship again and agreeing to visit him at his retreat in Norfolk.

So who had her mobile phone? Who could have sent those texts to Garnett?

Garnett had clearly believed the person texting him was Jill, so he couldn't have been aware of her death; he must've thought that she'd spent time at home, recovered and had gone back to Cambridge. The tone of his texts had changed too; he was suddenly back to being charming. He'd arranged for 'Jill' to drive down on the Thursday night and have dinner with him. Had he expected her to stay the night and drive him back to Cambridge the next day?

Except obviously that hadn't happened.

Because whoever had sent the texts had clearly visited Garnett, as arranged, and poisoned him.

But how had they persuaded Garnett to let them into the barn? The post-mortem had shown no evidence of wounds or blunt trauma: just the poisoning. If Garnett had been expecting Jill to turn up and someone had arrived in her stead, surely he would've reacted in some way? At the very least, he would've refused that person entry to the cottage.

Unless, Colin thought, Garnett had known the person who turned up at the door. But that still left no clues as to who it might have been.

He needed to check the whereabouts of Jill's phone. Much as he hated having to distress a bereaved family, there was no other way of finding out the information. He called Jill's parents; as he'd half-expected, the call went straight through to voicemail. 'Mrs Cassidy, it's Detective Inspector Bradshaw. We spoke a couple of days ago. I wonder if y—'

The phone connected abruptly. 'Hello?'

'Mrs Cassidy, I'm so sorry to trouble you again. I was wondering, do you have Jill's mobile phone, please?'

'No, I don't,' Mrs Cassidy said. 'Her sister wanted to keep it. She said there were some photos on it.'

A sister. If Jill's sister had sent the texts, and she looked like Jill, it would explain why Roland Garnett had let her into the barn – not realising his mistake until it was much too late.

'Could I trouble you for your daughter's name, number and address, please?' he asked.

'Yes. Jennifer – Jenny – Smith.'

'Not Cassidy?' Colin checked.

'No. She got married a few years ago, but it didn't last.'

'I see.' It was a name he recognised. Someone he'd already interviewed. He mouthed the address as Mrs Cassidy spoke. 'She lives at Number Four, Beech View, Little Wenborough, in Norfolk.'

Everything fell into place.

'Thank you, Mrs Cassidy,' he said. 'And I'm sorry to have troubled you.'

When he put the phone down, he said to Larissa, 'I think we have a poisoner to arrest.'

He explained his theory on the way to Little Wenborough. They parked outside Jenny's house, then rang the doorbell.

'Is Tom all right?' Jenny asked as soon as she opened the door. 'The hospital wouldn't tell me anything.'

'He'll recover. But you knew that when you poisoned him, didn't you, Jenny?' Colin asked. He nodded at Larissa.

'Jenny Smith, I'm arresting you on suspicion of the murder of Roland Garnett at Rookery Barn on Thursday, the twentieth of April, and on suspicion of poisoning Georgina Drake on Thursday, the twenty-seventh of April, and Tom Nichols on Friday, the twenty-eighth of April, because we have evidence that shows you may have been involved, and your arrest is necessary to question you about your involvement,' Larissa said.

Right by the textbook, Colin thought with relief as Larissa continued, giving the official caution.

'We need you to accompany us to the station to answer some questions, Ms Smith,' Colin said.

'But I haven't killed anyone! Georgina's alive, and so is Tom. And Roland Garnett was alive when I left him.'

'You live in Little Wenborough. I'm fairly sure you would have heard someone in the village mentioning the death of Georgina Drake's guest in Rookery Barn, so you know Roland Garnett died – and you know he died after ingesting poison,'

Colin said. 'You have the right to have a solicitor present at the interview, and I'd recommend that you do. Do you want to call your solicitor, or do you want to use the duty solicitor?'

She shivered. 'The duty solicitor will be fine. Thank you.'

'Do you still have your sister's phone?' he asked.

She nodded, looking defeated. 'Do you want me to fetch it?'

'Or tell Sergeant Foulkes where it is, and she'll get it.'

Jenny shook her head. 'I'm not going to try and make a run for it.'

'Go with her, Larissa,' Colin directed.

Back at the police station, they read her her rights again, made her a hot drink and waited for the solicitor.

When the solicitor arrived, Colin checked that Jenny was comfortable, and cautioned her again for the benefit of the tape.

'Tell us what happened on Thursday,' Colin said. 'And remember you're under caution. So you need to tell us the whole truth, Jenny.'

Jenny blew out a breath. 'Roland Garnett's a total bastard,' she said. 'My sister, Jill, is – was,' she corrected herself, 'really clever, but she was a bit fragile. She always had been. Being an academic would suit her – working in an ivory tower, away from anything horrible. When she applied to do her MA at Cambridge, I got a job in the botanical gardens, so I wouldn't be that far away if she needed me. When she finished her MA and started doing her doctorate, I thought she'd settled and was coping OK, and I got my job here at the Science Park.'

'How do you mean, coping OK?' Colin asked.

'Jilly had always been in a bit of a world of her own,' Jenny said. 'She was... naïve, I guess. Although she was the older one, I always felt older than her. And she'd been ill. She had glandular fever when she was seventeen, and she ended up having to retake her A levels. She got Covid in the second year of her degree; when it turned out to be long Covid, she ended up having to take another year out. Luckily she decided to go to

university at Bristol, where Mum and Dad moved to look after
our grandparents, so she was living at home and Mum could
look after her. But being ill for so long knocked her confidence
as well as her physical health.' Jenny spread her hands. 'Jilly
just needed a bit more support than most people. She was eighteen months older than me, but I was in the year below her at
school. With those two years she had to repeat, it meant I
finished my masters at the same time as she finished her first
degree.' She shrugged. 'Mum and I talked about it, and we
thought we'd all be happier if I was near Jill. Not living with her
– otherwise she'd never get her confidence and be independent
– but living close enough to be straight there if she needed me.
And it was OK for her master's year. Except then Garnett...'
Jenny grimaced. 'I wish she'd never had him as her tutor. He
took advantage of her.'

'Can you explain what you mean by took advantage?'
Larissa asked.

'He took her virginity, for starters,' Jenny said. 'He made her
think he loved her and wanted a future with her. He told her
they had to keep it quiet because, even though she was over
twenty-one, he was her tutor and it might make things awkward
for him at work. So she used to meet him in places where people
wouldn't recognise them, and they'd go separately so they
wouldn't be seen together in Cambridge.'

Which tallied with the texts Colin had read.

'It's...' She shook her head in what looked like a mixture of
anger and frustration. 'He's a bastard, and he didn't deserve
her.'

Colin, thinking of what Hayley Summers had told him,
wondered just how many times Garnett had done the same
thing to other vulnerable students.

'He was her tutor, so of course he knew all about her
research... and he used it to get a book deal. Jilly found out, and
she actually stood up to him – I'm so proud of her for that – but

he said she couldn't prove it, nobody would believe her and he'd make sure nobody would ever agree to be her supervisor if she tried to move and finish her PhD somewhere else. It was her word against his, and nobody would believe a student against a supervisor. I told her to go and talk to her personal tutor, but by then bloody Garnett had convinced her that nobody would listen to her. I was going to make an appointment with the head of college so I could put him straight about what was going on, and tell him that I'd go public with the information if he didn't stop Garnett. But then Jilly realised she was pregnant. She thought it would make a difference to Garnett – but of course it didn't. He just wanted her to get rid of the baby.' She dragged in a breath. 'I tried to convince Jilly to go back to Mum, but instead she took an overdose.'

'How did you find out about the overdose?' Larissa asked.

'The hospital rang Mum, and Mum rang me. I went straight to the hospital. The doctor treating her was really nice. He told me Jilly would be OK – they'd given her stuff so the paracetamol wouldn't do any damage to her and hopefully the baby would be OK, and he was going to refer her for mental health care.' She dragged in a breath. 'I was grateful for that – but when I saw Jilly lying there, pale as a ghost... She'd wanted to end everything because of Garnett. I was so angry. I wanted to make him pay for what he'd done to her,' Jenny said.

Colin could understand – sympathise, even – but people couldn't just take the law into their own hands. Vigilante justice wasn't the answer.

'I told my boss there was a family crisis, and she let me have a few days' unpaid leave,' Jenny continued. 'I kept an eye on Jilly while Mum packed the stuff from her room, and we took her back to Bristol. When Jilly was asleep in the car, I told Mum all the stuff Jilly had kept from her, and we agreed I'd stay at home for a while and sleep in the same room as Jilly so I could keep an eye on her, until she'd settled. For two nights, it worked.' She put her hands to her face. 'But the third night... I slept through. I still wonder if Jilly put something in my hot chocolate, sleeping tablets or what have you, that night. I woke up, the next morning, feeling as groggy as if I'd been to a first-year student party and spent the night drinking. And then I saw her bed was empty. She wasn't downstairs. She wasn't with Mum. We called the police, and then we went round the neighbours to ask them to help us look for her.' She swallowed hard. 'We found her in the river. She'd drowned herself.'

'I'm sorry,' Colin said, meaning it.

'It was Garnett's fault. He'd made her feel so worthless and hopeless that she killed herself. And I was going to make him pay. I knew the passcode to Jilly's phone. I was looking for photographs. His was one of her last texts – I couldn't help reading it and scrolling back through the conversation. And when I saw the stuff he'd texted her...' She grimaced.

'Did you tell anyone?' Colin asked.

She nodded. 'Tom Nichols. He's always been such a nice guy. I knew he was in love with my sister in sixth form, but she never noticed him.'

'Were you in love with Tom?' Larissa asked.

'No. I do love him,' Jenny said, 'but as the big brother I never had. I never fancied him or anything.'

'How did he react when you told him about Garnett?' Colin asked, wondering whether Young Tom had helped Jenny to kill Garnett.

'He said I should go to the college and show them what Garnett had done. Everything from stealing her work to getting her pregnant.'

'Did you go to the college?' Colin asked.

'No. I was going to, but Jilly's death knocked me for six. I could hardly string a sentence together, let alone make a proper coherent case,' Jenny said. 'I've been off sick from work ever since Jilly died. I was planning to go back to work next week, starting with three days a week and working my hours back up to full time. My car had conked out, so Tom was a sweetie and lent me his, so I could go and see my boss last week and get it all sorted out – and his mate Spike's a mechanic. He was going to fix my car for me before I went back to work.'

That, Colin thought, explained how Jenny had been able to get hold of Tom's car. Though Tom should've told them about lending his car to Jenny a few days before Garnett's murder.

'And then, on the Monday afternoon, I was with Tom at Rookery Farm. He's been brilliant while I've been off, making me get out of the house for fresh air and potter about in the gardens with him, and it's helped me so much. He's got nothing to do with Garnett,' Jenny said. 'It's all me, and I'm prepared to swear that in court. He was mowing Georgina Drake's lawn – and then this guy came out of Rookery Barn and had a go at him. I stayed out of the way, twitching out a few weeds, because I just didn't have the headspace to deal with someone else's aggro – but then I saw the guy's face and I realised it was *him*. Garnett.'

'You'd met him before?' Larissa asked.

'No,' Jenny said. 'But I'd seen the photos of him on Jilly's phone and I recognised him. When he'd gone, I asked Tom who the guy was, and he told me the guy was this academic from Cambridge. Dr Garnett. He was working on some book or other – and I know it was Jilly's research.'

'Did Tom realise this was the guy you'd told him was involved with Jilly?' Colin asked.

'I don't think so. He just thought the guy was being awkward and the sort who throws his weight around. But he didn't want to make trouble for Mrs Drake, so he backed off,' Jenny said.

'What happened then?' Larissa asked.

Jenny shook her head. 'I just lost it, I think. Garnett was in Rookery Barn, using my sister's work and pretending it was his, strutting around as if he owned the place – and my sister was dead because of him. He never even contacted Mum and Dad to say he was sorry she'd dropped out of her PhD because the work was too much for her – which is what everyone thought at the college. When she died...' She swallowed hard. 'I'm not sure if Mum told them at Cambridge. I was pretty sure he didn't know she'd died, and I wanted to make him hurt, the way he'd hurt Jilly. Make him face what he'd done to her, then make him apologise sincerely.' She took a deep breath. 'So I texted him, pretending to be Jilly. I made out that I'd changed my mind and I wanted to make up with him. I knew he was the type who thought he was wonderful – and untouchable – and I was right. He fell for it and asked me to come and see him. He gave me the address of the place where he was staying, not realising I already knew.'

'What were you going to do?' Colin asked.

'Jilly once told me he liked hot curries. So I made him one,' Jenny said. 'She'd told me all about her research, about poisonous plants in Ancient Greece, and how she thought Alexander the Great might've been poisoned with oleander.'

And that was the final piece of the puzzle: why she'd chosen oleander to poison Garnett.

'What do you know about oleander?' Larissa asked.

'Jilly told me there's a story that the Persians used it to poison Alexander the Great's horses, and possibly Alexander the Great himself. There's another story about Alexander the Great's soldiers skewering meat on oleander stems so they could cook it over the fire, and the poison killed them.' Jenny spread her hands. 'It sounded like an urban myth to me. Especially as not one single person survived.'

'I'd heard that story about a group of scouts eating sausages,' Colin said. 'I agree with you. It definitely sounds like an urban myth.'

'Jilly said there was another theory that scholars have

confused oleander with bay laurel, so it was actually oleander leaves that Pythia chewed to send her into a trance – or burned it and inhaled the smoke,' Jenny said.

'Who's Pythia?' Larissa asked.

'The priestess of Apollo at Delphi,' Jenny explained. 'She was known as the Delphic Oracle. People would consult her about an important decision; she'd go into a trance, have a vision, and say something ambiguous that they'd have to inter-pret to make the decision. The trance and the visions could have been symptoms of poisoning. And that's what gave me the idea. Poison a Classics teacher with something from Ancient Greece. Poison him with what he'd stolen from Jilly. I read up on it, and obviously because my degree's in plant biology I know that oleander's poisonous; but everything I've read said it was only fatal to sheep, goats, horses, dogs and cows. Humans who ate it would just get a nasty stomach-ache, with maybe a bit of diarrhoea and vomiting. That was good enough for me. Make him feel really rough, make him sorry – and make him admit what he'd done.'

Intent to harm, Colin thought with an inward sigh. That would count against her in court.

'Oleander's meant to taste very bitter, but I thought the spices in a really hot curry would be enough to disguise the taste. So I bought a cheap saucepan, a plastic jug and a wooden spoon – things I could throw away afterwards. I knew Sybbie – Lady Wyatt – had oleander in her garden, so I took some cuttings while I was helping Tom and his granddad at the Manor. I didn't damage the plants,' she added.

'Sybbie said the cuttings had been taken by someone who knew what they were doing,' Colin said. 'What did you do then?'

'I chopped up some oleander leaves, boiled them in water and made a chicken curry with the stock. I got rid of everything I'd used to cook it, so nobody would use any of it and accidentally be ill,' she said. 'I kept the bottle with the oleander liquid, because I was going to dispose of that in the hazardous waste at the lab. And then I went to Rookery Barn on Thursday evening, as I'd arranged.'

'When you arrived, did Garnett realise you weren't Jill?' Larissa asked.

'No. I guess because we're so close in age, and we look like each other, we could pretty much pass for each other.' Jenny put her own phone on the table. 'That's us together, on my lock screen,' she said.

Jill and Jenny were the same height and similar body shape; the only real differences were that Jenny's hair was shorter and she wore brighter clothing, and Jenny had the light tan of someone who worked outside whereas Jilly was pale.

'He noticed my hair, obviously, so I told him I'd had it cut because I wanted to look nice for him. And that's why I was wearing make-up, too – I was pretty sure he wouldn't notice that Jilly's skin is paler than mine because she spends all her time in a library, but I didn't want to take any chances.' Jenny shuddered. 'He made my skin crawl. But I managed to act all concerned and loving. Fluttery, the way Jilly is. *Was*,' she amended, and scrubbed away the single tear that spilled over her lashes.

'I know you hadn't met him, but hadn't he seen a photo of you?' Colin asked.

'Even if he had, he wouldn't have paid attention. He was a complete narcissist. Everything was always about him.' Jenny narrowed her eyes. 'He knew what he was doing wasn't OK. Yes, Jill was an adult, but she was his student. It wasn't an equal relationship. He made sure she didn't meet any of his family and friends, and he didn't meet any of hers.' She took a deep breath. 'What he didn't realise was that she'd told me about him.'

'And you made him the curry. Didn't he think it strange that you didn't eat it?' Larissa asked.

'Jilly's vegetarian. She would never have eaten chicken curry, even to please him. I was careful to reheat the veggie one first – and I told him it was so his would be properly hot and I didn't mind mine being a bit cold,' Jenny said. 'Which was the sort of thing Jilly would've done.'

'How long was it before he started to be ill?' Colin asked.

'About an hour and a half,' Jenny said. 'During which time I topped up his glass of vodka a few times and listened to him telling me about how clever he was. And I had to pretend to be all hero-worshipping, when I really wanted to punch him and tell him what a disgusting pig he was.' She grimaced. 'I honestly thought I was going to have to go through with going to bed with him. But then, thank God, the oleander started doing its stuff and he said he had a bit of a stomach-ache. I acted horrified and said maybe his chicken was off because I hadn't stored it well enough on the way from Cambridge, and I was so sorry because all I'd wanted to do was to make him a special dinner so we could make up again.'

'Cambridge?' Larissa asked.

'He thought Jilly was coming from Cambridge. He didn't know I live here.' She grimaced again. 'I told him to go and lie down, and I'd clear up in the kitchen then bring him a drink of water.'

'What did you do in the kitchen?' Larissa asked.

'I'd brought all the containers with me, so I put them in a plastic bag to get rid of later. I washed everything else – the plates, glasses and cutlery – with bleach to get rid of any traces of poison, so nobody else would be ill if they used them. Then I cleaned the kitchen,' Jenny said.

'Did you wear rubber gloves while you were cleaning?' Colin asked.

Jenny nodded. 'Of course. I was using bleach.'

It explained why there were no fingerprints. And it also explained the use of bleach. Not to hide what she'd done, but to make sure there was no collateral damage.

'What did you do when you'd finished cleaning?' Larissa asked.

'I took Garnett a glass of water,' Jenny said.

'What was he doing?' Colin asked.

'Lying on the bed, complaining that he felt terrible,' Jenny said.

That tied in with what he'd seen, Colin thought: the dead man had still been wearing his clothes and the curtains hadn't been drawn. 'Did he ask you to call a doctor?' he asked.

'No.'

'Did you offer to call a doctor?' Larissa asked.

'No,' Jenny said. 'That's when I told him who I was. That I'd put oleander in his food – just like my sister had written about, in the research he stole from her – and that she'd drowned herself because of him. I hoped a night with a stomach-ache would help prod his conscience to do the right thing and tell the truth. And I'd got plenty of proof of what he'd done. So, if he hadn't told the college by Wednesday of next week, I'd do it myself.'

'What was his reaction?' Colin asked.

'He called me a bitch and swore at me. I thought he was going to get up and maybe take a swing at me – but then I think his stomach started hurting a bit more and he fell back on the bed. So I walked out, made sure the kitchen door was locked – it was one of those locks that locks automatically behind you and you have to use a key to open it – and drove Tom's car back to his place.'

'Did Tom know you used his car?' Larissa asked.

'No.' She grimaced. 'I felt a bit bad – I'd forgotten to give him his key back when he lent me his car before. But I didn't think he'd mind me borrowing it again. I couldn't ask him if it was OK, because he was out at the pub quiz.' She smiled ruefully. 'He'd asked me to go and join his team, that night. I said no, because I was having the period from hell. I knew he wouldn't ask any more, because he's nice like that. He just asked if I wanted him to bring anything over. And I said I was fine.'

'Didn't you think there might be CCTV of the car and we'd trace it back to Tom?' Colin asked.

'Sort of,' she admitted. 'That's why I daubed a bit of mud over the car – especially the number plate. That's what Tom would've noticed, because he always keeps it clean. His grandad drilled it into him that a good workman looks after his stuff. I had just enough time to wash the mud off and get the car back in Tom's driveway before he got back from the pub quiz.'

'What did you do next?' Larissa asked.

'I walked back to mine. I kept all the stuff under the bed in my room until Spike brought my car back, the next day, and then I went to the lab and disposed of the curry containers in the hazardous waste, so I knew it wouldn't affect anyone else or wildlife – you can't just dump something like that in normal waste.' She looked at them. 'Garnett wasn't meant to die – just be ill, to give him time to think about what he'd done to Jilly.'

'But he *did* die, Jenny,' Colin said quietly.

Jenny wrapped her arms round herself, shaking her head. 'I... I'm sorry. That wasn't supposed to happen. I didn't mean to kill him. He was just meant to be ill for a day or two.'

'He choked on his own vomit. And that caused a fatal heart attack,' Larissa said.

Jenny's face paled. 'Oleander's not fatal to humans. It shouldn't have killed him.'

'There's a thing in law called the eggshell skull rule,' Colin told her gently. 'You take your victim as you find them.'

'Roland Garnett wasn't a victim. He was a horrible, horrible man who hurt my sister and stole her research and caused her death. But I didn't plan to kill him,' Jenny said again. 'I just wanted to scare him a bit. Make him feel ill. Make him apologise. And then I was going to tell the head of college about him so he'd never be able to take advantage of another student, ever again.'

'You killed him, so we'll need to put the case to the Crown Prosecution Service, and they're likely to charge you formally,' Colin said. 'What about Georgina and Young Tom? Did you make up another batch of poison for them?'

'No. When I went to get rid of all the stuff in the hazardous waste disposal, the bottle of oleander liquid fell out of the bag. I didn't notice it was still in the car until I got home. I stored it in Sybbie's potting shed until I could go back to work and get rid of it.' Jenny sighed. 'I overheard Mrs Drake talking about the CCTV and I knew I needed to warn her off. When she was sitting on the terrace... it just seemed an easy way to do it. Spill her coffee, apologise and get her another one, then add a couple of drops of the oleander liquid to her cup – enough to scare her, not to hurt her.'

'And Young Tom?' Larissa asked.

'He hasn't done anything wrong. And the only way I could think of to stop you suspecting him was to make him one of the victims. So I put a few drops in his flask of tea, that morning. He takes his tea sweet, so I thought the sugar would probably mask the taste. He is going to be all right, isn't he?' she asked, looking anxious.

'Yes – but no thanks to you,' Larissa said.

'We need to know precisely where you disposed of the curry remains,' Colin said. 'And the oleander liquid.'

'The labs usually get their bins collected by specialist hazardous waste contractors,' she said, 'so it might have already been taken, but I'll give you all the details so you can check with them. And the oleander liquid's still in Sybbie's potting shed. Hidden away at the back.' She dragged in a breath. 'I really didn't mean for Garnett to die – I just wanted to stop him stealing Jilly's work and treating his students as his personal little black book.'

Colin believed her, but you couldn't take the law into your own hands. He summarised what she'd told him. 'Do you want to add anything, or do you have any questions?' he asked.

'No.' Jenny said.

Colin gave the date and time for the benefit of the tape. 'We'll keep you in custody for a bit longer,' he said, 'because we need to speak to the Crown Prosecution Service. If they decide to charge you formally with the murder of Roland Garnett, then you'll be taken in front of a magistrate, who'll decide whether you'll be remanded in custody until the trial,' he added, as gently as he could. 'We'll make sure your family's informed.'

'Can you make sure the college sees his texts to Jilly? Just so they know what he did, and that she's completely innocent?' Jenny asked.

'Nobody's above the law,' Colin said. 'This is a bit of a grey area and, I have to be honest with you, a clever lawyer could make a case that Garnett did nothing wrong. But I agree that the college needs to know about it. If any of their other tutors are doing this sort of thing, it needs to stop.'

'Thank you,' she whispered.

FOURTEEN

Bea, satisfied that her mother was on the mend and having extracted a promise from Georgina that she'd take things easy, went back to London on Saturday morning.

Georgina was making notes about Trevor Taylor when she heard the doorknocker banging. She went to answer the door and was shocked to see Jack and Tracey Beauchamp standing there.

'I'm sorry to disturb you, but I haven't slept properly since you came over,' Jack said. 'I couldn't stop thinking about what you said.'

'I'm so sorry I hurt you,' Georgina said.

'Did you mean it? Have you *really* talked to my sister?'

She nodded. 'I know, it doesn't make any sense. I couldn't get my head round it at first. Please, come in, and I'll put the kettle on, and then I'll answer any questions you have, as best as I can.'

He tried not to flinch as he passed the spot in the hallway where his sister had obviously died, and she led the Beauchamps into the living room.

'Can I offer you some tea? Coffee?' Georgina asked.

They settled on tea, and she headed to the kitchen.

'My brother's here,' Doris whispered as Georgina busied herself making tea. 'He's actually come *here*.'

'I know,' Georgina whispered back. 'But you're really going to have to help me answer his questions.'

She put everything onto a tray, took it into the living room, set it on the coffee table and poured out three cups of tea. Tracey asked for milk and Jack asked for milk and half a sugar. Once she'd given them their mugs, Georgina sat so she could see both their faces clearly.

'So you're deaf?' Jack asked.

'Yes. Not from birth, though,' Georgina said. 'I could hear when I was younger, but it's got worse over the years. Even three or four years ago, I could still hear a conversation without my hearing aids, but I can't hear anything quieter than a phone on full volume, now.'

'But you can hear Doris.'

'Only since I got my new hearing aids. That first day, I could hear a woman's voice when I knew I was on my own. I thought I'd accidentally tuned into a radio play, but it turned out to be something I really wasn't expecting.' She blew out a breath. 'I'd never even believed in ghosts. Well, not until a few days ago.'

'But you believe in them now?' Tracey asked,

'Yes,' Georgina said. 'And I'm perfectly sane. Some of the things Doris said to me weren't on public record, and it wasn't just clever cold reading. Neither of us has worked out why she's here and why I can hear her, but I *can* hear her, and I want to help her. That's why I found you.'

'So you weren't researching the history of the house at all, then?' Tracey asked.

'Oh, I am,' Georgina said. 'But it was my priority to find Jack. I promise you, this isn't some elaborate con trick.'

'Is Doris... is she here now?' Jack's voice quavered slightly.

'Yes,' Georgina said.

'But I can't see her. I can't hear her. Doris? Talk to me,' Jack pleaded.

'Oh, Jack. My baby brother,' Doris whispered.

Georgina waited, her heart in her mouth; but the Beauchamps gave no sign of being able to hear Doris.

'Did you hear what she said?' Georgina asked.

'No,' Jack said, looking defeated. 'Could I hear her if I borrowed one of your hearing aids?'

'The mould won't fit your ear,' Georgina said, 'so all you'll hear is screechy feedback, and it's programmed to my hearing profile. But you're welcome to try.' She removed one of her hearing aids and handed it to Jack.

He held the end of the earpiece against his ear canal.

'Jack? Jack, can you hear me?' Doris asked eagerly.

Jack looked anguished as he took the hearing aid away from his ear and handed it back to Georgina. 'All I could hear was something that sounded like static and screeching. Did she speak?'

'Yes,' Georgina said. 'She asked if you could hear her.'

'Can she hear me?'

'Yes,' Georgina said. 'I know this is going to sound a bit weird, but could I... well, translate, I guess, for you? Repeat what she says?'

Tracey still looked suspicious. 'How do we know you're not making up whatever you claim she says?'

'You only have my word for it. And I can't prove that ghosts exist, either,' Georgina said. 'We tried taking photographs – I'm a portrait photographer,' she added, 'but there wasn't so much as a shadow in the wrong place or an orb. As far as I know, all the "ghost" portraits in history have turned out to be double exposures, a long exposure, dust motes or insects, or pareidolia – seeing patterns in things.' She smiled wryly. 'And I've already had that conversation with Doris.'

'Tell me something only she would know to prove it,' Jack said.

'I tried to tell you about the musket ball when I visited you,' she said. 'But I guess, as you're here, it's even better because Doris can help me be a bit more precise.' She gestured to the fireplace. 'OK. What she told me was that one of the stones in the fireplace – this side, not the dining room – was loose.'

'Which one?' Jack asked.

Georgina waited for Doris to tell her. 'The third row back, at the right-hand side as you look at it. It was back in summer 1965. Your dad took them all out so he could check the grouting, and there was all this packed earth underneath. He found an old coin and three musket balls. The coin was a George the Third halfpenny, dated 1774, and you thought the king's face looked like a Roman emperor. You thought the musket balls were just lumps of metal, until your dad told you what they were, and then you got so excited and you begged him to let you have one.'

Jack blinked. 'Yes, we did find three musket balls and a halfpenny. That last bit, though – that'd be true of any ten-year-old boy.'

'But the place is right?' Georgina checked.

He nodded.

'You never told me that story before,' Tracey said.

'I'd forgotten all about it,' Jack said, his voice cracking. 'But she remembered. All those years ago, and she remembered,' he repeated, clearly overcome by emotion.

'Your dad used to keep the coin and the other two musket balls in a matchbox in the kitchen drawer. The one where your mum kept the candles,' Georgina said.

'The only living person who could've told you that, apart from me, was my mum,' Jack said, his eyes narrowing. 'And I would've known if you'd visited her. You would've had to sign in with the warden – and they would've contacted me to let me know because you weren't one of her usual visitors. Unless there's a new receptionist who doesn't know the system.'

'They haven't contacted you, because I haven't visited your mum, Jack,' Georgina said.

He huffed out a breath. 'All right, then. What really happened to my sister?'

'This is going to be upsetting,' Georgina warned.

'I lost her when I was fifteen. How can it possibly get worse than that?' Jack asked.

'Tell him I love him, and I've never stopped missing him,' Doris said.

Tracey held Jack's hand very tightly. 'We're listening, Georgina,' she said.

Georgina swallowed hard. 'Jack, Doris wants you to know she loves you and she's never stopped missing you.'

'Same here,' he said softly, and Georgina heard a muffled sob from Doris.

'Doris and Trevor... let's just say they jumped the gun a bit in their relationship,' Georgina said. 'Back in February 1971, she was pregnant. About ten weeks.'

Jack's eyes widened. 'I had no idea. Did my mum and dad know?'

'Doris thinks she managed to keep it from them,' Georgina said. 'She and Trev talked it over, and they thought it wasn't the right time to have a baby. They both wanted to go to university – and, back then, there weren't the childcare options that we have now.'

'Dad would've made them get married, before she started to show,' Jack said. 'And Trev's mum was a bit of a snooty cow.'

'That's what she told me.' Georgina decided not to tell him about the potential threat of a home for unmarried mothers and having the baby adopted. 'So she went to the doctor. And he prescribed a hot bath, gin, and falling down the stairs.'

Tracey put a hand to her mouth. 'Oh, my God. That *poor* girl.'

'So you're saying she fell down the stairs on purpose?' Jack asked.

'Her memories are hazy,' Georgina said, 'and she doesn't remember Trevor coming over, or doing what the doctor suggested. But she knows that was what they planned.'

Jack shook his head. 'The doctor said it was an accident.'

'It must've been,' Georgina said. 'She didn't try to kill herself, if that's what you were thinking. From the little time I've known her, I'm absolutely sure that isn't what Doris would do.'

'It isn't. It wasn't deliberate,' Doris said.

'Oh, my poor sister. If only she'd told Mum. Mum would've known what to do,' Jack said. 'We lost her, all because of some stupid doctor giving her advice out of the ark instead of helping her.' He shook his head. 'What a waste. What a bloody *waste*. She had her whole life in front of her. She was going to be a teacher.'

'An English teacher. She loved Shakespeare,' Georgina said. 'We've kind of bonded over Shakespeare and Jane Austen, these last few days.'

Jack's eyes filled with tears. 'Doris, I want you to know you've never been forgotten. Not by any of us. Not by Mum, by Dad, by me. We've always missed you, and we've always loved you,' he said. 'And I wish you'd been here. I wish my Matt and Lucy had had the chance to know their aunt. I wish you'd gone to London and bought fancy clothes at Biba and seen George Harrison at a concert, the way you planned.'

Doris was crying. 'So do I.'

'It wasn't your fault. It wasn't anyone's fault. Well, except maybe that bloody doctor's,' Jack said. 'But at least I know now.' His hand tightened on Tracey's. 'I don't know if I should tell Mum.'

'That's your call,' Georgina said gently. 'But I do know your mum did exactly what I did when my husband died – she contacted a medium to see if she could get a message through to Doris.'

'And did she?' Tracey asked.

'No. Doris was there, but the medium couldn't see, feel or hear her,' Georgina said.

'So the medium was a con woman?' Jack asked.

'No. She told your mum things that made her feel better. I don't think she accepted any money.'

'You're not accepting any money,' Tracey pointed out.

'I'm not pretending to be a medium. I don't see or hear other ghosts. I just hear Doris. Who's actually laughing through her tears, right now, at the idea of me being a medium,' Georgina said wryly. 'But she's mostly glad you've had a happy life. That you have children.'

'Grandchildren, too.' Jack said. 'Matt has two boys, and Lucy has a girl. Lucy's middle name is Doris, and so is Scarlett's.'

'My brother *and* my niece named their girls after me?' Doris asked, sounding delighted. 'That's amazing!'

'Doris is really pleased to hear it,' Georgina said, smiling.

And she had a feeling that everything was going to be all right – at least for Doris's family.

* * *

When Colin had finished his paperwork on Saturday, he called in to see Georgina.

He knocked on her front door, and she raised an eyebrow when she opened the door and saw him. 'I thought we were friends. My friends use the kitchen door.'

'It's a formal visit,' he said, 'so I guess that means using the front door.'

She frowned. 'You've found more evidence?'

'Yes,' he said. 'I'm pleased to inform you, Mrs Drake, that you're no longer a person of interest in the Garnett case. We've made an arrest, and we'll ensure that Dr Garnett's belongings are returned to his estate.'

She looked surprised. 'Not to his family?'

'No,' he said. 'If I can collect his things now, I'll give you back the keys to the barn.'

'What I'd prefer you to do,' she said, 'is collect his stuff and then leave all the doors and windows in the barn wide open. With what happened, and it having been closed up for a week...' She grimaced. 'I'm feeling a lot better than I was, but I think that'll make me heave again.'

'We don't need the mattress for evidence – we already have enough from his clothes,' Colin said. 'I can move it out of the barn for you and open the doors and windows, if you like.'

'Yes, please,' she said gratefully. 'Then I'll arrange for it to be disposed of.'

'Stay here,' he said.

'Is that an official police order?'

'No. It's a friend talking – one who saw the results of you being poisoned, and who doesn't want you to be ill again,' Colin said.

The smell was appalling, and he was gagging by the time he'd hauled the mattress out of the barn. It took him a while to compose himself before he went back to the farmhouse.

'From the look on your face, I think I'm going to need to get a Hazmat suit before I tackle the cleaning,' she said ruefully.

'Not to mention a respirator. If it helps, I can recommend a specialist cleaner who deals with this sort of stuff,' he said.

'I'd really appreciate that,' she said. 'Thanks for getting the mattress out.' She looked at him. 'I'm going to offer you a cup of tea, and it's up to you whether you accept it as a policeman or as a friend.'

She was giving him the choice, and he knew what he wanted. 'A friend,' he said.

'Good.' Georgina busied herself in the kitchen, refusing his offer of help. And it was kind of nice, watching her potter about, he thought.

He followed her out onto the patio and sat on one of the wrought-iron chairs.

Her garden was a lovely spot to chill out. A place to think. Around the edges of the patio were terracotta troughs filled with pretty spring flowers and the occasional bee landing to take its fill of nectar; the warmth of the sunlight seemed to intensify the scent of the flowers. The road through the village was quiet, and anyway she was set back far enough that they couldn't hear traffic; all he could hear were birds singing.

'According to Young Tom, what you can hear are blackbirds, robins and finches. He thinks there's a woodpecker somewhere over the back, as well as the rooks that give the farmhouse its name. And he's going to take me and my camera to the spot on the River Wensum where I'm likely to see kingfishers,' she said. 'Unless, of course, you're going to tell me he's the one you arrested and is going to be charged with murder.'

'No. He isn't.'

'Good. I told you he was a sweetheart.' She looked at him. 'So who *was* the murderer?'

He coughed. 'You know I can't discuss a case.'

'Technically, you can't tell me anything, but I can talk to you,' she reminded him. She looked thoughtful. 'If it was Tom's car, then he wasn't the driver – because you just told me you haven't arrested him or charged him.'

'Tom is completely innocent of any wrongdoing,' he said.

'In that case, I'd say it was either the student Garnett was having an affair with, or someone who wanted her to take the rap for it,' Georgina said.

'You're not going to give up, are you?' he asked wryly.

'You've not noticed my "just call me Jane" T-shirt, then?' she teased, and he couldn't help smiling.

'All right, Miss Marple. I can't tell you who it was, but the person who poisoned him didn't intend to kill him. They meant to give him a severe stomach-ache – and then they were going to report him for inappropriate behaviour towards his student, and for stealing her research.'

'If the killer didn't mean him to die, does it still count as murder?' she asked.

'It's still unlawful killing. I'm not sure the prosecutor could prove an intent to kill – from the perpetrator's statement, it was intent to harm. If he hadn't died, then it would've been classed as actual body harm,' he said. 'A good defence lawyer could make a case for voluntary manslaughter, though not with diminished responsibility in this case. The inciting incident was the student's overdose, which clearly affected the poisoner's state of mind; but the perpetrator cleaned up the scene afterwards.'

'To hide their guilt?'

'No. So nobody else would accidentally ingest the poison,' he said.

She frowned. 'That doesn't sound like a cold-blooded killer to me; it sounds like someone who's normally responsible, and something went wrong.'

'The perpetrator obscured evidence so the owner of the car didn't get the blame,' he said. 'In my opinion, the perpetrator showed remorse, plus they had previous good character.' He shrugged. 'It's in the hands of the courts, now.'

'Was it the same person who poisoned Young Tom and me?' Georgina asked.

'You, to warn you off; and Young Tom, to stop us thinking he was the poisoner,' Colin confirmed. 'I really can't say any more than that, Georgina.'

'All right. Is Young Tom doing OK, though?' Georgina asked.

'He's going to be fine,' Colin said. He finished his tea. 'I'd better go and see Francesca, Sybbie and Jodie to let them know their names are clear. I'll wash up, first.'

'It's fine,' she said with a smile. 'Go and do your duty, Inspector.'

The teasing light in her eyes drew him. He badly wanted to ask her out again, but for now he'd have to leave that particular ball in her court. 'See you around,' he said. 'Take care.'

'You, too,' she said.

* * *

When Colin had gone, Georgina video-called Will and Bea to give them the good news that her name had been cleared, and they arranged to come and visit her the following weekend. She washed up the mugs, then leaned back against the sink and surveyed the kitchen.

Right at that moment, Georgina felt really flat.

Doris had gone quiet since Jack's departure. She probably needed to process the situation as much as Jack and Tracey did. Georgina had already spoken to her children; her local friends were busy; and she had nothing pressing to do.

Maybe it was time she went back to work instead of rattling around the house on her own.

She'd just about summoned up the energy to make a list of items she wanted to check for the house history research when there was a knock on the window, and then the kitchen door opened.

Sybbie raised the bottle of champagne she was carrying. 'Get your flutes out, Georgie, so we can toast the Musketeers having their names cleared.'

'That sounds good to me,' Georgina said, smiling. 'Have you decided which Musketeer is which, yet?'

'There are four of us. I think we can take turns in being D'Artagnan,' Sybbie said with a grin.

The absurdity was just what Georgina needed, and she burst out laughing.

Jodie and Francesca were waiting by the kitchen door.

'Cesca? Jodie? Aren't you coming in?' Georgina asked.

Francesca shook her head. 'I thought we could sit on the patio.'

'Good idea. It's a nice afternoon.' Georgina looked at Sybbie. 'Don't you start twitching weeds out,' she warned.

'As if I would,' Sybbie said, though they all knew she was fibbing. 'Though I'm glad I have secateurs in my handbag. Because I think that wisteria needs just a little bit of –'

'I give in,' Georgina cut in, laughing. 'I'll bring the glasses out.'

When she walked out onto the patio, she realised why Jodie and Francesca hadn't come into the kitchen. Between them was sitting a liver-and-white springer spaniel. 'Are you dog-sitting, Cesca?' she asked.

'Sort of,' Francesca said.

'Whose dog is it?' Georgina asked.

'Mrs Waring's. My neighbour,' Jodie said. 'The thing is – she's been getting a bit frail over the last few months. I've been W-A-L-K-ing Bert for her.'

The spaniel's tail beat against the flagstones of the patio at the sound of his name.

'Except,' Francesca continued, 'she's going into sheltered accommodation. And he can't go with her.'

'And she's terrified that, if Bert goes to a rescue centre for rehoming, she won't know what's happening to him,' Jodie said. 'Which means she won't settle. She'll just fret and get even more frail.'

'What the poor woman needs,' Sybbie said, 'is for him to go to a local home. And for Jodie to borrow him once a week so she can take him to visit – or even have a visit with his new owner.'

Georgina had a nasty feeling she knew where this was heading. 'I'm sure he'd have a lovely time romping around with Max and Jet,' she said, thinking of Sybbie's Labradors.

'I'm afraid I don't have the room for a third dog,' Sybbie said.

It was a blatant lie, and they all knew it. Sybbie would have half a dozen dogs, given the chance.

'I can't keep him,' Jodie said. 'With my cleaning jobs, my bar shifts and working in the farm shop, I'd have to leave him on his own too much.'

'And I'm at the farm shop all the time. The health inspectors would have my guts for garters if I had a dog in the kitchen,' Francesca said.

'So we were talking about the problem, and it occurred to us,' Sybbie said, 'that *you* might be able to help.' She gave Georgina a winsome smile.

'I'm planning,' Georgina said, 'to go back to work. I can't take a dog on a shoot.'

'Bert's six years old,' Jodie said. 'I know springers are normally bananas, but he's old enough to be sensible now.'

'He's *great* in the car,' Francesca added.

'He's lovely with people and other dogs,' Jodie said. 'He just wags his tail – well, his tail wags his whole body – and he wants to be friends with everyone he meets.'

Bert obliged by standing up and wiggling, his tail a blur.

'He comes when he's called, he *sits*,' Sybbie said, looking at Bert, who sat, 'he waits nicely and he's a total sweetheart.'

'Your son and daughter would also stop worrying about you, because he'll be company and security for you,' Francesca said.

Between them, Georgina knew they'd covered every single argument she could've made. When she opened her mouth to say no, three voices said in unison, 'Please, Georgie?'

Bert lay down with his chin on his paws, his golden eyes looking imploringly at her and the very end of his tail wagging hopefully.

A dog.

Georgina had never intended to get a dog.

But this was a dog who needed her. And maybe her children and her friends – and the ghost in the farmhouse, who might or might not return – were all perfectly correct when they said that she needed a dog.

'All right,' she said. 'He can stay.'

'You won't regret this,' Jodie promised. 'Cesca, shall we get his things?'

'What things?' Georgina asked, knowing they'd clearly worked out they could talk her into keeping the dog.

'Bed, water bowl, food, car harness, tennis balls,' Francesca said with a smile.

'What do you think, Bert?' Georgina asked. 'Want to come and live at Rookery Farm with me?'

His answer was a tail wagging so fast that it looked like a blur.

'There we are, then. You have a new home, Bert,' Jodie said.

'So did our dashing inspector tell you what happened?' Sybbie asked.

'Yes. Garnett was having an affair with one of his students, and he stole her research. She took an overdose and later drowned.' Georgina decided not to explain that Garnett's student had been pregnant by him. 'Colin didn't tell me who the murderer was, but it's connected. The murderer poisoned me to warn me off because I was getting too close to the truth, and then poisoned Young Tom so the police would stop suspecting him – he's completely innocent, too, by the way.'

'Garnett should've been brought to book,' Sybbie said, 'but killing him wasn't the answer.'

'It's all very sad,' Georgina said. 'And, actually, I feel a bit guilty that I'm sitting here drinking champagne when someone was murdered only a few metres away.'

'We need to celebrate life,' Francesca said. 'Roland Garnett didn't deserve to die, though he probably needed to be in court for what he did to his student. And the college definitely needs to clean up its act where its tutors are concerned.'

'You and Young Tom are both safe,' Sybbie added, 'Bert has a new home and we've all been cleared of suspicion. So, yes, we'll acknowledge Garnett's death – but Cesca's right. That shouldn't stop us being glad that everything else has been sorted out, and life can go back to being its normal quiet and pleasant self again.'

* * *

Later that afternoon, after Georgina had taken her new dog for a walk and discovered that her friends had told her the complete truth, they were curled up together on the sofa.

All of a sudden, Bert shifted and gave a little whine.

'Bert? What is it?' Georgina asked.

The dog appeared to be staring at something right in front of him – something she couldn't see.

'He's gorgeous,' Doris said. 'And he's just what you need.'

'Doris! You're still here!' Georgina said.

'And Bert,' Doris said, 'can see me. Can't you, boy?'

The dog gave another small whine, but it sounded more as if he was agreeing with her than as if he was upset. And he was wagging his tail.

'I'm glad you're still here,' Georgina said, 'but at the same time I'm sad that we clearly haven't worked out what's holding you here and stopping you – well, moving on.'

'Maybe I still need to work out the rest of what really happened, that night,' Doris said. 'It's a fair assumption that I took the doctor's advice and I hit my head when I fell down the stairs. But where was Trev? Why couldn't I see him?'

'I still haven't found him,' Georgina said. 'But I'm looking. And, when I've found him, we'll be able to ask questions.'

'Seeing Jack and knowing that he's happy – and that I'll see him again – has helped,' Doris said.

'Were you here when Colin came to tell me my name's cleared? Or when Sybbie, Cesca came round to talk me into keeping Bert?' Georgina asked.

'No,' Doris said, and Georgina filled her in on what she knew of the case.

'That's so sad for that poor girl and her family,' Doris said. 'Such a waste.'

Which was true of Doris's own death, Georgina thought.

'Life's so short,' Doris said. 'I've been thinking about why I'm here. Maybe it was for Jack, to reassure him that what happened to me wasn't his fault. But maybe also I'm here for you, to remind you that you need to make the most of life. You have so much to give, Georgie. And if your Stephen was here or could talk to you through me, I bet he'd say the same thing.'

He would, Georgina thought.

And maybe it was time to take that first step. To start unwrapping the grief she'd folded round herself like a protective cocoon. To see this second chance for what it was.

'Maybe,' she said.

'One more thing,' Doris said. 'I don't understand why, but I'm not stuck here at the farm anymore. I discovered that I can visit Jack. So I'm going to get to see my niece, my nephew and my great-niece and great-nephew, even though they won't be able to see or hear me.'

'That's lovely,' Georgina said.

'And I'm looking forward to going for nice walks with you and Bert. I know it's a bit cheeky of me to ask, but I'd love it if we could go to the beach,' Doris said. 'I loved paddling in the sea.'

'It's a date,' Georgina said.

'Dates. Hmm. You know, I really hope Trev found someone who'd love him as much as I did. And I bet your Stephen's thinking that about you, too. You don't want the one you loved to be alone and lonely for the rest of their lives. You want them to be happy. Cherished. You've been grieving him for two years. That's enough,' Doris said. 'Think of Christina Rossetti.'

Georgina knew the poem Doris meant. *Better by far you should forget and smile /Than that you should remember and be sad.*

But it was so much easier said than done.

'Be kind to yourself. For Stephen's sake. I think there might be someone you need to call, now you're no longer a suspect,' Doris said gently.

Georgina had been thinking something very similar.

'Don't just sit there. Do it. I'm disappearing, for now,' Doris said.

Bert settled back against Georgina on the sofa, signalling to her that Doris really had gone.

Georgina picked up her mobile phone, pressed a name in her contacts file and waited for the connection. The line rang once, twice.

'Bradshaw.'

'Hi. It's Georgina Drake,' she said, just in case he'd deleted her number now the case had been solved or her name hadn't come up on his screen. 'Are you busy?'

'What did you have in mind?' he asked.

'Someone,' she said, 'suggested having dinner. It's Saturday night, and I'm calling to say yes, I'd like to have dinner with you.'

'As a friend?' he asked.

'Perhaps,' she said. 'Plus I thought you might like to meet Bert.'

'Who's Bert?' He sounded wary.

'The new man in my life. Four paws. Waggy tail. Apparently rather fond of sausages.' There was a soft woof next to her, and she laughed. 'That's one of the words he definitely knows.'

'Then here's the deal,' he said. 'I'm driving over now to pick you both up. Find us a dog-friendly pub. And I'll buy you *both* dinner.'

'Done,' she said.

A LETTER FROM THE AUTHOR

Huge thanks for reading *The Body at Rookery Barn*; I hope you were hooked on Georgina, Doris and Colin's journey. If you want to join other readers in hearing all about my new releases and bonus content, you can sign up for my newsletter!

www.stormpublishing.co/kate-hardy

If you enjoyed this book and could spare a few moments to leave a review, that would be hugely appreciated. Even a short review can make all the difference in encouraging a reader to discover my books for the first time. Thank you so much!

This book was massively influenced by three things. Firstly, I grew up in a haunted house in a small market town in Norfolk, so I've always been drawn to slightly spooky stories. (I did research it when I wrote a book on researching house history, but I couldn't find any documentary evidence for the tale of the jealous miller who murdered his wife. However, I also don't have explanations for various spooky things that happened at the house – including the anecdote about Sybbie's dogs, which happened in real life with our Labradors and a tennis ball.) Secondly, I read Daphne du Maurier's short story *The Blue Lenses* while I was a student, and... I can't explain this properly without giving spoilers, so I'll say it's to do with how you see people. Thirdly, I'm deaf; after I had my first hearing aid fitted, once I'd got over the thrill of hearing birdsong for the first time in years, my author brain started ticking. The du Maurier story gave me a 'what if' moment: what if you heard something through your hearing aids that wasn't what you were supposed to hear? (The obvious one would be someone's thoughts; but that's where my childhood home came in.) It took a few years for the idea to come to the top of my head and then it refused to go away: *what if you could hear what my heroine Georgina ends up hearing?*

And so Georgina Drake ends up living in a haunted house in a small market town in Norfolk...

Little Wenborough isn't a real village, but the name is a mash-up of the town where I grew up and the river where I walk my dogs in the morning. But Norfolk is an amazing place to live. Huge skies (incredible sunrises and sunsets), wide beaches (aka my best place to think, and the Edit-paw-ial Assistants are always up for a trip there) and more ancient churches than anywhere else in the country (watch this space!).

Thanks again for being part of this amazing journey with me and I hope you'll stay in touch – I have so many more stories and ideas to entertain you with!

All best

Kate Hardy

ACKNOWLEDGMENTS

I'd like to thank Oliver Rhodes and Kathryn Taussig for taking a chance on my slightly unusual take on a crime novel; Emily Gowers for being an absolute dream of an editor – incisive, thoughtful, and great fun (and she makes great scones!); and Shirley Khan and Maddy Newquist for picking up the bits I missed! I've loved every second of working on this book with you.

A book is never written on its own, and I'm lucky to have good family and friends (both in and out of publishing) who are there to cheerlead through the good times and listen to me whinging/say something that sets off a lightbulb moment when things are tricky. Special thanks to those who've encouraged me to branch out with this book, particularly Kate Baker, Christine Brookes, Nicki Brooks, Jackie Chubb, Siobhàn Coward, Sheila Crighton, Liz Fielding, Sandra Forder, Philippa Gell, Rosie Hendry, Rachel Hore, Jenni Keer, Lizzie Lamb, Clare Marchant, Jo Rendell-Dodd, Fiona Robertson, Rachael Stewart, Michelle Styles, Heidi-Jo Swain, Katy Watson, Ian Wilfred, Susan Wilson, Jan Wooller and Caroline Woolnough. Thank you all for your friendship, book talk and the cake we've eaten and coffee/wine we've drunk together. (And apologies if I've missed anyone!)

Extra-special thanks to Gerard, Chris and Chloe Brooks, who've always been my greatest supporters and never minded me hijacking family days out for research purposes or dragging them off to the beach because I needed to think; to Chrissy and

Rich Camp, for always believing in me and being the best uncle and aunt ever; and to Archie and Dexter, my beloved Edit-paw-ial Assistants, for keeping my feet warm, reminding me when it's time for walkies and lunch and putting up with me photographing them to keep my social media ticking over while I'm on deadline.

And, last but very much not least, thank *you*, dear reader, for choosing my book. I hope you enjoy reading it as much as I enjoyed writing it.